D0091947

Other Books by Karen Baney

Prescott Pioneers Series

A Dream Unfolding

A Heart Renewed

A Life Restored

A Hope Revealed

Contemporary

Nickels

Prescott Pioneers Book 4:

A Hope Revealed

By Karen Baney

Prescott Pioneers Book 4: A Hope Revealed
By Karen Baney

Cover Illustration & Design by Brian Ring Designs

Publisher:
Author Services International, LLC
3317 S Higley Road
Suite 114-288
Gilbert, AZ 85297

www.karenbaney.com

Printed in the United States of America

ISBN-978-0-9835486-9-0

To my husband, Jim.
Thanks for being an
example of a godly husband.

For you have been my hope, Sovereign Lord,
my confidence since my youth.
Psalm 71:5

Chapter 1

North Texas

October 15, 1866

Mary Colter wiped the sweat from her forehead onto the rolled up sleeve of her dress. The hot water in the wash basin made the small laundry building into a steamy sauna. Her mother would have said it was good for her skin. She would argue against the notion, for once she left the steamy room, her skin dried out terribly from the harsh lye she used to scour the townsfolk's laundry clean.

A bell rang from the front of the building. Mary dropped the shirt she was scrubbing into the basin and dried her hands on her apron.

"Ma'am," Enoch Fowler greeted her.

She frowned in response, never trusting his motives. He had no need of laundry services as he was employed by Hiram Norton and all of his clothing was cared for by Norton's staff.

"They think they found yer man's—um—remains."

Mary bit back a snort of disgust. She couldn't count the number of times someone came into her business with similar claims in the past two years since Reuben's disappearance.

"The sheriff said you should stop by the mortuary. See if you can identify…"

She nodded, keeping a tight lid on the small hope that perhaps she would know once and for all if she was free.

"Iffen it is, boss says he'll come see ya in a few days."

"Tell Mr. Norton that my answer is still no."

"Ma'am." Mr. Fowler narrowed his eyes before exiting the building.

Mary made her way back to the steam room. She leaned against the wall and closed her eyes. Frustration and fear fought in her heart.

Two years ago, almost to the day, Reuben disappeared. Her

husband. Her provider. Her abuser.

While it had been hard to find a way to support herself and her two children, she managed to scrounge together enough money to rent out this old dilapidated building and start offering laundry services. It was a tough job that left her back aching and her hands roughened. But, it put food on the table, a roof over their heads, and clothes on their backs.

And, it came with freedom she hadn't known in twelve years of marriage to Reuben.

No longer did she fear the sound of footfalls entering her bedroom chamber in the middle of the night. He wasn't there to take whatever he wanted from her however harshly he wanted it. She didn't have to worry about burning dinner and receiving a beating for it later. No. She was free—even if that freedom could still be taken away.

Two years ago, Reuben got himself into serious debt with Hiram Norton. One afternoon in the middle of October, Reuben disappeared. A few days later, Hiram showed up on her doorstep giving her a choice—marry him or be evicted. When she asked if he could produce her husband's dead body, Norton shook his head. It was the only indication she had that Norton didn't know Reuben's whereabouts either.

Since then, every few months her husband's "remains" were found. She made each trip to the mortuary with the same conflicted feelings—hope that it really was him and that she was permanently free, combined with dread that it was not him and she would forever be looking over her shoulder in fear wondering if he would show up alive to reclaim her. Each time, Hiram Norton would show up within a few days to discover if she was finally free to be his wife.

She knew why he pursued her. For Norton, it was a matter of conquering the great Colter family. She was attractive enough—not that it mattered to Norton. Her looks were secondary to winning his ultimate goal.

Mary sighed. Why would she give up freedom from Reuben's abuse only to be chained under Hiram's? Nothing on this earth could force her to willingly accept that choice.

She moved back to the wash basin and hurried through the remaining clothing. If she moved fast enough, she would have time to go to the mortuary to identify the remains before Eddie and Beth returned from school.

Hanging the last item on the line, she wiped her hands on her apron and removed it. She pulled down her sleeves. If this had been her first trip, she might have taken the time to freshen up. She felt no need to do so now.

Grabbing her reticule, she walked down the board sidewalk to the mortuary, only a few doors down.

"Mr. Cawley," she greeted him emotionlessly. "I understand I am expected to identify someone in your care."

"Mrs. Colter. Yes. This way."

She held her handkerchief to her nose, prepared for any gruesome sight. She had witnessed all manner of men in all states of decay. Sometimes the images woke her at night. She prayed this would be more palatable than the last.

As Mr. Cawley pulled back the cover, Mary held her tongue. The skeletal remains of a man lay in a decaying sun-bleached suit that looked as if it might have been black at one time.

"How tall would you say this man was?" she asked.

"Probably between five foot eight and five foot ten."

Mary frowned. "Why do you insist on wasting my time? Reuben was well over six feet tall. You know this!"

"Ma'am. 'Twas the sheriff's request." Mr. Cawley's soft voice soothed some of the rawness from her anger.

"I know it's a difficult thing, Mrs. Colter, to come here so often. But, I must ask, do any of the personal affects look familiar?"

She allowed her eyes to roam over the dead man's clothing. The watch was not the same as Reuben's. The man wore a simple gold band on his left hand, as Reuben should, but neither ring was distinctive enough to say it was him. The height was most definitely wrong. Besides, Reuben had all his teeth, the last she saw him. This man looked as if he'd lost several.

"It is not him," she said the words with resignation. The little hope she tried not to let grow now vanished. She still didn't know if her husband was dead or alive.

The noisy chatter of her children bursting through the door brought Mary to the front room.

"Eddie, Beth, put your slates and pails away. Hurry!"

"Ma!" Eddie whined.

"Now, Edward," she cautioned with a frown and a hand on her hip. "Georgie Larson will be here any minute."

Eddie pouted. "I don't want to go out to the Larsons. They ain't got no boys!"

"Do not have any," she corrected his English. "Now go."

Eddie shuffled his feet to do his mother's bidding just as a knock sounded on the door.

"We're almost ready, Georgie."

"Ma'am," he greeted.

Georgie held the door open as Mary ushered her children out to the waiting carriage.

The drive to the Larson's ranch passed quickly. They lived relatively close to town. Once they arrived, Georgie helped her and the children down.

"Ma said to go on in," he said as he pulled the carriage away from the front of the house.

"Maggie?" she greeted hesitantly as she opened the door.

"In the kitchen, Mary. Come on back."

Mary gently nudged Eddie and Beth forward. Maggie's daughter, Helen bounded in from the kitchen.

"Come on Eddie and Elizabeth. Mama said we could watch Papa train the horses." Helen grabbed their hands and dragged them towards the door.

Eddie shook his hand free and scowled at Helen. Then a grin replaced his frown. "Race ya!"

"Be careful!" Mary shouted after the jubilant children.

When she entered the kitchen, Maggie Larson turned and gave her a huge welcoming hug.

"I'm so glad you decided to visit with us this evening. It's been far too long."

Mary nodded. "I'm glad for the break."

Missy, Maggie's second oldest daughter, pulled some biscuits from the oven and set them aside to cool.

"Missy, I think I've got everything under control in here. Would you mind going out and keeping an eye on the children? Take your sister with you."

"Yes, Mama."

Maggie sighed. "Now we can talk." Her green eyes sparked with a fire almost as brilliant as her red hair.

Mary smiled.

"Tell me how you're doing."

"Fine." Mary said.

"Hmm. Doesn't sound like it."

She gave in and began sharing her heart with Maggie—a longtime family friend. "The sheriff asked me to identify another body. It wasn't him."

"I see."

Mary fidgeted with the edge of her sleeve nervously. "Is it wrong that sometimes I wish one of these dead men were him? I mean, the alternative—that he's still alive and might come back anytime—is too frightening to consider."

Maggie looked up from the pan of gravy she stirred. "I know he was a mean man. It must be hard wanting to do the right thing. But, I also know the last two years have brought you peace and safety that you didn't know under his roof."

"It just seems wrong to hope he's dead."

Maggie walked over to the table and put an arm around Mary's shoulder. "I wish I had some advice for you."

Mary nodded as her tears rose to the surface. "It was awful living with him. Ten years of… The last two years of this marriage have been the most peaceful because he isn't here. If he came back… I just don't think I could live with him again."

"You thinking of divorce?"

Mary looked up as Maggie walked back to the stove. "Where would I get the money for that? If I had any, it would be better spent taking me and my children to Will's ranch in the Arizona Territory."

"So you are considering it. Divorce?"

Mary bit her lip. Her voice was a small whisper. "I have considered it. Many times. If it is the only way to be free from him…" She shook her head.

Maggie nodded. Her solemn expression hinted that she knew what a difficult decision that would be, should Mary ever be faced with it.

"It doesn't matter. I still don't know if he's alive or not."

Silence settled over the two women as Maggie turned her attention back to the meal for a few minutes.

"What about you? How are things with George?" Mary asked.

"As good as they can be. It's just the ranch we're worried about. George is talking about sending Georgie west to locate some new land."

Mary lit up at the news. "To the Arizona Territory?" It would make sense. Maggie had two children there—one lived on Colter Ranch.

"Yes. I miss Adam and Caroline so much. And we just received news. We're grandparents!"

"Adam?"

"Both Adam's wife and Caroline delivered both of our grandchildren on the same day. Adam and Julia have a daughter—Catherine."

"After her mother."

Maggie nodded. "And Caroline's son is named Drew after her husband's brother. From their letters, it looks like Drew was born first, with Catherine arriving a few hours later."

Maggie made direct eye contact. "Can you imagine? I'm a grandmother!"

Mary smiled. "Congratulations."

"With things not going well for our ranch, and with our grandchildren in Arizona, George keeps talking about moving there. The idea is that Georgie will take the stage out a few months before we leave so he can locate land. We hope it'll be near Will's ranch. But, we trust Georgie to make the best choice."

Sadness washed over Mary. She would have to say goodbye to her last friend. All others had forsaken her when she became a laundress—a position they deemed too far below their social standing. Maggie was the only one who stood by her side these last two years.

She wished she could go with them. But, she didn't have enough money to purchase the supplies for such a long trip. And she wouldn't ask for their charity. George and Maggie would need what resources they had left in order to care for their own family.

By the time Georgie dropped Mary and her children back home, the hour had grown late. The noise from the saloons at the far end of town escalated to a constant hum. She listened to Beth and Eddie's prayers before tucking them in for the night. Then she readied herself for bed.

A few minutes after she turned down the lamp, a loud knock sounded at the door.

Fear gripped her heart. What if it was Reuben?

Images of his dark scowl flashed before her eyes. The feel of his hands on her body became so tangible she almost thought he was there.

The knock sounded again.

"Mrs. Colter!" A woman's voice came from the other side of the door.

Mary threw back her fear with the covers of her bed. She lit a lamp and cautiously answered the door.

The ragged woman before her shook with deep coughs. After a minute rolled by, the woman regained her breath.

"Mrs. Colter, I've come to see my daughter. Doc says I ain't long for this world. I just want to see her once."

Mary's brow wrinkled in confusion. "I'm sorry, ma'am. I don't know your daughter. I don't see how I can be of assistance."

"You're Reuben's woman, ain't ya?"

"Yes."

"Then let me see my Elizabeth."

Mary's stomach knotted. She wished she would have thought to grab her revolver before answering the door. She had no way to defend herself or her children from this mad woman.

"I don't understand."

"Elizabeth—" The woman's coughing spasm interrupted her for a moment. "She ain't yourn. She be mine."

It was not possible. Mary remembered giving birth to her daughter six years ago. She remembered the night she held her in her arms. Soft brown eyes stared back at her. She had a difficult labor and the doctor kept her heavily medicated for the first few days. But, on the fourth day after her birth, when she held her in her arms, she immediately fell in love with her precious daughter.

"I see what yer thinkin'. Yer trying to figure it out. Let me save ya the trouble. See, you gave birth six years ago to a boy. Stillborn he was. Two days later, I gave birth to Reuben's daughter. It were his idea to switch them. Said life in a brothel weren't no place for a baby. Said it would be better for Elizabeth if he raised her."

Mary's ability to breathe faltered. Normalcy and reason shattered. She sank to a chair as the woman entered her home.

Chapter 2

"What are you saying?" Mary asked the woman as she took a seat across from her at the table.

"I'm saying yourn husband spent many a night in my bed. One of those nights he got me pregnant. I gave birth shortly after you did."

The part that Mary could easily understand was that Reuben bedded this soiled dove. But, how could Beth not be hers? The late nights comforting her when she was colicky. The tea parties with imaginary friends. The kissing away of every scrape or cut. Every precious moment with Beth was hers—not this woman's.

When the woman shifted in her chair, Mary saw it. The odd shade of brown eyes—lighter than Reuben's. Just like Elizabeth's. Nothing like her own violet eyes. In fact, her dear sweet Beth shared none of her characteristics. She always thought she more strongly resembled Reuben.

Until now. Now she saw the round face and pronounced chin in the adult face staring back at her.

"Name's Jasmine," the woman stated before another coughing fit shook her body.

Mary remained seated. Her legs turned to lead, pinning her in the chair. Her heart refused to slow to a normal rhythm. Her hands clenched in her lap under the table.

The longer she sat there, the more she believed the woman's story. She remembered having a very difficult labor. She knew she forgot a few days after the birth. Reuben had been the only one besides Julia that was home during those days. Will and his father were gone on some trip. Or perhaps they had been on the cattle drive. Julia would have been only twelve or so. She tended to spend much time out of doors. With Mary bedridden, she probably would have been so overwhelmed with putting meals on the table that she wouldn't have known if a switch had been made. Besides, Reuben was too cunning. He would have found a way to keep it from Julia.

"I see yer mulling it over," Jasmine said. "Look, all I'm asking is to see her. Just once afore I pass. Don't want nuthin' else."

Mary swallowed hard. Even if this woman was lying, what harm would there be in letting her see Beth as she slept? It would certainly get her out of her home sooner.

"Be quiet. The children are asleep," Mary said as she led the woman to the children's room.

Jasmine knelt next to Beth's side of the bed. She reached out a hand as if she was going to brush Beth's hair from her face. Instead, she pulled her hand back and dropped it in her lap. In a soft voice, she whispered, "You already done better'n yer mama, sweet child. You listen to her always. Be a good girl. I love you."

Suddenly, Jasmine stood and ran from the room, out the front door and down the street.

Mary followed only to the threshold to close the door behind the lady of the night. Then she dimmed the oil lamp and returned to her bed.

Sobs wracked her body. Another one of Reuben's lies cut her to the core. Her own daughter was a lie. How could he do this to her? Did he have no love for her at all? Had he ever?

She laughed—the kind of cackling laugh that is wrestled from a grief-stricken heart.

He never loved her. She should know that well by now. Lie after lie. Manipulation. Control. Money was the only thing her husband ever loved. Perhaps their son was a distant second. She, his wife, was just a pawn he used to get what he loved most.

The next morning, Mary woke feeling more somber than her worst morning after suffering one of Reuben's forceful nights. This was so much worse than him taking what he wanted from her body. He'd stolen her heart. He buried her son and left her with his whore's daughter—letting her believe Beth was her own.

This was the worst betrayal.

She knew he didn't love her. She knew he was not faithful. She knew he was capable of dark, unfathomable deeds—like what he had done to Julia—something she only learned of a few months ago.

This felt even worse.

He let her live believing Elizabeth was her own flesh and blood daughter. He even let her name her after her mother. Only to find out differently now.

As she set a bowl of grits in front of Beth, she studied the child.

Lord, forgive me! I cannot look at her now without seeing Jasmine. I can never look at my daughter the same way again.

But, Beth was still her heart's daughter. It mattered not a whit what Reuben had done. It mattered not what Jasmine had said.

Beth belonged to her. She was the only mother Beth had known. She certainly couldn't hand her over to a dying soiled dove. Why she would be drawn into unspeakable things at too young of an age. She could not. She would not.

No, she would do what she always did. She would pick up the shattered fragments of her heart. She would beg God to restore her and not leave her this time. She would move on.

Mary resolved that no matter what the truth was about Elizabeth, she would fight as hard as she must in order to make sure Beth never knew. She would fight with that same determination to make sure she never treated her as anything other than her own.

As the children finished their breakfast, she handed them their lunch pails and sent them off to school. Then she began stoking the fires under the wash basins, readying her next batch of laundry. While the fires warmed the water to temperature, she pulled the dried clothes from the line and brought them into the room where she ironed.

Her heart struggled to forget the events of the last day as she used her anger to press the clothing quicker.

She had to get out of this town. If Reuben did come back here, she didn't want to be here waiting for him. She wanted out. Out of this dreadful town. Out of her marriage.

Guilt pushed forward. She had vowed before God and many witnesses to cherish her husband, to remain faithful, for better or for worse. Marriage to him was about as bad as it could get. She didn't know his true nature when she said those vows. She had been living in numbing grief over the recent murder of her parents when she stood at the front of the church and made those promises. She had not been in her right mind and she was weary of honoring those vows.

Whether she decided to honor those vows or not, it didn't mean she had to stay in this town. If Reuben wanted to come back for her or his children, he surely would have returned by now. It had been two years. No, he was either satisfied with whatever new life he created, or he was dead.

If only she had the money to hop on a stage and head west to Colter Ranch. At least then she would be safe. She wouldn't have to fear anything there. No more late night surprises from Reuben's women.

A tear trailed down her cheek. It was hopeless to think of such things. It would never happen. She barely paid her rent and put food in her children's stomachs. There was no way she could hope to come up with enough to move west. She was stuck here.

Midweek, Mary closed up the laundry early. It was her shopping day. She pulled the door closed behind her and walked down the street towards Finley's Mercantile.

"Mrs. Colter!"

She heard her name being called as she walked past Mr. Gainsly's office. She turned as he caught up with her.

"Mrs. Colter, might you have a few minutes? I have some business I'd like to discuss with you."

"Certainly," she said, wondering what business the attorney could possibly have with her.

She followed him into his office and took a seat across from him.

"Are you aware that your father left some funds for your children?"

Her breath rushed from her lungs. "No. How is that possible? I wasn't even married when he and mother passed."

"He made a provision for any future children. He wanted to make sure they had something. I think he suspected you would marry

Reuben. He wanted it kept a secret. His instructions were very clear that Reuben or whomever you married should not be informed of the money unless the executor of his will deemed it necessary."

Mary shook her head. "I don't understand. Are you saying father left money for Eddie and Beth?"

"In a manner of speaking, yes."

"Why am I only now learning of this?"

"He left it to the executor's discretion."

"And who is he?"

Mr. Gainsly cleared his throat. "I am the executor."

Mary felt the blood rush from her face. Her breath shortened. Her hands grew sweaty. She wasn't sure she could withstand another shock.

"Mrs. Colter, it has come to my attention that you have been struggling these last two years to provide for your children. At first, I thought your husband might return to his responsibilities. As that does not appear to be the case, I felt now was the appropriate time to mention the funds."

"How much is there?" she asked, trying to keep her hopes from soaring.

"Not much. But certainly enough to purchase passage for you and your children to the Arizona Territory. I understand that is where your brother-in-law settled. Perhaps he is in a better position to provide for your family?"

She could hardly believe her ears. There was some money left. Enough to get out of this wretched town.

"Yes, Will should be able to take care of us."

"Very well. Would you like me to make the arrangements?"

"Um…" She hesitated. "Give me a few days. I'd like some time to think about it."

Mary hesitated only for a few days before purchasing passage on the same stage as Georgie. With a quick visit to the Larsons, all the arrangements were made. Georgie would help her with the children and make sure they arrived in Prescott safely. Though she sent a letter to Will before leaving Texas, she wondered if he would receive it before she arrived. Georgie told her he thought they would arrive in twenty-two to twenty-six days since stage travel was faster than going by wagon train.

Now on their seventeenth day into the trip, they arrived in Tucson in the Arizona Territory. After Georgie helped her and the children from the stage, he secured a room for them at a nearby hotel. He and Eddie shared a room while Mary and Beth shared another room. Secretly, Mary was thankful for the arrangement. Eddie had become increasingly difficult to manage the further they traveled from their home.

After a particularly trying day on the stage, she took a few extra minutes to help Beth wash up, before seeing to herself. Then she held Beth by the hand as they went back downstairs to the dining room.

She spotted Georgie by himself at table. He looked rather pale.

"Where's Eddie?" she asked as she approached.

"He's... Um..."

"Georgie?"

"Ah, there he is!" Georgie expelled the words in a rush as he stood to go get him.

Judging from the relief on his face, Eddie must have given him the slip for a few minutes.

As Eddie approached the table, Mary stood and propped one hand on her hip. "Did you run away from Mr. Larson?"

Eddie jutted his chin up and kept his lips sealed.

"Edward Reuben Colter! You answer me this instant."

His chocolate brown eyes narrowed in defiance—a look hauntingly similar to his father's. The stare down between mother and son continued for another few seconds before Georgie interrupted.

"It's fine, Mrs. Colter. I found him again."

She turned her anger on Georgie. "It is *not* fine. Eddie knows better than to just take off. Eddie, apologize to Mr. Larson."

He bowed his head and mumbled, "I'm sorry."

Mary decided to leave it at that. She didn't have the energy for a head-to-head confrontation with her son right now.

As the meal was served, Beth started in. "I'm tired of beans,

Mama. I want something else."

"This is what they are serving and you will eat it."

"But, Mama!" Beth whined.

Mary shot her a sharp look that finally silenced her. Beth picked up her fork and stabbed the mushy beans on her plate. One by one she ate the food in front of her until she was full.

Once the meal finished, Georgie stood. He ran his hand over his face nervously. Over the past few days she came to learn the habit meant he was stressed.

"Do you want me to take Eddie tonight?" she asked.

"No. We're fine."

"Then what's troubling you?"

"Just thought I saw a familiar face. Probably the lack of sleep getting to me."

He lightly clasped Eddie's hand and led him up the stairs towards their room. As Mary followed, she thought she heard her name.

She turned to look and found Enoch Fowler at the foot of the stairs. She called for Georgie to take Beth with him. He did as she asked.

"Mr. Fowler," she greeted stoically as she returned to the bottom of the stairs. "What brings you to Tucson?"

"Might ask you the same question. Rumor is that your husband sent for you—that you know where he is."

Mary frowned. "You shouldn't believe everything you hear."

"I don't ma'am. But I did hear something that I'm inclined to believe."

She narrowed her eyes and waited for him to continue.

"Heard tale of a wealthy rancher out near Wickenburg way. Rumor says he arrived in the area not too long after your husband disappeared."

"Your point, Mr. Fowler?"

"Curious. You wouldn't be headed to Wickenburg, now would ya?"

"Hardly. I'm headed to my brother-in-law's ranch outside of Prescott."

Mr. Fowler glared at her for several minutes, apparently weighing the truth of her words. At length, he finally nodded.

Mary started towards the stairs. Mr. Fowler grabbed her arm.

"Should ya happen to run into your husband, be sure to let him know that Hiram Norton is still looking for payment. No debt is forgiven."

She wrenched her arm from his grasp. "You'll have to tell him yourself."

Then she turned and ran up the stairs. She wanted to hold on to the hope that her husband was gone for good, but she feared this rancher in Wickenburg might be Reuben—especially if Norton was sending his men that direction.

Chapter 3

Colter Ranch

November 9, 1866

Warren Cahill slung his saddle into its resting place in the barn before grabbing a brush. As he brushed down his gray gelding, he frowned. He dreaded the coming conversation with Will. Though both he and Will suspected the head count was down, he doubted that Will expected it to be down by two hundred. That, along with the two hundred some head they lost on the drive in September, comprised a significant setback for the ranch.

Losses like that could bankrupt a smaller operation—like the one he used to own before life turned upside down and he became a drifter.

The image of a woman pressed on the edges of his vision. It was almost so real, he glanced over his shoulder. He saw nothing, confirming the image stayed confined to the recesses of his mind. It had been a long time since he thought of Dahlia or his ranch. Even now, just thinking her name resurrected the bitterness and anger he thought he released years ago.

The gelding snorted, causing the image to fade. Warren resolved to worry only about his present troubles. He could do nothing about the past—about Dahlia.

"Give it back!" Jed's voice echoed through the barn.

"If ya want it back you'll have to take it," Owens replied.

Warren sighed as the sound of a scuffle filtered down to the stall where he stood. Stepping from the stall, he tossed the brush on Adam's work bench and hurried toward the sounds.

When he came into view, he saw Owens holding a small bag in his hand behind his back. As Jed lunged toward him, he shifted to the side, keeping the item from Jed's reach. The dance between the two men went on for a few steps, until Jed plowed his shoulder into

Owens's stomach. The force was enough to jar the bag from Owens hand. It landed on the barn floor.

Owens charged toward Jed. He swung his fist and made contact with Jed's jaw. Jed held his ground. His fist caught Owens hard on the temple.

Warren stood by watching. As foreman, he would step in and break it up when necessary. Though Ben would have done so by now, Warren felt it was better to let the men work out their differences.

Jed brought up his other hand hard against Owens's jaw. Owens reached for his revolver. In less than a second, he had it pointed at the center of Jed's chest.

"That's enough," Warren said, training his gun on Owens.

Owens made no move to stow his weapon.

"Put. It. Away." Warren emphasized each word.

When Owens kept his gun on Jed, Warren cocked his revolver. "Unless you want to cause a lot of extra work for Mrs. Colter this evening as she patches the hole in your leg, I suggest you holster your weapon."

Slowly, Owens returned his gun to his side.

"Jed, get on up to the bunkhouse. I'd like a word with Owens."

Jed nodded. He bent over and picked up the small bag then darted out of the barn.

"Next time I catch you drawing your weapon on a Colter cowboy, it better be 'cause you caught them rustling or harming one of the women folk. Is that clear?"

Owens narrowed his eyes and jutted his chin forward. "You saying someone here's involved in rustling."

"I'm saying you need to check yourself or find another place to work."

Owens frowned, but held his tongue.

"Get on up to supper."

As Owens turned, Warren added, "And I better not hear of any issues when I get up there later."

Once Owens disappeared, Warren shook his head. Owens was downright out of control. If there was an inside man involved in rustling, he was sure Owens had something to do with it.

Will rode up as Warren was about to leave the barn. He

followed Will back in and waited as he cared for his horse.

"How was the meeting with Jacob Morgan?" Warren asked, hoping to delay the conversation he knew was coming.

"Good. Hay crop is looking real good." Will unsaddled his horse and began brushing him down. "Asked if he'd seen anything unusual lately. He said there were some tracks through the far north end of the pastures."

"Really?"

"Looked like they were about a day old."

"How long ago did he see them?" Warren asked, wondering if the rustlers might be skirting around the Morgan property. He thought they would have headed west, then south. But it sounded like they may have headed east and then south.

"Yesterday."

Warren's stomach tightened.

"How was the head count?"

"Not good."

He darted his gaze away as Will frowned.

"Lost at least two hundred head."

Will looked up from brushing his horse. "Two hundred?"

"Yup."

"Since the count last month?"

Warren nodded.

"We've got to get to the bottom of this. I know we've tossed around some ideas of who's involved, but do we have any proof?"

"Nothing concrete."

Will finished caring for his horse and put away the brush. Warren fell into step beside him as he headed toward the ranch house.

"I was thinking," Warren started. "Maybe I should talk to the sheriff tomorrow."

"Let's both head into town in the morning."

"Even though you're leaving on Monday?"

Will nodded. "I think the sheriff will want to talk to me. Ben can finish getting everything ready for the trip to Mohave."

Ben, Adam, and Julia joined them on the porch. As Will pushed the door open, they were greeted by the screams of an infant.

As soon as Will stepped into the ranch house, Hannah sighed in relief. “Here, take him,” she said, thrusting Samuel into his arms. “I need to get back to the kitchen.”

“What do you want me to do?” her husband replied, still holding their screaming son at arm’s length.

She bit back a frustrated sigh. “Just watch him until Betty and I get supper on the table.”

“Is he hungry? Is that why he’s crying?”

She turned and headed back toward the kitchen. “I don’t know,” she shot over her shoulder.

When she stepped back into the kitchen, she grabbed the bowl of mashed potatoes and the serving tray of pork chops. Then she entered the dining room and placed the items on the table.

“Does he have a fever, dear?” Betty asked as they both went from the dining room back into the kitchen for the next round of items.

“He felt warm, but I couldn’t tell if he has a fever or if he is just warm from crying so much.”

“Do you think he’s teething?”

“I don’t know.” She sighed. Was four months old too early to start teething? James hadn’t started teething until six months old. Her nerves were too frayed from the constant cries that she couldn’t remember what was normal.

Just as she entered the parlor, James started crying. For a few brief seconds, she closed her eyes, gathering strength to face both of her upset sons. When she opened her eyes, she took Samuel from Will’s arms. Betty scooped James up from the floor.

“Supper is on the table,” Hannah said. “Please start without us.”

As she headed for the stairs, Julia asked, “Where’s Catherine?”

“In the bassinette in the kitchen. She slept through all our noise making dinner and even Samuel’s crying.”

Not waiting for Julia’s response, Hannah climbed the stairs. She went into her bedroom and shut the door. Then she sat on the edge of the bed, rocking Samuel back and forth in her arms.

“What’s wrong, little one?” she whispered.

She placed her wrist on his forehead. He felt warm. Maybe he was coming down with something. After a few minutes, he finally calmed and fell asleep. She stood and moved to the crib in the corner of the room. Gently, she laid him down.

Letting out a slow deliberate breath, she closed her eyes again. *Lord, help.* She couldn't manage much more than the simple plea.

She opened her eyes. Moving to the doorway, she left the door open and went back downstairs. Hopefully she would be able to hear him over the noise of supper conversation, if he stirred.

As she entered the dining room, she apologized. Will smiled reassuringly at her. At least he wasn't upset. James sat in his high chair—the one Will lovingly hand crafted—next to Betty, having calmed from whatever upset him earlier. She didn't see Julia's Catherine in the room, so she must have decided to let her sleep in the bassinette.

Hannah took her seat next to Will, thankful that he had taken the time to fill her plate with food. As she reached for her fork, he extended his hand and gave hers a squeeze.

"Is he alright?"

"He's sleeping now."

A frown formed over his eyes. "Is he sick?" The question came softly, only loud enough for her to hear.

"I think so."

"Should I send for Doc Hank?"

"Let's see how he is tomorrow?"

Will nodded.

As the conversation hummed around the table, Hannah began to relax. It seemed like most suppers at Colter Ranch. Adam and Julia sat next to her, talking excitedly about the horses they were training. Then Julia asked how Catherine was for the few hours she left her daughter in Hannah's care. Warren sat across from her and to Will's right, occasionally engaging Will in a discussion about some part of the ranch business or another. He seemed rather withdrawn this evening. Betty sat next to him, with baby James next to her. Ben sat at the foot of the table making silly faces at James in between bites of his meal.

She loved this odd assortment of people that she considered to be her family. It was so far from what she had grown up with—

feeling abandoned and rejected by her father after her mother passed. This is what she always dreamed family would look like.

Catherine fussed from the kitchen and Julia excused herself. Hannah could hardly believe the two month old slept uninterrupted for the past few hours. Though Samuel was a few months older than his cousin, he never wanted to sleep for more than an hour at a time during the day. At least he was starting to sleep better through the night.

"Warren and I will be heading in to town tomorrow morning," Will announced.

Hannah looked up from her meal with her eyebrow raised.

"Seems we've lost a fair number of cattle. I'll need to report it to the sheriff."

"Since last month?" Ben asked.

"Yes. Two hundred head."

Hannah stifled her gasp. Even though the herd stayed around three thousand head, she understood that two hundred was a significant loss.

"Snake will be in the butcher house nearby. Adam, you weren't planning on heading into town, were you?"

"No. My next meeting with Thomas isn't until next week. He said the express owner couldn't make it to town before then. He is going to let me know at church on Sunday which day I should head in."

"Good. Just want to make sure we've got some men close to the house."

Hannah smiled. Will always made sure she felt safe. Since Samuel's birth, he had grown even more protective—if that was possible.

"I'll be around, too," Ben said. "Just gettin' ready for our trip next week."

As everyone finished their meal, Hannah started to rise, but Betty stopped her. "I'll bring out dessert. You finish your supper."

Ben grinned as Betty brought several pies to the table. "Got any apple?"

Betty bent down and kissed his cheek. "Of course, Benjamin. I know it's your favorite."

She began slicing the pies and passing pieces around the table, serving her husband first.

James grew fussy again. Hannah stood and lifted him from his chair. His soft cries grew louder and he squirmed in her arms. She moved from the dining room into the main living room, so as not to disturb the family. She tried bouncing him up and down. Still he cried. She tried rocking him in the chair. Nothing seemed to calm him.

She touched his forehead and it was hot. Her heart sank to the floor. Both James and Samuel were sick?

As she paced back and forth, she thought she heard Samuel fuss.

"I'll get him," Will said. He bounded up the stairs and brought him down.

Worry squeezed her heart. She wasn't sure how to help either of her children. A fever could be the start of any number of illnesses.

Betty and Ben headed back to their cabin. Warren took his leave to the bunkhouse. Julia assured her all the dishes were done. She held Catherine in her arms and followed Adam out the door, back to their home, leaving Hannah and Will alone with two crying sons.

She tried to nurse Samuel twice more throughout the evening. Both times he refused to eat. Will held James and then rocked him. Nothing seemed to calm either one.

Will looked worried. His jaw clamped tightly shut and she caught the slight tick on the right side. Over the varying degrees of screaming and cries from their sons, she learned that he was very concerned about the missing cattle. He was certain someone at the ranch was helping the rustlers.

"Who could it be?" she asked.

"Possibly Owens. Maybe Bates. Warren is pretty sure it is Owens. Regardless," he looked her in the eye, "be careful around the men—especially Owens, Whitten, and Bates. I don't want you around any of them alone while I'm gone next week. Make sure Adam or Warren or Snake are around when they are. Let Rosa handle feeding the men at the bunkhouse."

She nodded. She hated to think that any of the cowboys would be working against her husband.

As the hour grew late, both James and Samuel quieted. Hannah and Will retired to their room. She placed Samuel in his crib as Will did the same with James.

She let her shoulders sag once she finished unpinning her hair.

"Hey." Will came up next to her. "They'll be fine."

She turned fearful eyes towards her husband. The tears started to fall. "I don't know how to help them. I don't know if they have the flu, or a cold, or something worse like pox."

Fear crossed Will's face. "Small pox?"

Shrugging her shoulders, she answered, "I don't know. It can start with a fever. So can Scarlet fever."

"Whoa. Now you're scaring me," he said, pulling her to his chest.

"It could be nothing."

"What do we do?"

He was looking to her for answers. She had none. Though she helped Drew many times in his clinic with all of the diseases she mentioned, she couldn't remember ever treating infants. Besides, most of the time, his patients had been suffering milder symptoms for days.

"Wait and see if they develop other symptoms or if it passes."

She stepped from his embrace and changed into her night dress. Then she sat on the edge of the bed and started brushing her hair. Will's gentle touch on her arm stopped her. He took the brush from her hands. Then he ran it through her long locks for several minutes.

He set the brush aside. Then he repositioned her hair over one shoulder, exposing the side of her neck. Softly he kissed her neck. Slowly she turned toward him and his lips met hers in a gentle kiss.

When he ended the kiss, he ran his fingers along her cheek. "I know you're worried."

A half-smile titled up one side of her mouth. "Maybe a little less than a few moments ago."

He smiled. "If they're still sick tomorrow before I go, I'll bring Doc Hank back with me."

"Thank you," she whispered as she pulled his face towards hers for another kiss.

Chapter 4

The next morning, a groggy Will saddled his horse. He'd barely gotten four hours of sleep. Every time he fell asleep either James or Samuel woke up crying. Hannah tried to get them to settle quickly, but it was obvious both boys were very sick.

He mounted his horse and followed Warren up the road to town. This morning, Hannah looked very worried. With all of the medical knowledge she acquired working with her first husband, if she was worried… Well, that made him twice as worried—enough that he decided he would bring Doc Hank back with him.

It had taken him longer than most to find a wife and when he married Hannah, they wasted no time starting their family. He loved both his sons so much. If anything happened to them, he would be crushed.

His sons gave him renewed purpose. He wanted to build up Colter Ranch to be the best outfit it could be, not only to provide for them now, but to leave them a legacy for their future. He wanted to watch them grow up. He could hardly wait to teach them how to rope and ride. He would teach them everything they needed to know to take over the ranch one day.

But first, there was this matter of the rustlers he needed to deal with today. He wasn't looking forward to speaking with the sheriff since he had nothing more concrete than missing cattle and suspicions. Neither he nor Warren knew for certain if someone at the ranch was involved.

Will rubbed a hand over the stubble of his beard. A nagging feeling settled into his gut yesterday at supper and it hadn't left. Something was wrong. He didn't know what. He hated when he got these feelings. It was like danger was coming or already here and he didn't know enough about it to clearly identify it.

Maybe he was just being paranoid about the missing cattle. Or, perhaps it had to do with his upcoming trip to Mohave next week?

He held back a sigh as he realized he was no closer to understanding the premonition this morning than he had been last evening. Hannah and the boys were safe. Snake and Adam would watch for trouble today. They would be there next week, too. Maybe he would ask Warren to stick close to the house while he was gone—just to be safe.

Warren pulled his horse to a stop in front of the sheriff's office. Will followed suit, pushing his fears from his mind. Time to deal with his current troubles and stop borrowing them from tomorrow.

"Morning, Colter, Cahill," the sheriff greeted as they entered his office. "What brings you to town?"

"Missing cattle," Will replied.

"I'm guessing more'n a few if you're here to see me."

"Two hundred head unaccounted for."

The sheriff let out a low whistle. "That's the biggest loss I've heard of yet."

Warren jumped in. "So other ranchers are having trouble, too?"

Nodding, the sheriff said, "Got reports of missing cattle from every ranch from here to Wickenburg. On the mountain. Down in the valley. Seems everyone is having troubles these days."

Will frowned.

"Though, no one else has had more'n seventy or so missing. Course you're running the largest ranch in the area. Don't know if that has anything to do with the larger missing numbers."

"Any idea who's responsible?" Will asked.

The sheriff shook his head.

"We think someone on the ranch is helping them," Warren said.

"Got any proof."

"None yet."

The sheriff looked Will's direction. "You agree with his opinion?"

"Yes. I think it could be one of three of my men. The rest I trust completely."

"Let me guess. Owens is on that list."

Will nodded.

"He'd be my first guess, too. Gives me enough trouble when he's in town. That boy don't know how to stay out of it."

The sheriff went silent. He crossed his arms over his chest and appeared to be thinking. "Got any tracks or anything through your land?"

"Jacob Morgan had some tracks across the northern section of his property. Damaged some of his crop," Will said. "Nothing as obvious on my ranch, though."

"I hate to leave town on a Saturday. Seems it gets pretty busy 'round here then. How 'bout if I stop by on Monday."

"I'm headed off to Mohave for the week. Warren will be around. He can take you out to where Jacob saw the tracks."

"Fair enough. I'll see you Monday then."

Mary smiled as the town of Prescott came into view, despite Beth's whining and Eddie's constant squirming. She wasn't the only one eager to settle into their new home.

The stage pulled to a stop in front of the livery. Georgie exited first. Then he held out his hand for Beth. Eddie bounded down from the stage and darted off towards the livery.

"Eddie! Stay close!" she hollered after him. Georgie helped her down.

Solid ground. At last. Just a short trip from Prescott out to Colter Ranch and she would be home.

"Georgie!" A young woman shouted. Then she shoved her baby into Mary's arms. It took her a second, but she recognized a squealing Caroline Larson as she hugged her older brother tight.

"I can't believe you're here!"

"Linny."

Mary ignored the rest of the conversation. A young man came up next to her and took the baby from her arms, thanking her for her help. She smiled, but moved around him.

Her eyes darted around the area until she spotted both Beth and Eddie. Relief washed over her. On the trip west, she could scarcely count the number of times Eddie slipped from her view. It seemed he was getting better at it the further they got from Texas.

A light touch to her arm brought her attention back to the conversation.

"You remember my sister, Caroline?" Georgie asked.

"Yes, of course." Mary smiled.

"This is her husband, Thomas Anderson, and their baby boy, Drew."

Mary greeted both Thomas and Caroline before introducing her children.

"Are you hungry?" Caroline asked.

Mary nodded.

"Come have dinner with us at Lancaster's."

Taking hold of her children's hands, Mary followed as Caroline led the way.

"Papa!" Eddie screamed, letting go of her hand.

Mary's heart stopped in her chest as she frantically searched the crowded streets for some sign of anyone resembling her husband.

Robert Garrett stepped back into the shadows as the breath left his lungs. She hadn't seen him. But her son had.

He counted out the seconds in his mind as he waited for the boy to return to his mother's side. The boy looked right at him for what seemed like minutes. Eventually he frowned and listened to his mother's pleas to come with her.

As they walked towards Lancaster's, his heart rate returned to normal.

Then his anger burned. Her presence here could ruin everything. All his plans. He waited over a year for the perfect time to strike at Will Colter and Adam Larson. The time was almost at hand.

He wouldn't let her ruin this. He waited too long. He would do whatever was necessary to make sure she didn't interfere.

Then it became abundantly clear to him. He could not keep his appointment with Adam Larson early next week. He would need to have his associate conduct the meeting on his behalf. He needed more time to think about how to deal with Mary Colter and how to keep her from saying anything if she did recognize him.

He pushed the frustrating thoughts aside. He had business to attend to.

As he opened the door to Zach Drake's office, he was greeted by the attorney's secretary. Drake appeared a moment later and led him back to his office.

"What can I help you with today?" Drake asked as he motioned for Robert to take a seat.

"I need a bill of sale for one hundred head from Will Colter. Then I need one for twenty head from Perry Quinn."

"I see your man has been busy," Drake replied as he pulled a folder from the locked drawer in his desk. "It will be a few minutes. Would you like to come back later?"

Robert thought for a moment and decided to wait. He wasn't ready to brave the public streets just in case Mary Colter decided to snoop around where her son had been looking earlier.

As Drake wrote up the papers, Robert rolled his dilemma around in his head. How could he make sure she didn't say anything? How could he bribe her to keep her mouth shut? Threatening her children might work.

Then again, it might not. She might call his bluff. She knew him well enough to know that he wouldn't harm her son. Her daughter, on the other hand, would be easier to dispose of if it came to that.

Only, he doubted if threats alone would be enough. They never had been before.

Oh, he was brilliant. Why hadn't he thought of this before?

He would send his associate to Colter Ranch to meet with Adam Larson. While his associate was there, he could do a little digging. See if he couldn't find out what it would take to purchase Mary Colter's silence.

"Here," Drake said, as he pushed the completed paperwork across the table.

Robert took them and folded them neatly in his coat pocket. He smiled as he left the attorney's office. This situation with Mary Colter could be managed. And his plans could still be carried out. Plans to make Colter and Larson pay.

Once seated inside the large dining hall, Mary breathed a sigh of relief. Whomever Eddie thought looked like her husband either disappeared or Eddie had been mistaken. Perhaps he saw Will. After all, it would be entirely possible that he might be in town today.

"Uncle Will!" Eddie shouted and waved his arm in the air.

So much for her hope.

"Mary?" Will said with wide eyes. "Eddie? Beth? What are you doing here?"

Georgie scooted down the bench to give Will and his cowboy room to take a seat.

"I..." Mary suddenly felt very nervous. Obviously her letter hadn't arrived yet. What if he didn't want them here?

Instead of taking a seat, he moved around the table and stood before her. Then he pulled her into a gentle embrace. When he released her, some of her nervousness left—until she got a better look at the man standing next to her brother-in-law.

Her voice fled as she studied his silver blue eyes. His sandy brown hair was only partially obscured by his brown cowboy hat. His sun bronzed skin gave him a mysterious appeal. He was holding out his hand to take hers.

"Ma'am," he said as his fingers lifted her hand to his lips for a polite kiss.

"Mary, this is Warren Cahill, my foreman."

She smiled and managed a greeting as she quickly drew her hand back to her side.

"When did you arrive?" Will asked as he motioned for her to take a seat. Then he sat across from her and the children. Warren sat next to him.

"We only just arrived. I had hoped you would receive my letter prior to our arrival."

"Might be this," he said patting the envelope in his pocket. "Didn't have a chance to read it yet."

"Oh. Well, I hope you don't mind that we're here." She fidgeted with the coffee mug a young woman set before her.

"Hannah will be thrilled that you're here. She's always eager to receive your letters and I know she's wanted to meet you and the children."

Their food arrived. Mary debated how much more she should say in front of this stranger. Deciding not to reveal more about her circumstances, she redirected the conversation.

"Is Ben Shepherd still around?" she asked.

"Sure is. He's running the meat company now."

Meat company? Obviously Will was doing better than his letters let on.

"Uncle Will," Eddie interjected. "How far is it to your ranch? Will we get there this afternoon?"

"About an hour from here."

Eddie sighed heavily. Then his eyes lit up. "Will I get my own room?"

"Edward," Mary cautioned.

"We'll see what Aunt Hannah says when we get home." Will looked directly at her now. "Where are your things?"

"At the livery. Mr. Anderson said we could leave them there until after dinner. Then we could borrow a wagon and head out. He suggested that he and Caroline might come with us for a visit."

"Hmm. Probably not the best timing for a visit. Both James and Samuel are sick. I'm planning on asking Doc Hank to come back with us."

"Samuel?" she asked.

Will smiled and his face lit up with fatherly pride. "Our second son."

"Two Colter brothers," she whispered.

His smile dimmed some. It seemed he understood that her comment had been rooted in fear. She would hate for his sons to grow up and become like he and Reuben.

When they finished their meal, Will led the way back to the livery. "Warren, can you get Mary and the children settled in a wagon while I go speak with the doctor?"

Warren nodded. Will turned and walked toward the building with the doctor's placard overhead.

"Can you show me to your luggage?" Warren asked.

She started to move toward the stack of trunks and carpet bags when Eddie darted out into the street. A scream tore from her throat as she saw a wagon moving quickly in his direction.

Chapter 5

Warren's head snapped to attention at Mary's scream. He saw the flash of brown cloth as her son darted into the street in front of an oncoming wagon.

With only a few seconds to react, Warren ran into the path of the wagon. His heart raced frantically. He grabbed the boy. Then he tucked him to his chest. He dove for the ground. Just as the wagon arrived at his position, he drew his legs up toward his torso. The dust from the wagon choked the air from his lungs. Thankfully, neither his body nor the boy's made contact with the wagon.

He stood to his feet, hauling the boy to his.

Mary came running toward them. "Eddie!" She knelt down and drew him into a hard embrace. "What were you doing?"

"I thought I saw Papa again."

Warren didn't miss the fear in her eyes as the color drained from her face. In a heartbeat, she recovered. She frowned at her son.

"Don't you ever do that again. You could have been killed," she chastised, her voice thick with emotion.

"Yes, Mama." His chin wobbled with silent sobs.

She grabbed his hand. Looking both ways, she paused before crossing the street. Warren followed behind.

As he loaded Mary's things into the wagon, he couldn't help but wonder why she suddenly showed up on Will's doorstep. Any mention of her husband sent fear marching across her face. Not the sadness of a widow. It was most definitely fear. No, she believed her husband was alive—and it didn't look like she would be pleased to see him again.

Very odd.

But, none of his business. As long as her presence didn't bring harm to the ranch, it mattered little to him why she was there. Maybe he could forget how much she reminded him of Dahlia, with her wide violet eyes, ebony black hair, and creamy porcelain skin. The resemblance was frightening. At least he would have little interaction with her—only at the crowded supper table.

He shook off the thoughts as he hefted another trunk into the wagon. No sense in letting a woman get to him. He traveled that road once and it only brought him pain.

By the time he had the wagon loaded, Will returned with the doctor. Georgie Larson offered to drive the wagon. Doc Hank agreed to drive it back to town after he checked on the Colter boys. With everyone settled, Warren mounted his horse and led the way back home. The wagon followed behind and Will brought up the rear.

As they neared the ranch, Warren felt inexplicably warm. Beads of sweat broke out on his forehead, though the day was overcast and the breeze felt cool against his skin. After a few moments the feeling passed. Hopefully he wasn't catching what Will's sons had. He could not afford to get sick with Will headed to Mohave on Monday.

Mary smiled as Georgie helped her down from the wagon. She made a mental note to write to Maggie Larson and tell her what a fine young man she raised. He had been so thoughtful and helpful on the trip west. Maybe she would bake a special dessert for him as her way of showing her gratitude once she got settled.

A short woman with reddish blonde hair stood in the shade of the porch. Was this Will's Hannah? She looked different than Mary pictured her from the few letters they exchanged.

Eddie darted off toward the stables.

"Eddie!" she lamely shouted after him.

She hoped he would start listening to her again once they settled in their new home. Maybe Will would be a good influence for him. Living without a father for the past few years had taken its toll on her son. She saw it in the moody outburst. It was probably what prompted him to look for his father in a crowd of strangers in town earlier. Some days she wondered if he was better off without a father than he would have been if Reuben were still around.

Will led her and Elizabeth toward the house and up the porch steps. Georgie followed behind.

"Don't worry about Eddie," Will said. "Adam and Julia are always at the corral or in the stables. He'll be fine."

When he stopped in front of Hannah, he made the introductions.

"I am very pleased to meet you, Mary. We have three open rooms upstairs. You are welcome to your pick."

"One room will be plenty for us."

Hannah's brow arched. "At least take a separate room for yourself. Your children are old enough, and it would do you good to have some privacy."

Mary hesitated. She would love the luxury of having her own space, but she felt guilty for doing so. She would be living off their charity for the foreseeable future. A brief image of her son as a teenager flitted through her mind. It was enough for her to agree to a separate room for herself.

"Thank you for your kindness," she said.

A baby's cry shattered the stillness. Hannah's eyebrows drew together in worry.

"I brought Doc Hank," Will said.

"Doc Hank," Hannah greeted. "I'm concerned that the boys might have the pox."

Mary's heart went to her throat. A few years ago, small pox hit the Star C. Both of her children had it. She remembered watching them suffer for weeks with the painful sores. She almost lost Elizabeth then.

Again a brief stab pierced her heart as the soiled dove's claim echoed in her mind. Elizabeth was not hers. She maintained her composure despite the rawness of the thought.

Hannah's voice jarred her from the memory. "I'm concerned about your children."

"They've had the pox before."

Sighing heavily, Hannah said, "Oh, good. I've never known a child to contract the disease twice."

Doc Hank spoke up. "They should be fine. So should any of the adults that had it as a child."

"Georgie," Will said. "Would you mind taking Mary's things upstairs while Hannah and I show the doctor to our children?"

Georgie nodded.

Will and Hannah led the doctor up the stairs. Mary, with Beth in tow, followed behind them. At the top of the stairs, Hannah pointed to the two rooms on the right.

"Perhaps those will work for you?"

Mary agreed.

Will, Hannah, and the doctor entered one of the rooms on the left, leaving Mary and Beth alone.

"Shall we take a peek?" she asked Beth.

"Yes Mama." Beth's voice was soft and sad. Mary hoped that in time both her children would adapt to living here.

She pushed the door open to the room towards the front of the house. There was a small window along one wall. She noted the absence of furniture. With Beth still holding her hand tightly, she entered the second room. The slightly smaller room also boasted a window along one wall. It was as empty as the first. Perhaps Will would make them each a small bed and dresser in time.

"Where do you want this?" Georgie asked from the doorway.

"Anywhere is fine. You can just bring everything up to this room," she said, as she stood in the smaller room. She would take this one, for now. As Eddie and Beth got older, she would move Eddie into the smaller room and share the other with Beth.

"I think you lost someone," a deep voice said behind her.

She slowly turned around to face Warren Cahill. His hand rested firmly on Eddie's shoulder. The hint of a smile played at the corners of his eyes, but his mouth remained steady in a firm line.

"Yes. Thank you."

Warren released his hand from her son's shoulder.

"Ma'am."

He didn't wait for her response before he left. The rapid thuds of heavy footfalls dimmed the further down the stairs he went.

"Eddie, see if you can help Georgie bring the rest of our things up."

"Yes Mama."

She took one last look around the room before she considered unpacking. There wasn't any place to put anything, so she decided on organizing their trunks. At least then it would be easier to find what they needed.

"Chicken pox."

Doc Hank's diagnosis brought a wave of relief over Hannah. She much preferred chicken pox to the much deadlier small pox.

"Here's some dusting powder," Doc Hank said, handing her a small tin. "Use it on the spots to help soothe the itching. If that doesn't seem to help, then try an oatmeal bath a few times a day."

She nodded, glancing at Will. He still looked worried.

"Treat the fever like you would any other. You said they aren't eating?"

"Yes. Samuel takes very little when I nurse him. James turns away from any of the solid food I put in front of him, though he did manage to take some meat juice this morning."

"Try to get Samuel to nurse. If he refuses, then try some bread soaked with cow's milk. For James, meat juice or beef broth will be fine until his stomach feels better."

"Thank you so much, Doc Hank," she said.

Will cleared his throat. "Would you care to stay for supper?"

"Oh, no thank you. I need to be getting back. I did have a few patients expected this afternoon." Doc Hank shook Will's hand and followed him down the stairs.

Hannah sank onto the bed. Chicken pox. Though not as dire of a diagnosis as small pox, with her sons' young ages, it could still be dangerous. *Lord, please protect my boys.*

Tears pooled in her eyes. She could not bear it if anything happened to her sons.

Heavy footfalls sounded on the stairs. Then Will appeared in the doorway.

"Will they be okay?" he asked.

She brushed the tears from her eyes as she nodded, trying to hide her doubt for his sake.

He moved into the room and took her hands in his. Then he pulled her up from the bed and into his comforting arms. For several minutes, they stood there, drawing strength from each other.

"Maybe I should cancel my trip next week."

Hannah leaned back and looked up into his golden brown eyes.

"I know how important this trip is. Don't worry about us. We'll be fine."

He raised a hand and gently cradled the side of her face. When he spoke, his voice sounded heavy. "Are you sure?"

She nodded.

He lowered his head then lightly brushed his lips across hers. "I need to check in with Ben. See if he's got everything under control. I'll try to be back before supper to help with the boys."

She forced a smile to her lips to chase away the gloom in her heart. She felt so helpless watching her children suffer.

"I'd appreciate that."

A few seconds later Will left. She hovered over Samuel's crib, hoping that both of her sons would make it through this illness.

"Welcome, Dear!" Betty Shepherd said as she pulled Mary into a bone crushing hug.

Thankfully, it hadn't lasted long. Mary sucked in a deep breath. She liked this woman that Ben married.

A smile played at the corner of her lips. She still couldn't believe Ben was married. He had worked at the Star C long before she married Reuben. He always seemed reserved and mostly kept to himself, even though Edward Colter and he were close. At family meals, he said little.

Now, here he was—engaging others around the table. It was obvious he adored his wife.

Mary glanced at Julia again. Her welcome hug seemed very stiff and anything but welcoming. When Julia looked up from her food, the smile faded from her lips. An icy stare froze over her eyes.

Surely Julia didn't blame her for Reuben's actions. She hadn't known about the utterly repulsive thing he did to Julia until months later. By then, Julia was gone. There was nothing Mary could have done to help or to prevent it. If she had any inkling he would do such a thing, she would have sent Julia off to the Larson's or someplace safe.

Mary lowered her eyes. She had known about the beatings and

she had done nothing.

What could I have done? She faced similar—even worse cruelties—under Reuben's wrath. She couldn't stop him from harming her, how could she have stopped him from hurting Julia?

Sadly, she doubted if Julia would understand. It seemed none of the Colters knew the private abuse that Mary suffered under the same roof as them. Edward turned a blind eye when he was alive. Will hadn't noticed. If he had, he did nothing. Neither had Julia noticed, until she tasted a brief sip of Reuben's anger.

The conversation around the supper table hummed. Smiles and laughter. Something she missed. Aching loneliness threatened to swallow her. When was the last time she laughed?

She thought back to the days living at home with her parents. She had been happy then. Her parents loved her dearly. Too bad they had been fooled by Reuben's silver tongue.

As supper ended, Mary stood to help clear the table.

"I've got this," Julia snapped.

Mary frowned, but acquiesced. She didn't want to cause trouble or upset the peaceful balance of Colter Ranch.

She managed to keep her memories from invading her thoughts as she watched her children play in the living room following the meal. The memories even stayed suppressed as she put her children to bed—rather on the floor in their room with a blanket. It wasn't until she lay on the floor in her own dark room that the memories took control.

Twelve years ago, she had been only sixteen then, she somehow managed to snag the elusive and dashing Reuben Colter for her beau. She had been so naïve then. Many women tried and failed to capture his heart. Yet she managed to capture it without even trying. Or so she had thought.

Their courtship had been rather short, at his insistence. He charmed her father and her mother. He even charmed her, despite their twelve year age difference.

Her tears began to flow as she thought back to just how much he had charmed her.

His kisses had been sweet and very compelling that night. It wasn't the first time he kissed her, but it was certainly the most ardent. She thought she loved him—had been sure of it then.

"Marry me." The words came as a whispered breath in between heated kisses. He consumed her lips again, not giving her a chance to respond.

When he finally pulled back, he said it again. As she looked back now, she realized, he never really asked. Later she would learn that he never asked for anything. He only took what he wanted or commanded others to action.

But, she was drunk from the taste of his lips and the feel of his hands. She could not say no. Certainly, this was love.

She said yes.

Abruptly he ended his ardent pursuit for the evening. He pointed the carriage toward her home as night began to fall. She would never forget that night—not because it was when she agreed to marry the man that would make her life a living hell. No, it was for what came next.

As he pulled the carriage to a stop in front of the large ranch house, Mary thought it was odd that the building had been so dark. Her parents did not normally retire so early. Reuben seemed nervous. Perhaps he had picked up on her anxiety.

"Shall we tell your parents the good news." Again, it was not a question.

She nodded.

When she went to place her hand on the door knob, she realized it was not latched. Carefully, she pushed the front door open. The house was dark and growing darker by the minute as dusk retired for the night. She reached for the lamp on the stand by the door, only it was gone.

She moved forward into the house, tripping over something rather large on the floor. She managed to step over it. The sound of glass crunching beneath her boot, brought fear to her heart. She took another step, then another until she felt the wall. She followed it to the living room, searching for the next closest lamp.

"Mary." Reuben's voice came from the front entryway. "Light a lamp." His voice was short.

"I'm almost there."

She felt the lamp on the end table. Her fingers connected with the matches nearby. With the flick of her wrist she coaxed a small light from the match then transferred it to the lamp. As the flame grew brighter she turned back toward the front of the house, unprepared for the horrific scene that awaited her.

The thing she tripped over—it was her father's lifeless body lying in a pool of blood. Shards of glass lay next to him. Her mother's sickening death stare glared at her from a nearby chair. She had been brutally beaten in the head. Dried blood trailed down the side of her face.

Mary remembered little of what followed immediately afterwards. Only that the next morning she woke up on the Star C.

She remembered a few bits and pieces from the subsequent days. She buried her parents. She sent a letter off to her sister in New Orleans. It went unanswered. She inherited all of her father's wealth—a staggering sum. She married Reuben. He loved her. He was the only one left to care for her.

Mary burrowed her head into a wadded up corner of her blanket to muffle her sobs. It wasn't until much later, sometime around her sixth year of marriage, that she learned that the sheriff suspected her husband had something to do with her parents' murder.

Even then, she had denied it.

Now, she could see her life for what it was. She had been a pawn in Reuben's schemes to further his wealth. He knew her father left her as sole heir to the Ross family fortune. The only way to secure the fortune for himself was to kill her parents and marry her.

That was the awful, revolting truth. She knew it in her heart. For, if he would lie and deceive her about what happened to the birth of her second son—a son she never got to hold in her arms—and replace him with Beth, the daughter of a whore—then he absolutely could have orchestrated the circumstances that tied her to him for life.

Her sobs diminished as cold hatred filled her veins. She hoped he was dead, rotting in hell to pay for his crimes. All she wanted was to be free from him. She couldn't see beyond that one desire. To hope for any kind of meaningful or happy life—well, Reuben beat that hope from her long ago.

Chapter 6

Colter Ranch

November 12, 1866

Warren wiped the beads of sweat from his forehead onto his shirt sleeve. When he escorted the sheriff around the property that morning, he felt warm despite the cool breeze. The feeling only worsened throughout the day. He was definitely coming down with an illness.

Despite feeling less than perfect, he assured Will this morning that he would look after things at the ranch this week. He wanted to prove worthy of the trust Will placed in him. It wasn't easy filling Ben's shoes, but he thought he was doing a good job. For Will to leave his family in Warren's care—well, that showed just how much his boss depended on him.

The sound of the supper bell echoed across the valley. He pointed his gray gelding toward the ranch. Once at the stables, he rushed through caring for his horse. As he walked toward the ranch house, his stomach cramped, forcing the air from his lungs. He stopped and waited for the feeling to pass.

"You don't have to wait for us," Adam said as he and Julia caught up with him.

"No trouble." Warren managed to answer without giving away his real reason for stopping.

A baby's cry sounded from the other side of the closed door. Julia pushed the door open and ran inside.

"Catherine is sick, too," Hannah said, holding the infant toward Julia.

Julia took her baby and cooed loving sounds over her daughter. Adam followed, leaving Warren standing in the doorway alone.

He closed the door and turned to head back toward the dining room. Suddenly, his head felt like it did when he drank too much as a young man. The room started to spin. He closed his eyes and waited for the feeling to pass.

By the time he made it to the supper table, everyone else was seated. He took his usual seat, next to Will's empty chair. Tonight, Mary and her children sat across from him with Georgie sitting at the end. Adam and Julia now sat to his right. He wondered if this was to be the new seating arrangement.

He wasn't sure he liked it. He was trying to avoid Mary as much as possible. It wasn't anything she did. In fact, she had been very pleasant. She seemed to have a sweet disposition and often kept her thoughts to herself.

No, it was nothing she did or said. It was simply that she reminded him too much of Dahlia. He did not think he could sit across from her every meal being reminded of the wife who had left him.

She bowed her head. Her dark lashes rested softly on her rosy cheeks. At the sound of Adam's voice, Warren closed his eyes and bowed his head for grace. When Adam finished, he lifted his head once again, his eyes meeting hers. She offered a hesitant smile. She was even lovelier than Dahlia had been.

Warren rallied from his thoughts and took the platter of chicken that Hannah held out. He grabbed a few pieces and passed the platter to Adam. Food moved around the table until everyone's plates were full.

"Samuel and James seem less fussy today," Betty commented.

"Yes," Hannah said. "It looks like the fever is gone. Their appetites are returning too."

"I hope it passes as quickly for Catherine," Julia said.

"It'll be several days yet before the spots fade. The dusting powder the doctor gave us seems to help ease the itching." Hannah giggled. "Though, I don't think Samuel is old enough to understand what itchy feels like."

Betty laughed.

As Warren bit off a piece of fried chicken, it turned to gravel in his mouth. He swallowed and his stomach cramped again. He felt the perspiration pop out on his forehead and neck.

"Are you alright?" Mary's soft voice drew his attention.

He took a deep breath. "Fine."

She gave a slight nod and turned her attention back to cutting up Beth's food.

Other conversation buzzed around him, seeming so loud that it hurt his ears. Every noise grated on his nerves. He took a look at his barely touched plate.

His stomach roiled and he shot to his feet. "Excuse me."

Then he ran for the door. The horrible feeling that washed over him ended with him falling to his knees in the grass just a few feet from the door. He retched as his entire body warmed. When he tried to right himself, dizziness swarmed him.

"Warren?" Mary looked up from the meal just in time to see a very sickly looking cowboy dash from the room. Without thinking, she stood to her feet and followed him from the house.

When she caught up with him, he sat on the ground bent over and clutching his stomach. He lost his dinner.

She came up behind him and laid a hand on his shoulder. He stiffened at the touch. He closed his eyes. She could tell he was fighting for control.

"It's okay," she said reassuringly.

He retched again.

She waited for a minute to see if he looked like he would be sick again. Sweat soaked the back of his shirt. His body shook slightly. She placed her hand on his elbow.

"Let's get you to the bunkhouse."

He groaned, but did not resist when she helped him stand. She looped her arm around his waist. He lifted his arm and rested it on her shoulders. They walked slowly toward the bunkhouse. As she reached to open the door, he shook his head.

"I can manage," he said.

He looked like he would wither to the floor as soon as she let go of him, so she reached for the knob a second time. He put his hand over hers, keeping her from opening the door. When he looked down at her, she stopped breathing. A tender look passed over his face, but it was quickly stamped out by a frown.

He removed his arm from her shoulder and pushed her arm away from his waist. Then he opened the door and stumbled toward his bunk.

The laughter of the cowboys as they ate supper died abruptly. Mary felt every eye follow her as she moved towards Warren's bunk. She reached out a hand to place it on his forehead. He grabbed her wrist stopping her short.

"I'm fine."

He released his grip quickly—something Reuben never would have done. No, he would have squeezed harder, turning his dark eyes on her in warning. Warren did none of those things. Instead he closed his eyes.

She waited a few seconds then gently touched his forehead. He was burning up!

"Warren?"

He opened one eye.

"Have you ever had the chicken pox?"

"I don't know." His eye flitted shut.

"I think you do now."

He groaned and rolled on his side so his back faced her.

She stood and turned to face the crowd of cowboys staring at her. Though she'd never been able to handle Reuben, she had always been able to command some respect from his men. *Maybe it was because they feared him.* The thought almost shook her confidence. She took a deep breath.

"If he gets worse, please come get me or Hannah."

Most of the cowboys nodded. Jed was the only one that answered. "Yes ma'am."

She headed back to the ranch house. Once she sat at the table again, she explained what happened to Hannah. She agreed with Mary's assessment. Warren probably caught the chicken pox from the children. They would know for sure when the spots appeared in a few days.

Warren's breath came in shallow, ragged bursts. He opened his eyes to the moon's silver light shining in through the west window of the bunkhouse. His stomach knotted.

He closed his eyes again to clear away his confusion. When he opened them again, he remembered that he got sick after supper.

A creak of the floor boards drew his attention. One of the men, with boots in hand, moved toward the front door and opened it. When he stepped through the door, he carefully pulled it shut behind him.

Warren's heart began to race. Was this the rustler's inside man?

If so, he couldn't lose a minute. He slid from his bunk. As he reached for his boots on the floor, his head swam. No matter how much he wanted to fall back into bed, he couldn't. He had to follow the cowboy—see where he was going.

He swiped his hand under his pillow to grab his revolver and gun belt. Awkwardly, he strapped it on while sitting. Slowly he stood, with boots in hand, and left the stillness of the bunkhouse.

He spotted the figure moving toward the stables. Warren moved off the porch. Leaning against the railing, he put on his boots before running after the figure, careful to stay in the shadows until he made it to the barn. The cowboy left the barn with saddled horse in tow. Then he mounted the horse and took off towards the herd.

Warren hurriedly saddled the first horse he came to, ignoring the waves of nausea washing over him. He mounted the horse and headed in the direction of the rider, thankful again for the full moon.

As he neared the herd, he found the rider near the base of the mountain. He couldn't tell if the rider had seen him or not. He moved around the herd to get closer to the rogue cowboy.

Once he was as far as he dared go on horseback, Warren dismounted and tied the horse to a tree. He proceeded on foot, begging the dizziness to subside. He almost had the traitor identified.

"Owens!" A voice whispered up ahead.

The cowboy stopped. "Pete, is that you."

"Shh!"

The voices grew too quiet for Warren to distinguish. He carefully made his way to a closer vantage point.

"Where's my money?" Owens asked.

"You'll get it soon 'nough. You still owe us a few more head before ya get paid."

"I've done my part. Now pay up."

"Two hundred head ain't quite the same as two fifty. Boss ain't gonna pay until we get the rest."

"How can I be sure you'll pay me at all?"

The clink of some coins sounded in the crisp night air.

"That ought to hold ya for a bit. The rest will be paid when you deliver."

"I don't think I can get too many more," Owens said. "Colter is getting pretty suspicious."

"If ya want the rest of the money, you better find a way to make it happen."

Owens cursed. Then the brush rattled and he appeared a few feet from Warren.

Warren ducked behind a boulder. He listened to the sound of Owens's feet move further away from him. His stomach tightened and bile rose in his throat. He was going to be sick again. He couldn't be. Not here. Not with Pete and Owens still out there.

He clamped a hand tight over his mouth and hurried to where he tied his horse. He mounted it and set the horse at a gentle pace towards home. Within a few hundred yards, he couldn't hold back the bile clogging his throat. He leaned over the side of the horse and threw up.

Wiping the back of his hand across his mouth, he begged God not to let him be discovered. This information was too important. It was enough to haul Owens off to jail and stop Will from suffering any more losses.

The sick feeling soon passed. Warren made it back to the stables before Owens. He removed the saddle as quickly and quietly as he could. Then he hurried back to the bunkhouse and fell into bed.

As soon as the sun rose, he would head into town to talk to the sheriff.

When Warren didn't show up for breakfast this morning, Mary volunteered to check on him. She already figured out that he probably wouldn't want solid food, so she decided to prepare some meat juice for him. She retrieved the iron meat juice press from its resting place on the shelf. Then she placed it on the work table in the kitchen. Taking a large piece of beef from the boiling pot on the stove, she placed it on the lower cup of the press. Then she turned the crank on the top of the press until the heavy flat iron surface made contact with the meat. She kept turning the crank until the juice started to flow from the meat.

She double checked to make sure the bowl sat flush against the spout of the cup on the press. Then she continued turning the crank of the press until she squeezed all the juice from the beef that she could.

Once she was done, she cleaned up quickly. Then she took the strong concentrated beef juice in the bowl with her to the bunkhouse. She knocked softly on the door. No answer.

She assumed Warren and the night shift were the only ones in the bunkhouse, as all the other cowboys already left to care for the herd. So, she opened the door.

Warren's still form lay on the same bunk where she last saw him. All of the other bunks in the front room were empty. She glanced toward the back room. That must be where the night shift slept.

She set the bowl down on the floor near Warren's bunk then she moved a chair from the long chow table and placed it next to his bunk.

"Warren." Mary touched his arm. When he didn't rouse, she called his name again.

His eyes blinked open. Tears formed rivers from the corner of those blue eyes down the side of his cheeks.

"Dahlia." He reached a hand up and cupped her face in it, running his thumb over the high points of her cheekbone.

Mary froze at the gentle touch. Even though she understood that it wasn't for her, she savored it—so foreign it was from the way she was used to being treated.

"You came back. You came back for me."

The words jolted her back to reality. She was a married woman. She shouldn't let him touch her that way, even if he was delusional. She clasped his hand in both of hers. Then she gently laid his hand by his side.

"You're sick," she reminded him. "I've brought some meat juice." She leaned down and retrieved the bowl from the floor.

"I've missed you," Warren said. "I always hoped you might not mean what you said. I hoped you would come back."

Mary's face heated. He didn't realize he was confessing his deepest feelings to a complete stranger. Whoever this Dahlia was, she had hurt him pretty deeply—she could see it in his eyes.

"Hush, now. Drink this," she said, lifting a spoonful of the juice to his lips.

He obediently swallowed. She repeated the routine several more times until he refused more. Then he closed his eyes.

Unconsciously, he began to scratch at his arm.

"Warren, stop."

His eyes flew open. "Mary?"

"Let me see your arm."

He held it out. She unbuttoned the sleeve and pushed it up his arm. Sure enough, he had pox marks all along his arm. She took a closer look at his face and neck. They were small, but visible there as well.

She was glad she brought some of the dusting powder with her. "Remove your shirt."

He frowned at her.

"So I can put some of the powder on the marks. It will help soothe the itching."

He still didn't move.

She narrowed her eyes as a challenge.

"I can put the powder on myself."

"No you can't. Not if you have marks on your back. Besides, it's much easier if someone else helps you."

"Fine." Warren sat upright in his bed. Leaning forward, he pulled his shirt over his head, careful not to smack his arm on the bunk above him. "How long have you been here?"

She placed the bowl on the floor and retrieved the dusting powder as she answered. "Awhile. I gave you some—"

The words piled up on her tongue as she looked at his bare chest. Strong muscles bulged in all the right places. The sight left her mute.

A smirk settled onto his face. "That bad?"

Mary stammered. "Ah... Turn around. Let me... See your back."

His back, equally attractive, was also covered in pox marks. She remembered the dusting powder and began sprinkling it on his back. When she finished, she handed the tin to him.

"I think you can manage the rest."

She stood, wanting to run from the building, terrified by how he affected her. As she moved away, he reached for her hand.

"Thank you," he said, before giving her hand a squeeze and letting it go.

Without looking at him she replied, "You're welcome."

Then she bolted for the door.

Chapter 7

A few days later, Warren finally left the confines of the bunkhouse. Will was due back today and he felt guilty for not going out with the herd for the entire week. He had several things that needed his attention before he could ride out for the day.

First on his list, he needed to fix a hole in the chicken coop. As he neared the building with the cackling chickens, a flash of gray passed the corner of his eye. He turned to catch Mary hurrying from the area.

He jogged a few steps to catch up to her, certain now that she had been avoiding him.

"Mary. Mrs. Colter. Wait."

She paused and turned slightly—only enough that he could see half of her face. As he studied her now, he wasn't entirely sure why he thought she looked like Dahlia. From this perspective, they barely shared any similar features—nothing more than hair and eye color. Yet, she had a certain charm and quiet beauty about her.

"Have I offended you in some way?" he asked, trying to get to the bottom of her strange behavior over the last few days.

She shook her head slightly.

He frowned, perplexed. He didn't remember much from the first few days he was sick. He'd been delirious with the fever. But, he was pretty sure she hadn't attended him after the first day. He tried to recall what he might have said or done to cause her to fear him.

"I didn't… I didn't treat you poorly when I was sick, did I?"

Again, nothing more than a slight shake of her head.

Warren stepped closer and gently touched her arm. She withdrew it from his reach with incredible speed before she turned fiery eyes toward him.

"Don't touch me," she said through gritted teeth.

"Is that what I did? Did I touch you?"

Red settled over her high cheekbones. Her gaze darted away.

He had touched her.

Then a foggy memory became clearer. He thought she was Dahlia. He remembered caressing her face.

"I'm sorry if I mistook you for someone else. I wasn't in my right mind. I hope you can forgive me?"

The scarlet on her cheeks faded to a light pink. She nodded.

An awkward silence settled between them. He glanced at the empty egg basket on her arm. Odd that she would head back to the house with no eggs. Then it dawned on him. She had been avoiding him. She was going back empty handed because he was there. He reached for the basket.

"Let me carry that for you."

She slowly released the basket.

"I was just headed that way myself. Wanted to patch that hole before Will gets back."

Once at the coop, he handed her the basket. She started to go inside, but stopped and looked back at him.

"Who's Dahlia?"

The name broke open the deep wound in his heart. He bit down hard to stem the flood of emotions her name always evoked. At last, he managed to say, "My wife."

Mary studied him with narrowed eyes for a second. "But not anymore."

The fact that it wasn't a question bothered him. Had he been so easy to read?

"No."

"I'm sorry she hurt you."

The softly spoken words took nearly a minute to register in his mind. Mary disappeared into the coop to gather eggs before he fully felt the impact. Those words were spoken from an equally wounded heart.

As he set about mending the coop, he couldn't shake the feeling that he forgot something else from earlier in the week. Something important. Something related to the missing cattle.

Mary bit her lip to hold back the tears. She hadn't expected to feel such compassion for Warren's pain. It surprised her that she had any left—especially since she felt nothing but jealousy toward the woman she never met.

For the past few days, she could think of nothing else. The way he gently cradled her face. What kind of woman would reject such love? Yet, Warren's wife had. She didn't have to know all of the details of what happened to piece that one thought together. He loved her. She left him. He still held out pointless hope that she would return.

Yes, Mary was deeply, bitterly jealous. If her husband loved her even a small fraction of the way Warren obviously loved his wife, she would be overjoyed. She would try to find him—to reunite with him.

Instead, she dreaded the possibility of ever seeing Reuben and being subjected to his brutality again.

She hated him. Feared him.

The only thoughts she had of her husband was escaping him once and for all.

A tear plopped down on the top of her hand as she reached for the next egg. She took a deep breath. She would not cry. Breakfast hadn't even been served yet. She needed to pull herself together.

Taking a deep breath, she forced herself to think on other things. Her children. They often provided the best distraction from her thoughts and things she could not control.

Though they had been on the ranch for only a week, she needed to think about schooling them. She hadn't asked Hannah if there was a school in town, or if it made sense to send her children there. It was something she needed to decide soon so their learning didn't lapse.

Once she collected enough eggs to fill the basket, she returned to the ranch house. Rosa and Hannah already hovered over the stove, frying potatoes. Mary set the basket on the small table in the kitchen. She began cracking eggs into a large bowl.

"Will and Ben should be back today," Betty said as she bounced baby Samuel on her hip.

"Yes. I can hardly wait to have him home," Hannah said.

"Does he travel much?" Mary asked, trying to make polite conversation.

"In the two years we've been married, he hardly leaves the ranch for more than a trip into town. This is only the second time he's traveled for more than a day. Never been gone this long before."

Mary found the wistful tone in Hannah's voice hard to relate to. The times Reuben traveled away from the Star C had been some of the best times of their marriage. For a few days, she didn't have to fear his harsh correction or late night visits to her bed. It was the only time she experienced peace.

She shouldn't be surprised that Will's wife would miss him. She always knew he was very different from his brother. In just the few short days she watched the couple interact, Mary figured out that Will treated his woman far better than Reuben had.

"You haven't said much of your husband," Betty commented.

Hannah turned her direction with sympathy in her eyes.

Mary frowned. She didn't want their pity.

"There's not much to say."

"Because he's dead!" Eddie's voice screeched from the doorway. "Papa is dead!"

The hatred and anger dripping from her son's eyes scared her. It too closely resembled a look she'd seen often on her husband's face.

"We don't know that." She was surprised by her own soft response.

"It doesn't matter." Eddie kicked the doorframe with his foot. "He left us. I wish he were dead."

Betty's round chocolate eyes softened as she reached out a hand to Eddie's shoulder. He shrugged it off.

"I hate him!" Eddie screamed before running from the room. The front door banged open then shut. "I hate him!"

Searing pain rooted Mary's feet in place. She hated that her son was hurting, but she had no words of comfort to offer him. She hated Reuben far more than he did. She didn't trust herself to say otherwise at the moment.

"I could go after him," Betty suggested after a minute.

Mary bristled, feeling judged as a poor parent. "He just needs some time."

Sounds of sizzling potatoes and frying eggs kept the room from falling into complete silence.

Her heart churned within her chest. How much of Eddie's anger was his own and how much was a reflection of hers? She didn't want her son growing up to hate his father—whether or not Reuben deserved it. She didn't want him to be angry and bitter. If he stayed this way, would he turn out just like his father?

Guilt warred with regret. At length she finally wiped her hands on her apron and wordlessly left the room. She headed toward the barn.

As she neared, she heard Warren's distinct deep voice.

"Why do you wish he were dead?"

Mary's stomach lurched. She stopped her forward progress and stayed out of sight just outside of the barn entrance.

"Cause he hurt Mama."

A tear slid unbidden down her cheek. Sadness mixed with motherly pride.

"Because he left?"

"Naw. She don't miss him."

Guilt pierced her heart again. She had done such a poor job of hiding her real feelings.

"He hurt her. Before he left. He always made her cry. A lot. Left marks on her arms. I seen 'em. She tried to hide them. But I knew."

How? He couldn't have been more than six or seven when Reuben left. How had he seen? How had he known?

"And that's why you wish he were dead?"

Eddie's voice quivered as he answered, "I wish he were dead so I could have a new Papa. One that would make Mama smile instead of cry."

Moisture covered her cheeks. She lifted a sleeve to her eyes as her heart broke over the protective love of her son. Sobs pressed at the back of her throat, but she swallowed them away. She'd had much practice hiding her sobs, though perhaps she was not as good at hiding them as she thought.

Warren whispered something to Eddie then silence fell over the barn. She quickly moved to the side just out of sight as Warren and Eddie emerged.

"Why don't you go on up for breakfast?" Warren suggested. "Let Mrs. Colter know I'll be up in a minute."

"Yes sir."

Then Eddie darted off as a carefree young boy again.

"How much did you hear?" Warren asked.

Mary took a shaky breath and emerged from her hiding spot. "Enough."

"So you're not a widow then."

The words came out hard. A wave of defensiveness surged within her chest. "No. I'm an abandoned wife who has done her best to make a life for her children on her own for these past two years."

"Then what brought you here, now?" The narrowing of Warren's eyes hinted at distrust. She wondered how much of his distrust was against women in general or her specifically.

"I was tired. Am tired. I need help. Eddie needs a man to look up to. I knew Will wouldn't refuse us. I knew he would be a good influence for my son."

"So you're here to live off of his charity."

"What have I done to cause you to distrust me so?"

"Nothing."

Rosa emerged from the ranch house and headed towards the bunkhouse, distracting him for a moment.

"Yet." Warren added under his breath.

She heard the unspoken warning loud and clear. If she did anything to cause trouble on this ranch, she would have to deal with him.

Jutting her chin in the air she marched toward the ranch house, hoping she looked more confident than she felt. She wouldn't let Warren Cahill control her. She was done with men trying to change the course of her life.

Chapter 8

A deep pang of homesickness settled into Will's stomach as he pulled the wagon to a stop in front of the ranch house. He missed his wife. He missed his sons. His arms felt achingly empty.

The door opened as he jumped down from the wagon.

"Will!" Hannah ran down the steps, launching herself into his arms.

The sweet smell of his wife's hair tickled his nose as he held her close to his chest. Oh how he missed her. It had been only a few days, but it seemed much longer.

She leaned her head back and looked up at him, blue eyes shimmering with joy and love. He leaned down, ignoring the growing audience, and swallowed her lips with his. A fire ignited in his chest and he longed for later in the evening, when they could be alone. She broke off the kiss and stepped back.

With a shy smile, she whispered, "I missed you."

A roguish smile curled up one side of his mouth in response.

The rest of the family pressed in for a greeting.

"Welcome home, Will," Julia said, giving him a hug.

"Come," Hannah said, taking his hand. "We just set supper on the table."

He groaned. "I need to take care of the horses first."

"I'll see to them," Warren volunteered. "You go on in with your family."

Will nodded. As Warren started to walk away, he took a second look. Did he have chicken pox marks on his face and neck?

Hannah must have caught his surprise. "He was sick earlier in the week," she explained. "He's doing a lot better than he had been."

A surge of protectiveness overtook him. He frowned. "What about you and the children? Who took care of you?"

"We managed just fine. Don't worry."

He allowed Hannah to lead him into the house and back to the dining room. "Paww paw!" James squealed in delight from his highchair. Will walked over and kissed him on the top of his head before taking his seat at the head of the table.

Following grace, the family started asking questions. He interrupted them with his own.

"James and Samuel?" he asked looking at his wife.

"Other than a few lingering spots, both are well."

"Good." He had been terrified of leaving them while they were sick. It nearly broke his heart. But, this meeting in Mohave was important. It proved to be good timing that he and Ben arrived when they did.

"And the meeting?" Adam asked.

"It went well."

"Very well," Ben added.

"We'll be supplying beef to the military fort and the town. Hardyville, too."

Adam let out a low whistle. "Wow."

"It opens up an opportunity for us to sell further down river. We could drive them to Hardyville and ship whatever is needed down the Colorado."

Warren entered and took his seat. "Sounds like it was a good trip."

Will nodded. "I'll fill you in on the details later. How were things while I was gone?"

The question from his boss was to be expected. "Fine," Warren answered, despite the nagging feeling that something important had happened earlier in the week and he just wasn't remembering it.

As the conversation hummed around him, he chanced a glance at Mary. She looked at him at the same time. Her gaze quickly darted away.

He didn't trust her. Plain and simple. Something was not as it appeared to be with her. He wondered why she let them all believe she was a widow, when she clearly wasn't. Something about it bothered him.

He mentally shrugged it off as he took another bite of his food. An image from a moonlit night invaded his vision. He was on horseback. Sick. Following someone.

Was this what he couldn't remember from earlier in the week?

Two voices. A stranger. And…

"Owens." The name leaped from his lips unbidden.

Every eye turned towards him. Concern wrinkled Will's brow.

Warren cleared his throat. "Sorry, I was thinking out loud."

Then he turned toward Will and kept his voice low. "We need to talk."

Following the meal, Ben and Will joined him in the front parlor—away from the women's hearing while they cleaned up after supper. Throughout the meal, the foggy images from the other night solidified. Owens was helping the rustlers.

"I was delirious with fever," he began. "So, I wasn't sure until this evening if what I remembered was a dream or real. Something you said at supper triggered it.

"On Monday night, I woke to him sneaking from the bunkhouse. I followed him out to the edge of the herd, where he met some guy named Pete."

"What'd he look like?" Ben asked.

"Not sure. It was hard to tell in the dark. Didn't impress me as someone familiar."

"Go on," Will said.

"Anyway, I heard him tell Owens he'd get paid when he delivered another fifty head. He paid some money that night. Owens complained that it would be hard. That we were watching more closely now than we had been."

Will rubbed a hand across the stubble of his beard. Ben frowned.

"I think we should watch him. Follow him to see if we can get to whoever is running the rustling operation."

Will shook his head. "I want to take him into the sheriff tomorrow. Let the sheriff deal with the bigger problem. I'm not going to let Owens spend one more day on this ranch risking my family's safety."

"I understand."

"First thing in the morning, we restrain him and take him in."

Warren nodded his agreement. It wasn't his ranch. Even though he'd rather get to the rustlers, it was Will's call. He had a traitor in his midst and he wanted him gone as soon as possible. Maybe he'd feel differently if he had a wife and children to protect. He held back a snort of disgust. Dahlia saw to it that he'd never be in that position.

Hannah smiled as Will entered their bedroom. The sweet scent of soap from his bath earlier lingered on his skin. Oh how she missed him!

She watched as he slipped out of his trousers and shirt and slid into bed next to her.

He turned to face her. She moved closer, pressing her lips against his. The kiss was short lived. Soft and gentle. And distracted. Something was weighing on his mind.

He cradled her against his chest with one arm wrapped around her shoulder. He leaned over and turned down the lamp, then settled back into place.

Rubbing his hand up and down her arm, he breathed a heavy sigh.

"I'm so glad to see our sons are healthy." His voice caught.

"God answered our prayers."

He groaned. "I confess I did a poor job of asking for His help. I was so worried."

She snuggled closer. "Regardless, they are well now."

Silence stretched and Hannah closed her eyes, thinking he was ready to sleep. She startled when he spoke.

"How have Mary and the children been getting along?"

She hesitated. "Well enough, I suppose."

"Hmm. Something happen while I was gone?"

"She's not widowed. Did you know that? Your brother just left her."

"You know, with the boys being sick, I'm not entirely sure I remember if she said one way or the other."

"Well, Betty, Julia, and I were certain she said she was a widow."

"It doesn't matter. Not really," Will said. "She needs our help. She can stay as long as she likes. Chances are that life with us is far better than with Reuben—wherever he may be."

Hannah sighed. "Eddie is very bitter and angry. He said several times that he wished his father was dead."

Will snorted. "I'm not surprised. It's no secret Mary and Reuben did not love each other. I'm sure Eddie picked up on some of that."

"What was he like? Your brother? Do you think he hit Mary?"

Will sighed heavily. The bed vibrated up and down as he turned on his side. "I used to think he wasn't that way. But after… After what he did with Julia, I'm afraid I may have credited him with more honor than he has."

"Then it's possible."

"If she says he did, I would be more inclined to believe her."

Sadness weighed down her heart. Poor Mary. Living with a harsh husband.

"What do you think would happen if Reuben knew you were here?"

She felt his body stiffen next to her. Several seconds ticked by.

"I think he'd try to take away everything I worked for—everyone I love."

Silence fell. She worried that her husband sounded afraid. He was always so strong. He always protected them.

She tried to shake off her own fear.

"Let's not worry about what we cannot control," she suggested.

He sighed heavily. "You're right, dear wife. God will protect us all."

Then his lips searched for hers. She returned his kiss with all the longing of the days spent apart. She loved her husband and relished showing him as only a wife can.

The next morning came too quickly. Will wanted to stay in the sweet embrace of his wife. It was so much more pleasant than the task that awaited him for the day.

For almost three years, Owens worked for him. There had been a few times when Owens gave him trouble, like on the drive west. But, for the most part, he had been reliable.

He remembered an incident on the drive west when Owens bucked his authority. He considered leaving him in Santa Fe. At this moment, he wished he had.

Instead of eating breakfast with his wife and family, Will followed Warren out to the bunkhouse. They agreed last night that it might be better to take Owens by surprise while there were other loyal men around to help.

He touched the Colt .45 holstered at his side. He hoped it wouldn't be necessary, though he feared it would. Owens always had a temper.

Warren swung the door to the bunkhouse open with little fan fare. "Owens. We'd like a word with you."

Owens eyes went wide. Panic covered his face. His eyes darted around the room as if he were a caged animal. His hand went to his side.

Will and Warren both trained their guns on him.

"I wouldn't do that," Snake's voice came from behind Owens as he pressed a knife to Owens's throat.

Owens's hand froze, hovering over his side arm.

Warren nodded and Snake shoved Owens up against the wall. Warren tied Owens's hands behind his back as Will explained.

"We know you sold out. We know you've been helping the rustlers."

Owens cursed. "Watcha gonna do about it?"

"Take you in and let the sheriff deal with you."

Owens kicked his feet. Snake pressed the knife closer.

"Ya ain't gettin' out of this," Snake said.

Finally, Owens stopped squirming. Warren took his arm and led him from the bunkhouse where Ben waited with three saddled horses, one of which had a long lead tied to the horn of Will's horse. Warren helped Owens mount. Then Will and Warren mounted their horses, with Will in the lead.

"You want an extra man?" Snake offered.

Will shook his head. He and Warren could manage.

The ride to town seemed longer than normal. Will scanned each tree and shrub, looking for any accomplices. He hadn't thought bringing Owens in would be easy.

Only, it was just that. He and Warren arrived uncontested at the sheriff's office. After the sheriff took down Will's statement both Warren and Will returned to the ranch.

An uneasiness settled over Will as he brushed down his horse. This wasn't over. Somehow he instinctively knew it, even though he didn't know why.

Chapter 9

Hannah tried not to think about Will's mission this morning as she scrubbed the laundry. It made her nervous knowing one of the cowboys betrayed her husband.

The hair on the back of her neck stood on end. For the second time in the last hour she couldn't shake the feeling that she was being watched. She let the shirt slip from her wet fingers into the wash basin. Then she wiped her hands on her apron. Slowly she leaned down to make sure the rifle was within reach—if she needed it. Then she scanned the area around her, like Will taught her. She looked for anything that seemed even slightly out of place.

For several minutes she looked around. Finally, after seeing nothing other than Mary heading her way, she dismissed her earlier notions as foolish. She was just overreacting to the news that they had a betrayer in their midst.

"Need some help?" Mary asked as she moved toward the wash basin.

Hannah still hadn't figured out her mysterious sister-in-law. Mary had been rather quiet since arriving. This was the first time she offered to help with laundry.

"Sure," Hannah said, welcoming a break from the washboard.

Mary nodded in response. Then she picked up the bar of soap and shirt and began the routine of lathering the shirt, plunging it in the water, and scrubbing. Hannah marveled at the speed with which she washed the clothing. When the shirt was clean, she handed it to Hannah to wring out and hang on the line.

"This is how I supported us for the last two years." Mary's statement came so softly and without warning that Hannah almost thought she imagined it.

"Washing, ironing, mending. Long hours over a wash basin. I'll admit it's why I've been reticent to help before now."

She turned sad eyes toward Hannah.

"So, I apologize. I will do my best to help you in whatever way I can. I don't want to be a burden to you."

"You're not a burden," Hannah replied. How could she think that?

"Still, I don't expect your husband to provide for me and my children. But, I do sincerely appreciate his willingness to do so." Mary glanced away. "And yours. I don't deserve such kindness."

Hannah's heart broke at her words. Of course she deserved their kindness. "You're family. You're always welcome here. We're happy to have you."

Mary let out a slow long breath as she handed Hannah the next shirt.

"You have no idea what it was like. Living in fear. What had I done this time to deserve such harsh treatment?"

Hannah was confused. "It must have been hard living without your husband."

Mary snorted. "I was talking about what it was like living *with* him. He was a harsh, cold man. There was only one thing important to him and that was wealth. Not just money, but large sums of it which he hoarded for himself."

Silence fell as Hannah wondered how to respond or if she should at all. The bitterness that coated Mary's words left her treading carefully.

"The past few years without him… The only fear I had was that he would come back. Each time the local sheriff or his men found an unidentified man or his remains, he requested that I come to see if it was Reuben. And each time, I hoped it was. I wanted to be free from him. Only the body was never his. He's still out there somewhere."

Hannah wrung out a pair of trousers. Her heart hurt for this stranger before her.

"I even considered divorce. That way I wouldn't have to go with him if he came back. I never had enough money—not beyond what we needed to survive, so I couldn't afford a divorce."

She took the next item from Mary's hand, a frown creasing her forehead.

Mary held onto the garment for a second or two, until Hannah looked her in the eye. "I know it sounds cold, uncaring. But, if you met Reuben you would understand. He has a way of driving all feeling from a soul until only numbness and compliance remain. Please don't judge me by my disdain of my husband."

As Mary released her hold on the garment, Hannah considered her words. She hoped she didn't come across as judging, even if she couldn't fathom such a heartless reaction to one's spouse. Though, she had the love and devotion of her own husband, she simply could not understand.

Opting to change the subject, Hannah asked, "Are you thinking of schooling your children?"

Mary sighed deeply, the heaviness of their previous thoughts visibly slinking away. "Yes. Is there a school nearby?"

"Some of the children travel to town for schooling, though most out our way are taught at home."

"I suppose I should purchase some materials then."

Hannah thought for a moment. She had some materials that might be appropriate for Mary's children, though she wasn't sure if she should explain why she had them. She decided to plunge forward anyway.

"I have some primary readers. They are probably better suited for Beth, but there may be a few that would work for Eddie."

At Mary's frown, she continued, "Will has been trying to regain his ability to read after an accident a few years ago. He found it too frustrating, so he let it go. But, I still have the books we purchased. You can use them if you like."

"Thank you."

Pete Vance smiled, pleased with his perfect hiding spot near the lake. He was close enough to overhear the two Mrs. Cotlers talking. When Robert Garrett commanded him to spy on the women, he wasn't sure he would be able to find much useful information.

Oh, but he had been pleasantly surprised. It sounded as if Mary Colter wanted nothing more than a divorce from her husband—a Reuben Colter. He was sure Garrett could arrange the necessary paperwork. It would provide the leverage he needed to keep her quiet—about what, Pete wasn't sure.

He learned early on not to question Garrett. The man had a short temper and was no stranger to inflicting violence. Though Pete could take care of himself, he felt it was in his best interest not to ask questions.

Besides, Garrett hired him to be his eyes and ears. He also hired him to take care of any number of situations. It was a great job that suited him and his many disguises well.

His current identity, Pete Vance, was perfect for working with Owens and the rustlers. Oh, he wasn't directly involved in the rustling. He believed, as did Garrett, in keeping a degree or two of separation between him and the end crime—unless it came to killing. Then he was all in.

He wondered for a moment what Garrett might want to do about Owens. From best he could tell, Will Colter and his man took Owens into the sheriff this morning. Perhaps Garrett would have him tie up that loose end. Or maybe he would just ask that Pete Vance fade away to be replaced by a younger, more business-like man?

Pete smiled again. He had so many disguises. Really any would work well.

After the women finished laundry and went inside, Pete waited a few more minutes. Then he left as carefully as he came—in broad daylight, nonetheless. Colter was a fool for not keeping better watch over his womenfolk and children. It would come back to hurt him in the end.

And it would make Robert Garrett very pleased indeed.

Pete never failed to be amused by the uppity righteous crowd and their complete oblivion to danger. It's why they were the easiest targets of all—the thought that they were presently in danger never even crossed their minds. It was almost too easy. Almost.

The next afternoon, the sound of an approaching rider stole Mary's attention from her children's studies. She moved to the front window, more out of curiosity than concern. She was still acclimating to what a typical week was like on Colter Ranch. She knew Will stayed close to the house today, since he promised to finish a dresser for her by evening.

A man in a fine suit dismounted. Something about his stance—the way he carried himself as he met Will coming from the barn—was eerily familiar. She knew this man.

Her mind frantically searched. Her heart raced.

Then the fear settled in the back of her throat, restricting her breath.

It can't be. That's impossible.

Her instinct argued ferociously with her mind.

When they turned toward the house, she stepped back from the window. She rushed from the parlor, back into the dining room.

"Children, that's enough studying for the afternoon. Why don't you go outside and play for awhile."

Eddie wasn't fond of schoolwork, so he jumped up first.

"Wait for me!" Beth darted after him.

"Stay close to the house!"

Mary sighed. She hoped they would make it out of the house before Will and his visitor entered. She couldn't fathom what the children would say if they recognized Will's guest. She wasn't sure what she would say.

How had he found them? Had Will been in contact with him before? Is that how he knew where to find her?

None of it made sense. She and the children arrived at the ranch less than two weeks ago. That was not long enough for word to get around that they were here.

What if he ran into Hiram Norton's man, Enoch Fowler?

No. Enoch Fowler would have killed him or dragged him back to Texas.

The door to the ranch house opened.

It was time to face him.

She squared her shoulders and forced a smile to her lips, though she felt no such amiable feelings at his presence. Every muscle tensed in her body as her mind begged her to run.

"Hannah, we have a visitor," Will announced as he moved toward the dining hall.

Hannah stepped from the kitchen, through the dining room—where Mary remained hidden—and into the living room.

"Mr. Garrett! This is unexpected."

The rest of Hannah's words were drowned out by the loud rushing sound in her ears. Confusion settled over her. She was certain he was…

"Mary, please come meet Mr. Robert Garrett," Will was saying. "Robert, this is Mrs. Reuben Colter."

Robert Garrett extended his hand, waiting for her to place hers in his for the courteous kiss demanded by polite society. As she placed her hand in his, their eyes met.

There was no denying the icy cold glare in those chocolate brown eyes held a threat—one meant only for her. He knew she recognized him. Her husband. Reuben Colter.

The fear consumed her. Her head floated above her body. Dizziness ensued.

He found her.

Blackness pressed in.

Chapter 10

"Pleased to meet you."

The kind greeting barely penetrated Mary's mind as she gripped the back of a chair to steady herself. She almost fainted. Almost.

He would have loved that.

She managed some appropriate response. Barely.

As Will offered a seat to Robert Garrett, Mary studied him. His hair was lighter. His accent masked. He wore his facial hair in the favored style of the day, no longer clean shaven. There were many more deep wrinkles around those dark foreboding eyes.

His eyes. She hated his eyes the most. He commanded and threatened and coveted all with subtle variations that only she knew. She married the monster twelve years ago. Of course she would recognize him.

She couldn't believe Will didn't.

Then as she studied him more, she began to understand why Will didn't. He wasn't looking for his brother. He never thought of Reuben. Never glanced over his shoulder searching every face in a crowd to see if he was there.

No. The accent was convincing. Even she might be fooled if she wasn't constantly fearing his return—watching vigilantly for the moment of escape.

The conversation between Will and Reuben—er, Robert—buzzed in her ears. She only paid partial attention. He was here to secure more horses for his ranch. It was near Wickenburg. He would be in town for a few more days.

Then he looked at her again.

"Unfortunately, I won't be able to stay for supper. I would have enjoyed getting to know Mrs. Reuben Colter much better." His words were in response to Will's invitation while his dark eyes threatened her if she spoke. "Perhaps she would be so kind as to see me to my horse?"

She should have prepared herself for that. Of course he would find some way to have a private conversation with her. He always had been good at subtle manipulation.

"Certainly," she replied.

She led him to the door. She felt his intense stare boring through her skull.

"Surprised, my dear?"

She ignored the question, setting a brisk pace to his horse which was tied near the barn.

"There was a time when you understood an indirect command. Have you forgotten already?"

The northern accent did little to hide the sinister tone to his voice. It was the same regardless of what accent shrouded it.

She slowed her pace at his warning.

"Look at me," he commanded as they reached his horse.

Though she faced his direction, she refused to look into his eyes.

He grasped her hand in such a way that it would appear as a polite gesture to others. Yet, the force he applied crushed her fingers in an all-too-familiar way.

"You're hurting me."

"Mary, Mary, Mary. You know me well enough to know that was entirely the intent."

"What do you want from me? Come to take me to your ranch?"

He laughed. A deep throated laugh hinting of disbelief.

"You are penniless and have nothing that I want."

"Except silence. You want me to keep quiet about your true identity. How do you intend to convince me to keep quiet?"

He laughed again, enjoying what only he could find humorous about her words.

"I have the one thing you want more than anything. That alone should be enough to buy your silence."

"And what is that?"

All joviality fled from his features. "Divorce papers."

Mary swallowed hard. He was offering her freedom—the one thing she desperately wanted, needed, craved.

It wouldn't come without a price. Nothing ever did with Reuben.

"Come to my room at the Juniper House after dark. Be sure you aren't followed."

He finally released his crushing grip on her hand and mounted his horse.

"You better come or I'll make sure the ones that are dearest to you suffer."

Reuben Colter kicked his horse into motion.

As the dust faded behind him, Mary knew she had no choice. She was at his mercy. She couldn't tell Will or he would harm the children. She knew that's what he meant. If she went, who knows what he would require of her before giving her those papers—or if he would even go through with his end of the deal.

This could all be a trap. He may lure her to the hotel only to have her killed on the way there or on the way back.

Numbness took control of her body. Hours from now whatever happened would change the course of her life forever.

Or end it, leaving her children without a mother.

Mary barely touched her food at supper, trying to reason through her pending meeting with Reuben. A dozen times she considered telling someone—Warren, Ben, Will. Each time she convinced herself that she must face this alone. It was her cross to bear. It was the only thing to keep her children safe.

She went through the routines of the evening. She sat in the living room following supper, watching Beth and Eddie play. She lovingly tucked each into bed before retiring to her own.

Beth and Eddie. It was for them that she would go to face Reuben tonight. It was for them that she would gladly accept those papers from his hand.

Freedom would mean she could stop looking over her shoulder. Freedom would mean she could find a good man to be a father to her children. She wouldn't hope for love. She gave up on that fantasy a long time ago. Surely there were good men that would treat her and the children well. Any one of them would do.

She turned down the lamp next to the bed, still fully clothed.

Then she waited. One hour. Then two. Then three.

Mary stood and walked to her window that faced the bunkhouse. No light came from the building. The boys settled in for the night.

Night.

She took a sharp breath. Just leaving and wandering around town at this late hour was dangerous, Reuben aside.

Her hand shook as she reached for the door knob. She carefully crept down the stairs, avoiding the steps that were prone to protesting. She made special note of them on her way to bed earlier in the evening.

Slowly, she unlatched and pushed the door open, just barely enough to squeeze through.

The cool night air bit her cheeks and stung her lungs. Not quite cold enough for snow, but close.

Mary moved quickly to the barn. She had followed Adam out after supper, asking a few questions she hoped appeared innocent. Which mare was the most gentle? Was there one he would recommend for her—for the children—should she wish to take them riding soon?

Third stall on the left was the mare Adam said he would suggest for her. Gentle. Steady. It was the horse Hannah took when she rode, though it had been awhile.

Growing up on a ranch was good for a few things. Even though she was a prim and proper young girl, her father made certain she knew her way around a horse. Reuben never let her ride, but some lessons could never be forgotten.

She quickly saddled the mare and led her from the stable outside. She found an empty crate and turned it over, using it as a step up so she could reach the stirrups. Then she mounted the horse.

In no particular hurry, she set the pace at a gentle walk. Her heart raced from fear, anticipation, and even a little excitement. After tonight she would finally be free from Reuben. He would no longer hold any control over her life or the children's. From this night forward, her children would no longer call him father. She would no longer call him husband.

As she neared town, she directed the horse to the side of the street furthest from the saloons. She slid off the mare's back then she looked around. The street was quiet. The only noise came from the row of saloons to her left. She quickly tied the horse to a hitching post and scurried toward the hotel door.

When she entered the hotel, a man glanced up from the front desk. He smiled then turned his attention back to reading the paper.

Mary sighed in relief. He either thought she was a guest here—or that one of his patrons ordered a lady of the night. The second thought disturbed her, yet her arrival at such a late hour must seem suspicious. She made her way down the long hallway of rooms until she reached the back stairs. She climbed them quickly, despite the quivering of her stomach. Then she stopped at the first door on her right.

Reuben's room.

What if he tries to bed me? Her hand stopped abruptly before knocking on the door. The thought terrified her.

She hadn't considered the possibility until now. Yet, it was surely part of his plan. He would never give her the papers without some sort of payment from her.

She turned back toward the stairs. A man stood in the shadows near the top of the stairs, blocking her escape.

"Goin' somewhere?" His voice remained low as he took a step toward her. "I believe Mr. Garrett would be a mite miffed if you decided to take your leave without seeing him."

Mary's breath went shallow. Her mind raced. This had been a terrible mistake. One she was about to pay for.

Robert Garrett heard the voices coming from the hallway. Mary was here. A deep sense of satisfaction warmed his body. He still controlled her. Even after all this time, he knew just what to say to get her to show up.

What a fool she was!

He swung the door to his room open. She gasped. Then he grabbed her wrist and yanked her into the room.

"Stay close," he commanded his associate.

Then Robert closed and locked the door.

He turned his eyes on his wife. Fear paled her skin and widened her eyes. The sight only served to stoke the fire in him. He would have her. He would manipulate her. He would make her regret wishing to divorce him.

And he would ensure her silence.

He approached her like a mountain lion stalking its prey. Her pale ivory skin shimmered in the lamp light—which he would leave on so he could fully enjoy his revenge on her. It would be the last time he would be with her.

A hint of sadness quickly dissipated as he remembered he would be free of her after tonight. Oh, he didn't love her. Never had. But, he did take great pleasure in her beauty and her body.

He ran fingers down the side of her face and along her neckline, stopping at the edge of fabric. She stiffened at his touch. A smile spread across his lips.

"After all this time apart, you wouldn't deny your husband, would you?"

Her eyes grew cold.

"Don't touch me."

Robert laughed. Then he crushed her body to him. He ate hungrily of her lips. As she tried to force him away, his appetite grew. In one swift motion, he had her hands pinned behind her back. The weight of his body kept her frozen. He grabbed the small length of rope from his pocket and tied her wrists together behind her.

As she took in a deep breath, presumably to scream, Robert clamped his hand around her throat. He loved the look of shock as it crossed her face, quickly replaced by desperation. The fight left her.

He dropped all pretenses about what his intentions were and he abandoned the northern accent in favor of the one she would remember.

"Mary, you know me well enough to know, I will take what I want from you. Just what exactly did you think would happen tonight? You would come with nothing more than your body to offer and walk out of here without paying for those papers?"

He loosened his hold on her throat. She didn't move. She didn't respond.

His hands moved to her bodice and ripped it open sending buttons clattering to the floor. He made quick work of removing her corset, her skirt, and her under garments.

"Reuben, don't."

"You are still my wife. Don't fight me."

Then he dragged her to the bed and began undressing himself. The fire in his veins grew to a height that matched his desire for revenge. He would take her. He would give her the papers. Then he would make sure she would stay silent about his true identity.

Chapter 11

Mary struggled against Reuben as he moved toward the bed. She would not let him take her without a fight. She sucked in another deep breath, ready to scream. His fist pounded hard into her thigh. The other fist connected with her stomach, forcing all the air from her lungs.

He grabbed a handkerchief from the stand next to the bed and tied it tightly over her mouth. With her hands bound behind her back, the only thing she had left to fight with was her legs.

She kicked at him, but he clamped forceful hands down on her thighs. He squeezed hard over the bruise already forming on the one thigh where he punched her.

Mary's heart sank as his body pressed down on her. She stilled.

Old habits returned. She ignored the sensations of what he was doing to her. Instead her mind drifted to sweet memories from her childhood. She thought of picnics with her parents under the shade of a large tree. She thought of chasing after her father in a playful game of tag. She thought of the flowers she gathered in the spring and gave to her mother.

A hand smashed the sides of her cheeks together, causing her lips to pucker open, despite the handkerchief over her mouth. Her eyes opened. It was one of Reuben's favorite controlling holds.

"I want you here. I want you to keep your eyes open. Look at me. Know it is your husband."

Her gaze moved from his dark sinister eyes to his bare chest. The jagged scar on his left shoulder left no doubt as to his identity.

When he was satisfied, he lifted himself from her body.

She closed her eyes as the pain settled over her. She hoped she wouldn't end up pregnant from him again. Not now. There would be no way to explain that to Will and Hannah.

Mary started to sit up.

"Stay right there. You're not free to go quite yet."

She sat up anyway and began working the rope from her hands.

Reuben finished dressing. Then he pulled some papers from his jacket pocket and set them on the night stand.

"These," he said, pointing at the papers, "are what you just paid for."

Then he switched back to his northern accent. "My associate will be in shortly. What he does with you? Let's just say, it is far less than what he'll do to your children should you say anything about this night."

Her throat went dry. She was still naked, hands bound behind her back and mouth gagged. He wouldn't let this other man do that to her…

A smile spread across Reuben's face. "Yes I would let him do exactly what you're thinking. You're no longer my wife. I don't care what he does to you as long as it keeps you quiet."

With a haughty laugh, Reuben opened the door and left as his associate entered—the man from the hallway.

Reuben's associate moved toward her. He cut the rope loose from her hands. "Hurry up," he said as he tossed her clothing at her. "I gotta get you out the back while the desk clerk is gone."

Mary's hands shook as she tried to clothe herself again. Most of the buttons from her bodice ripped off. She had no way of covering her undergarments completely. She tried to force the events from her mind. *The feeling of Reuben's body pressed against hers. His hands all over her.*

He shoved the divorce papers into her hand.

"That's good enough."

He grabbed her arm and dragged her from the room and down the stairs. Then he led her through the dark dining room, through the kitchen, and out the back door of the hotel.

"Stay here and I'll bring your horse around. Don't move, unless you want to leave your children motherless."

She did as he commanded, too weary to run. Too sore to move quickly.

He came back with her horse in a few minutes.

"We're watching the ranch and the house. We'll know if you say anything. So keep your mouth shut and your brats will be fine."

He leaned in so close his hot breath warmed her face. "If you don't, I'll kill them with my bare hands and I'll be sure to make it slow and painful."

Then he helped her onto the horse. He slapped the horse's rump sending it off at a trot.

As soon as she was out of town, she slowed the horse's pace. Her skin crawled with memories of tonight. She needed to scrub them away. She needed to be clean—be free from the stench of her evil husband.

Once she was back at the ranch, she tied the horse near the barn. Then she stripped off each layer of clothing as she approached the lake, still under the cover of darkness. She submerged her body up to her neck in the icy water, scrubbing fiercely over every inch of her skin.

Her mind splintered. The only thing she could think about was removing all traces of him from her. She didn't feel free.

Warren stirred from a restless sleep. He thought he heard something outside. Quickly, he donned a shirt and pair of pants. Grabbing his gun, he headed for the bunkhouse door.

As soon as he stepped from the building, he caught movement near the barn. He approached cautiously since he could see little from the small sliver of moonlight.

Suddenly he stopped. It was Mary!

He stilled as she began undressing. She dove into the lake—perhaps the most bizarre thing he'd seen a woman do in the middle of the night, especially since the water would be freezing.

He went into the barn and searched for a wool blanket. Finding one, he threw it over his shoulder and headed for the lake.

When he arrived, Mary was still in there thrashing about frantically. Her clothes lay strewn along the shore. He gathered them into a pile.

"Mary," he whispered loudly.

She stilled.

"It's me, Warren."

She made no move to get out of the lake.

"Please come here. You'll catch your death."

Slowly she made her way toward him, the reflection of moon shifting in the moving water. He averted his eyes, though he doubted if he would see much in the darkness surrounding them. He held the blanket up in front of him.

Then he waited.

Just when he almost thought she would never reach him, a small body pushed the blanket into his chest. Instinctively, his arms came around her, wrapping her with the blanket.

She made no sound, though her body shook. His arms remained securely around her.

"What happened?"

He felt her head shake against his chest. She wasn't going to talk.

"Let me take you up to the house. Get you near a fire."

"No." Her voice sounded small, frightened.

"But, you're shivering."

"No."

He rubbed his arms up and down over her back trying to get some warmth to return. She stiffened at the movement.

"At least come to the barn, to get away from the breeze."

She nodded.

He released his hold on her. When he started to kneel to gather her clothes she stopped him. Instead, she picked them up and hugged them tightly.

Warren led her to the barn and had her sit on a stool. When she was settled, he went back outside to retrieve her horse. Both of them remained silent as he lit a lamp.

Her ivory skin had a gray cast to it. He studied her face for a moment. Fear devoured her eyes. Her shoulders slumped. There was a small cut at the corner of her mouth.

The blanket covered every inch of her from her chin down to her ankles. Only her head and feet were visible.

"Tell me what happened."

Her gaze drifted to a stall toward the front of the barn as her lips pressed together in a hard line.

"Did someone attack you? Try to kidnap you? What?"

"Stop."

With one word spoken softly, she communicated her deep pain—a pain that reminded him of his tormented Dahlia. He wasn't sure if there was anything he could do to help. He hadn't been able to help Dahlia either. Words hadn't helped. Neither had good intentions. Her inner pain grew until it overwhelmed them both.

He sighed and turned away from Mary to go care for her horse, leaving the memories behind. By the time he returned, she was gone.

Warren turned down the lamp and returned to bed, very disturbed by the strange behavior from Mary Colter that night.

Had she gone to town? Had she met with someone? Would she betray Will? Would she betray him?

Wait a minute! Why would he think she would betray him? Warren had no claim to her. Besides, the events of the night should be more than enough to convince him he couldn't trust her.

Just like he couldn't trust Dahlia.

He rolled over on his side facing the wall. The entire strange scene replayed in his mind. But, it was the feel of her in his arms that lingered on into his dreams.

Mary woke long after the sun rose the next morning. Her throat burned. Her legs and back were sore.

She threw back the covers and tentatively lifted her night dress over her head. As she surveyed the damage to her body she cringed. Deep purplish marks covered her stomach and the insides of her upper legs. Finger shaped purple dimples marked her upper arms.

Images from the hotel room tried to break through to a conscious thought. She forced them back. Out of long habit, she almost succeeded.

Mary looked through her wardrobe for a high collar to cover the bruises she felt on her neck. She selected a long sleeved navy bodice and a matching skirt. The ensemble would leave her face as the only exposed skin. No one should question it, given the chill in the air.

She dressed slowly, sore from her attacker. Every part of her body screamed in pain.

Once she finished dressing, she hid her clothes from the day before. She would find a way to burn them and the memories they contained. As she shoved them behind her trunk, her hand brushed the papers that cost her far too much.

Reaching out for them, she paused. What if he had done all of that and the papers were blank? What if they weren't divorce papers?

She snatched them up from the pile of clothes. Unfolding the papers, she scanned through them. A tiny bit of relief flirted with her heart. They were indeed divorce papers. Dated a year ago with an envelope that looked like it had been mailed to her in Texas.

There was only one problem. She couldn't tell Will or Hannah or anyone at the ranch about these papers—especially since they were dated a year ago. She never hinted that she was divorced. Perhaps she tried to imply she was widowed, but she told Hannah that she didn't know if her husband was dead or alive. Nothing about the way in which she talked about Reuben would ever lead anyone to believe she had been divorced from him already.

She must be careful with what she said. Perhaps she could manage to stage receiving the letter sealed inside one from Maggie Larson. Surely Maggie would send something soon. Yes, that might be the best way to handle this—for she did not want anyone believing she was still tied to Reuben in any way. She needed others to eventually see that she was free.

At what price? What was Reuben planning that he needed her to keep his presence silent? What harm would come to Will and his family—or even Julia and hers—if Mary stayed silent?

No. She couldn't tell anyone about Reuben or what he did last night. His associate made it very clear that the ranch was being watched. They would find out she said something and hurt Eddie and Beth. She couldn't risk that. No matter what happened she had to keep them safe.

She made her way downstairs. Eddie and Beth sat at the dining room table with their slates in front of them.

"I hope you don't mind. I started them on their studies this morning," Hannah said from the kitchen doorway.

“Thank you.” When she spoke, the words came out scratchy sounding, no doubt the result of her tender throat.

Hannah frowned. “Is your throat sore?”

Mary nodded.

“Does your head ache?”

She nodded again.

Hannah placed her wrist on Mary’s forehead. “You don’t feel hot. Are you feeling achy all over?”

“Yes.”

“Hmm. Sit. Let me make you some willow bark tea with your breakfast. Then, I think we’ll send you back to bed for some rest.”

“No food, please. My stomach…”

Concern creased Hannah’s forehead. She turned and went back into the kitchen. Within minutes she set a cup of willow bark tea in front of Mary. “Drink.”

She did as Hannah requested. The bitter taste matched the bitterness welling in her heart. When she finished, Hannah agreed to watch the children for the day. Then she sent her back upstairs.

Mary crawled under the covers, fully clothed and let sleep numb the ache in her heart from all she endured in the last day.

Chapter 12

Colter Ranch

January 12, 1867

Will entered the ranch house mid-afternoon. The house seemed rather silent except for hushed whispers from the kitchen. At first he thought Hannah and Mary were putting the final touches on Julia's surprise birthday party.

"What do you know of Robert Garrett?" Mary asked.

At her question, he stopped just outside of the dining room. Something about it put him on edge. Especially since it had been two months since Garrett came to the ranch.

"Not much," Hannah replied. "He's got a ranch in Wickenburg. Buys horses from Will every now and then. He seems like a nice man when he visits."

As silence fell, Will waited, feeling a little guilty for eaves-dropping. His gut told him Mary wasn't done.

"How much do you know about Reuben?"

"Your husband?"

"And Will's brother."

"Will doesn't talk about him," Hannah said. "Only that he forced him from the ranch after their father died."

Mary's voice charged with anger. "He's a dangerous man. If he knows—er, knew that Will was here…"

A shiver ran down's Will's spine. Protectiveness surged through him as he stepped into the dining room. "Is Reuben here?"

She jumped at the sound of his voice. She turned frightened eyes on him. Then her gaze shifted toward the window, refusing to return to him.

"Do you know something?" Will asked moving into the kitchen.

At length, she shook her head.

"Then why the sudden mention of him?" Will wasn't going to

let her off that easily.

"I… I received divorce papers from him."

Will's heart nearly stopped beating in his chest. If Reuben was here… His family wouldn't be safe. None of them would be. Especially if Reuben's twisted mind found a way of blaming him for the loss of the Star C back in Texas.

"When?"

"From… With Maggie's last letter. She sent the unopened envelope with her letter."

Will frowned. That was over a week ago. Why was she only mentioning this now?

"The papers were dated over a year ago. It looked like they were mailed from some place in California or Arizona. They must have arrived in Texas after I left."

Mary's gaze remained locked on the window overlooking the grassy area in front of the lake.

"Why didn't you say anything before now?"

She turned sharp eyes on him now. "Do you think it's easy being discarded? I needed time before saying anything."

He tightened his jaw. Her feelings aside, he needed to know if there was any chance Reuben knew where he was.

"Does he know you're here?"

Her gaze moved back to the window and her voice softened to a whisper. "I… I don't think so."

Moving his focus to his wife, he studied her reaction for a minute. Hannah shook her head, which meant that she didn't know anything else.

"If you hear from him, let me know immediately."

When Mary gave no indication of hearing him, he added, "Mary, let me know."

At last, she nodded.

The silence grew thick. After a tense minute, Mary excused herself. "I need to put some finishing touches on Julia's present," she said, darting from the room.

Will closed his eyes and counted to ten. She was hiding something. Her refusal to look him in the eye convinced him of it.

A light touch to his arm stirred him from his fears. He opened his eyes to find Hannah standing close. She said nothing. She just moved her hand lightly back and forth across his arm. He pulled her into an embrace and settled his chin on top of her head.

Sucking in a deep breath he let it out slowly.

"What is it, Will?"

"If… If Reuben is here, I'm afraid that you won't be safe. The boys won't be safe." He gazed out the window and tried to stifle his mounting fear. "None of us will be."

Hannah leaned back to look up at him. "Why?"

Will swallowed hard. "He hates me. I know how he thinks. He'll find a way to blame me for losing his ranch. Somehow in his mind it will be my fault. If so… He's not the type of man to let go of a grudge."

She snuggled against his chest again. "Is there anything we can do?"

"I"— Will tightened his arm around her protectively. "I don't know."

Mary held her tears back until she reached the safety of her room. Guilt pressed in. She should tell Will. She should warn him.

But, if she did, Reuben was certain to find out. He would harm Eddie or Beth. She couldn't let that happen.

What an awful woman she was lying for him! Will and Hannah welcomed her and the children into their family with open arms. They gave her a place to stay. They treated her as if she mattered—as if they cared about her. Now she repaid their kindness by hiding the truth from them.

Yes, she was a wretched woman indeed. For the first time she felt truly worthy of the disdain she felt from Reuben. And all of it was because she kept his secret.

The supper bell rang, pulling her from her self-loathing. She took a deep breath and went to the wash basin to clean the dried tears from her face. Then she retrieved her gift for Julia from her dresser. She made her way back down the stairs to the dining room. Eddie and Beth already sat in their chairs at the table. Quietly, she slid into the chair next to Eddie.

The heaviness of her heart distracted her from the normal chatter. Sensing someone's eyes on her, she glanced up. Warren stared at her. Then red flushed his cheeks and he looked away. A little of her foul mood lifted.

Over the months since his chicken pox, this was the little game they played. She would catch him staring, he would look away. Never anything more. Yet, somehow a connection developed. This dance left a warm sensation radiating through her body.

Will asked him a question and the flush faded from his cheeks. His eyes grew serious and he spoke with confidence.

An odd thought struck her. Something seemed out of place with Warren. The way he carried himself. The way he answered Will's question. It almost seemed like he should own the ranch, not play second fiddle as the foreman. Perhaps it was his confidence that gave her that impression. Could he be trusted? Was he really all that he seemed?

She shook off the thought.

The meal finished and the children were sent off to the living room to play. The women cleared the dishes from the table, but left them to be cleaned later. It was time to celebrate Julia's birthday.

Warren excused himself from the gathering at the table, shooting her a brief smile.

Mary leaned down to retrieve her small gift from its resting place beneath her chair. She set it in her lap. It was nothing overly special, but she hoped Julia would enjoy it all the same.

The energy of the room heightened.

"What did you get me, Adam?" Julia's eyes lit with excitement as she looked at her husband.

"Be patient."

"You've been teasing me for weeks. Come on. I want my gift now."

He shook his head. "Saving the best one for last. You'll just have to be patient."

She pouted, bringing a smile to Mary's lips. It was so good to see Julia happy.

"Are you two done?" Will asked.

Julia nodded.

"Good. This is from Hannah and me." He stood and slid the

brown wrapped bundle in front of her then stooped to place a kiss on her cheek. "I hope you like it."

Julia ripped the paper from the gift in a flourish. "Oh!" She lifted a pair of kid leather gloves from the paper, gently caressing them. "They are so nice. Thank you, both!"

"You're welcome," Hannah answered.

Next Betty and Ben presented their gift. "A new cowboy hat! Oh, I love it!" Julia laughed. "But, maybe you should think about one for Will. That old hat of his is nasty." She winked playfully at Will, looking over her shoulder toward the front of the house where his hat rested on a peg by the door.

"Hey. Don't even think of touching my hat. It fits my head perfectly."

"Probably because you would sleep with it on if you could."

Will chuckled. "Certainly have on occasion."

Mary smiled as everyone laughed. Julia and Will had always been close—something she loved watching, even if it came with a little jealousy. She wished she had family that close.

She cleared her throat and handed her simple gift to Julia.

Julia frowned. "I don't want anything from you."

Her heart sank. She thought she was getting along well with her sister-in-law. But the dark frown that settled over Julia's face told her otherwise.

"Julia." Adam's soft voice broke through the simmering tension. He reached for the gift that she refused to take.

Julia folded her arms over her chest ignoring him and glaring at Mary.

"Look, she made you a nice reticule that will go perfectly with your Sunday dress." Adam tried to hand the gift to Julia.

She grabbed it from his hand and threw it at Mary. "Do you think this makes up for anything?"

Mary swallowed hard and sank into her chair.

"You knew Reuben was beating me. But you did nothing. Nothing!"

"I—"

"Do you know what he did to me the night I left? Do you?"

Mary looked around the table. Accusing eyes stared back at her. Julia. Adam. Will. Ben. Only Hannah and Betty offered a sliver of sympathy.

"He raped me. Your wretched husband raped me!"

Mary closed her eyes. "I know."

"And you did nothing!"

Her eyes flew open. She pushed back her chair and stood. "I didn't know until much later—after you left. What did you expect me to do?"

Her hands shook and tears welled in her eyes.

"Why didn't you stop him?" Julia shot to her feet.

"I couldn't stop him from using me." She wrung her hands in the folds of her skirt. "How could I stop him from hurting you?"

Tossing the unwanted gift aside, Mary ran from the room out the front door into the chilly night air.

As he left the outhouse building, Warren stopped at the sight of Mary running from the ranch house. She ran to the barn, yanking the door open hard—well, as hard as her small frame allowed. She should have been celebrating Julia's birthday with the family. What happened?

He glanced back toward the house. No one followed her.

For a split second, he hesitated. A part of him wanted to run back to the bunkhouse. Stay out of her life.

Yet, compassion rose in his chest. She shouldn't be alone. She was distraught.

The first step felt forced, but each consecutive step he took towards the barn became easier. He pushed open the door and stepped inside. He paused, listening for the muffled sound of crying. He heard nothing.

Clearing his throat, he debated whether he should just leave.

"Mary?"

Silence.

A horse snorted. The sound came from the back of the barn. He followed it. As he neared the last stall, he saw her curled up in the corner, leaning one shoulder against the wall. Her knees were pulled tight to her chest with her head buried behind them.

The scared posture brought a lump to his throat. She was hurting.

Approaching quietly, he stopped in front of her. He knelt down to her level and reached out a hand, resting it on her shoulder.

She stilled and lifted her head slightly. Red rimmed her lovely violet eyes. Regret and fear crossed her face before being stamped out by despair.

He offered a sympathetic smile.

"You… Should go." Her whispered voice barely registered.

He waited.

She lifted her head. "Warren, just go."

He shook his head. "What happened?"

The tears rushed down her face like a mighty waterfall. "I'm a horrible woman. I don't deserve your kindness. I don't deserve to be alive."

The words rammed through his chest bruising the deepest, hidden part of his heart. How many times had Dahlia said the very same thing?

"It can't be that bad."

"You have no idea what I've done."

His legs began to numb, so he shifted to sit on the floor Indian style. "Why don't you tell me?" As the words left his lips, he wondered for a brief moment what possessed him to stay and draw her out—especially after the connection his mind made between her and his wife.

Her eyes darted away. "I couldn't stop Reuben from… From hurting me. Hurting Julia. Doing awful…" A sob broke from her throat.

Warren studied her small frame. He pictured a time when she stood next to Will. Though she wasn't significantly shorter, her narrow shoulders and petite form would have stood no chance of fighting off her husband if he was anything similar in stature to Will. From the bits and pieces of conversations over the last few months and what she revealed now, he was certain Reuben had been abusive.

His gut wrenched. How could some men treat their women so poorly? Look at her. She was beautiful, fragile. She needed protected, not…

What if he came back and found her?

The urge to hold her and keep her safe overwhelmed him. "I won't let him hurt you again." Oh foolish man! He had no grounds for making such a bold claim.

Mary tilted her head to the side. "Legally, I'm no longer bound to him."

Warren wrestled with the emotions that stirred. Had she divorced him? Was she more like Dahlia than he wanted to believe?

"I… He sent papers. Dated a year ago."

His heart broke. She had been cast aside. Just like him. He reached out to touch her arm, but she shied away.

A stuttered breath left her lungs. "Julia is right. I should have done something to protect her. To protect myself. I should have taken her and the children and left. I could have found some way. I should have."

Warren remained silent. His own churning emotions thickened his tongue so it felt like dead weight inside of his mouth. His heart was still raw from what Dahlia had done—even after all these years.

"I was strong once. Before I met him. I knew how to run both the ranch and the house under my father's watchful eye. I could have found some way to break free from him… His heavy hand. His…"

Mary swiped at the moisture coating her cheeks.

"He broke me. Just like a wild horse, he destroyed my will to fight. Year after year, a little more of me slipped away. Each time, I became less willing to stand up to him. Less willing to do anything other than conform. I was better off bending to his will and desires. It wasn't as… As bad. I learned to be what he wanted me to be."

She dropped her arms from her knees to the ground. Her fingers dug deep into the layer of hay on the floor at her side.

"I don't want to ever see him again."

"None of us will let him harm you. You're safe here."

She released her hold on the hay. Then she reached up to pat her hair, leaving behind a stray piece of hay clinging to her dark locks.

Without thinking, Warren reached up and removed the piece of hay. His hand betrayed the thoughts running through his mind by resting softly against her cheek. When had Mary Colter snuck into his heart?

Her breath caught. Fearful eyes connected with his. He immediately dropped his hand, chiding himself for thinking, hoping there might be something else in her gaze.

She jumped up and brushed the hay from her skirt before heading towards the door. As she neared the entrance, she said, "I am… Sorry to… Thank you for listening."

Then she was gone.

Warren sat still in the barn for a few minutes, gathering his wits. What just happened?

Chapter 13

"I think Julia loved the saddle from Adam," Hannah said.

Will continued readying himself for bed, picking up on her attempt to end the day on a lighter note. "Too bad for him."

"Why?"

He chuckled. "How is he ever going to find her a better gift next year?"

Jumping under the covers, he dodged his wife's swat.

"I'm sure she'll love any gift from him, even if it is smaller."

He turned down the lamp and snuggled close to her warm body. What just happened at supper? And what should he do about it? Soft snores from his two boys filled the silence. Soon he felt Hannah relax against him, indicating she fell asleep.

It wasn't just Mary and Julia's harsh words at dinner that kept him awake. Mary's conversation with Hannah earlier in the day troubled him. If Reuben knew he was here, he would surely cause trouble. Would he go so far as to kill?

What could he do to keep his family safe?

Do not fear.

Conviction chained his heart. There was nothing he could do—except rely on God to keep his family safe.

Still, he would talk to Warren in the morning. They could at least be more vigilant.

Though far from being at peace, Will fell asleep.

Sometime in the middle of the night, he woke with a start. What had Mary asked Hannah? What did she know about Robert Garrett?

He sat upright. As shock smacked him hard across the face, his heart plunged. Why hadn't he seen this before now? How had he been so blind?

Robert Garrett was Reuben.

His brother, his enemy.

The man dined at his table. He tousled his son's hair. He

graciously thanked his wife for her hospitality.

He shook his brother's hand as he sold him horses.

So many signs had been there. The sharp angled jaw line. The shuffled stride. Even the way he awkwardly dismounted his horse—it was all the same as Reuben.

Oh, his hair was lighter. He wore facial hair, good old mutton chops. The accent. It had been very convincing.

What a fool he'd been!

He believed every lie, letting Reuben get close to him—close to his family. He had plenty of time to study them. Why hadn't he struck yet? What was he waiting for?

Mary.

Anger burned through his veins. Was she helping him? She had to be.

He jumped up from the bed.

"What's wrong?" Hannah's voice came as she stirred.

He strode to the bedroom door and swung it wide, slamming it against the wall. In two steps he was across the hall in front of Mary's room.

"Mary!"

His sons' cries came from the room behind him, but he pushed forward determined to get some answers.

Mary startled awake at the sound of the door crashing open. Old instincts kicked in. She mentally prepared for the blows that were to come at Reuben's hand. Or worse. She could never prepare for that.

Had he been at the saloon again? Her foggy brain couldn't remember.

"Mary!"

The sound of her name cleared her mind. She was at Will's. It was his voice that woke her. Reuben wasn't here.

Relief rushed over her for a few seconds. She reached over to the night stand and lit the lamp with shaky hands.

When she turned to face Will, she cowered back in fear. The anger on his face matched that of his brother's.

"Where is he?"

He strode forward and placed his hands on her shoulders, giving her a forceful shake. "Where. Is. He?"

"I... What are you talking about?"

"Reuben. Robert Garrett. Your husband."

"I don't know." Fear closed her throat.

Will released his hold and stepped back from her. He paced back and forth across the length of her room. Hannah appeared in the doorway, confusion written on her features.

"Robert Garrett is Reuben. You know this."

He turned ferocious eyes on her.

"I... I don't know." She lied. If Reuben found out she told him...

"What did he do to get you to come here and pretend to need our help? Is he asking you to spy on us? I always thought you were better than that."

"He... He didn't know I was here. He doesn't know. He..."

Will stopped in front of her, his eyes wild. "He knows now, doesn't he? When he came to purchase the last round of horses, you were here. He asked to speak to you alone. What did he say to you? Did he offer you money? A divorce?"

The harsh truth of his words broke down her defenses. "He threatened to kill the children. If I said anything he would send someone for them. I... I had to be silent."

Will's jaw tightened. She'd seen that look before. He was beyond angry.

"I want you gone first thing in the morning."

"Will," Hannah's soft voice came from behind him.

He turned on his wife. "You stay out of this." He turned back towards Mary. "You are not welcome here any longer."

"Please, Will. Don't send us away. We have no other place to go. I didn't know he was here. I didn't know. When I recognized him, he found a way..."

She paused. She had to be careful how much she said. She couldn't admit that Reuben bought her silence with the promise of a divorce. She couldn't tell him that she met him in his hotel room. It wouldn't help her cause.

"He told me he would kill the children if I said anything."

A small gasp came from the doorway. Eddie stood behind his sister with loving hands steadying her shoulders. Mary's heart fractured. How much had they heard?

"So it *was* Papa that I saw," Eddie said. Deep anger creased his forehead. "You said he couldn't be here! You lied!"

Her son darted from the doorway. Rapid footfalls echoed down the stairs. Mary lurched forward, but Will caught her.

"Sit. I'm not done with you yet. Hannah, go get the boy."

Hannah turned from the door as requested, leaving Beth standing alone. She didn't move. Fear widened her eyes, breaking Mary's heart as Will refused to let her go comfort her daughter.

"Talk."

The word from Will still held anger, but it seemed softer than before. Mary forced the words from her lips.

"Reuben recognized me immediately the day he came to visit. When he took my hand in greeting, he crushed my fingers—a warning not to say anything.

"Will, I lived ten years with his control and wrath. I understood the subtle looks and I knew that grip meant so much more than be quiet. It meant be quiet or else."

"Or else what?"

"Or else I'll hurt you. I'll hurt the children. I'll come back and drag you to my ranch. Subject you to… the horrors you knew during the first ten years of marriage. That's what he meant. He meant to remind me of his power and remind me to fear him."

Will leaned against the wall and crossed his arms over his chest.

Would she have to tell him everything?

"Later, he… I went to see him. I wanted to beg him to leave. To leave me and the children alone. Only he had other ideas." She choked back a sob. Her voice found even footing, though her heart continued to slam her chest. "He found the right way to ensure my silence. And he had his man make sure I understood that those I loved wouldn't be safe if I said anything."

Will frowned, and for a second she thought he guessed what she hadn't quite said. Only that could be worse.

Nervously, she twisted her fingers in her lap. She had to tell him something. Make him believe in her again. "He has a man watching the house."

Will dropped his arms to his side and stood tall. The anger on his face faded to fear. "He what?"

"His man told me they were watching the house. Had been for some time. He told me he would know if I said anything."

The silence between them seemed deafening.

"Please don't send me away. If you do, he'll know I said something. He'll come after the children. After me. I can't live with him again." Desperation clawed at her heart. She dropped to the floor on her knees in front of him. "Please don't send me back to him."

Hannah cleared her throat from the doorway. Mary looked to see that Eddie was with her. Beth still stood there silently. She turned her head back towards Will.

"You may stay."

He moved toward the door. "But only because of them."

At the doorway, he turned back toward her. "You are not to leave these walls unescorted. Either me or Warren or Ben will walk you where ever you need to go."

A prison. He offered his version of a prison. One that was better than the one she would have with Reuben, but a prison nonetheless.

She nodded her head accepting the punishment, wondering just what he was going to tell his men.

Warren clenched a fist at his side. She was a betrayer just like Dahlia—only worse. She betrayed an entire family. A family that took her in and treated her as one of their own.

He held back the words pressing at the back of his throat. As he slowly inhaled a deep breath through his nostrils, he tried to keep his face impassive.

"During the day, I want you to follow her any time she leaves the house," Will said. "If you can't at any time, make sure Ben is around to keep an eye on her."

Warren gave a curt nod.

"I don't know how much of her story I believe," Will said as he stood from the table. "She didn't come down for breakfast, but I had Hannah check. She's still up in her room."

He began pacing back and forth. "And if she isn't lying, given half a chance he… God forgive me. I never saw it—the way he treated her. I should have. I lived under the same roof!"

Warren kept his trap shut as he tried to follow Will's scattered thoughts.

"I'm gonna take Hawk out and see if we can find any signs of this man who's been watching us. I told Hannah to keep the rifle handy."

"What do you think your brother is planning?"

Will glanced toward the window. "I don't know. Back in Texas, I always suspected he was involved in some pretty underhanded dealings. Father never wanted to hear it so I let it drop. Now…"

Warren clearly saw the worry in Will's face. "Think he'd go after your family or just you?"

"He would hit me where it hurts most—Hannah, James, Samuel."

"Then I'll keep an eye on them too."

Will reached out a hand and squeezed Warren's shoulder. "Appreciate it." Then he turned and headed out the front door.

Warren followed, but only to the front porch. Anger churned, mixed with regret and embarrassment. He couldn't believe he fell for Mary's pretty eyes. The way she looked at him. He started feeling something for her. Something he thought had died when Dahlia left.

The image of Mary cowering in the barn last night softened his heart again. He forced it from his mind.

Pacing back and forth on the porch, he vowed he would extract her from his heart. She betrayed Will. She misled him. She probably wasn't even divorced. Those papers were probably forgeries.

A soft clearing of a throat sounded behind him. He turned and unmasked his anger as he faced the object of it.

"I need to…" She nodded toward the outhouse.

He motioned for her to head that direction and he followed behind.

It would hurt to evict her from his heart. But, he had to. He couldn't trust her and he would be spending a lot of time with her now, doing his best to protect Will and his family.

Chapter 14

Prescott

February 20, 1867

Robert Garrett sipped his whiskey, keeping an eye on the door of the saloon. Any time now his associate would arrive. He hoped he would recognize him since he would probably wear a different disguise.

One of the saloon girls stepped into his view. She sauntered toward him twirling a fan in her hand. She stopped next to him and looped her hand through the crook of his arm just as he set his whiskey glass down on the bar.

"Hon, you looking for a good time?"

Robert hesitated. He really needed to wait for his associate before indulging.

"Might be."

She leaned closer and whispered in his ear. "Pete said you should follow me."

Then she leaned back and took his hand in hers. "Come on up and I'll show you that good time."

He wasn't sure how or when Pete managed to get past him, but he understood the ruse well. As he suspected, when the soiled dove opened the door to her chamber, Pete sat on a stool near the window. He turned to face the pair as they entered the room.

Winking at the girl, he said, "Be a sweetheart and get us some drinks. But take yer time."

She snatched the coin from his finger tips and flashed him a knowing smile.

Robert stood near the closed door. He scowled at Pete. "You better have some good news."

Pete pushed his cowboy hat back on his head. "Better'n good."

Letting out his breath in a rush, Robert said, "Out with it."

“Seems Colter is planning a trip to town in three days. He’ll be making a delivery out to the fort then making the rounds in town.”

Robert rubbed the mutton chops on his face. “What about Ben?”

“Leaving him behind. Seems Larson will be with Colter. Has some business with the stagecoach line.”

Anticipation throbbed in Robert’s veins. “Cahill?”

“Just him and Ben will be at the ranch. It’ll be easy enough to get around Cahill. Seems he’s guarding yer woman.”

“She isn’t my woman.”

Pete waved his hand in the air, brushing away the comment. “This will be the time to move. Larson’s wife will be on her own with the horses. Ben’s wife will likely be baking up a storm in their little cabin like most days. That leaves the Colter women at the main house with Cahill. Ben might be there too but he ain’t moving fast these days. Be easy to overtake him. ‘Specially with a couple of men with me.”

Slowly a smile slithered across Robert’s face. The moment he had been waiting for was almost here.

“Make sure you get the two Colter boys and Larson’s baby. I want all their kids.”

“And the wife?”

“Her too. You’ll need someone to keep the baby quiet. Besides, it will tear Colter apart knowing his family was taken right out from under his nose.” Robert had other reasons for wanting Colter’s wife. There was no better way to make Colter pay than what he had in mind for her.

“You got the money?”

Robert reached into his vest pocket and counted out half of the payment. “The rest you’ll get when you deliver them to the shack out on the fringes of my place.”

Pete nodded.

A knock at the door announced the saloon girl returned. Pete opened the door and stepped into the shadows down the hall as the saloon girl entered carrying just one drink.

Robert grabbed her by the waist and pulled her toward him, kicking the door shut with his foot.

“Good girl. Now how about that good time you were telling me about?”

He took the whiskey from her hand and downed it in one fluid motion. Then he shoved her toward the bed.

Excitement coursed through him. The sweet taste of revenge was on the tip of his tongue. Just a few more days before Colter and Larson would regret stealing everything from him. He waited so long for this moment. Planned it so carefully.

Mary had kept her mouth shut. She didn't ruin his plans. In fact, she unknowingly helped them along. From what Pete told him on another occasion, it seemed Mary was doing a good job of distracting Cahill without trying. He'd be too focused on her that it would make Pete's job easier.

He laughed and the girl looked up at him in confusion. She didn't need to know the reason for his glee. But, she would be a part of his early celebration.

Chapter 15

Colter Ranch

February 22, 1867

Warren held back a frustrated sigh. He was getting tired of following Mary around the ranch. Going on five weeks now. He'd had enough. If Will's brother was going to strike, surely he would have done so by now.

Yet, there had been small signs around the place that indicated they were being watched—maybe. The broken blades of grass near the back of the ranch house. The traces of campfires on the side of the mountain. Could be someone was watching them.

Or could be they were all paranoid.

He sighed as he finished cinching the strap of the saddle on Mary's horse. He bit his tongue to hold back another sigh, annoyed that he gave in to her this morning.

"The children are antsy," she had said. "They need to get out."

When he hadn't responded she put on the pressure.

"Will didn't say we couldn't go riding. Just that you had to watch me. My children shouldn't have to suffer for it."

The way she crossed her arms—melted his heart. He saw how agitated the children seemed. Today was the perfect day for a ride. The weather warmed slightly. The sun was out. If he were in Eddie's position, he'd be eager for a ride too.

So, he caved.

Taking the reins on the three horses, he led them to the ranch house. Okay, so he'd let Mary out of his sight for a few minutes. It was the first time. But, there she and the children sat, waiting patiently on the front porch, right where he left them.

Eddie smiled as Warren approached. "I get my own horse?"

He nodded.

When Eddie started to dance around, Mary touched a hand to

his shoulder. "Be still or you'll frighten the horses."

Warren helped Mary up on her horse, then handed Beth up to her. Then he helped Eddie up on his very own horse before swinging onto the back of his gray gelding.

"Ma'am. Lead the way."

He waited for her to move her horse. Eddie followed behind. Warren brought up the rear, keeping a close eye on Mary. His eyes fell to her waist.

Heat crept up his neck when he realized he'd been watching the sway of her dainty body on the horse with too much interest. He didn't have to watch her *that* closely.

For the past five weeks he had been by her side constantly. During that time, his anger faded. He began to see what her motivation had been for keeping quiet. Her children.

After a few short days, her love for them was hard to ignore. Every action, every movement, every step she took—everything was for Eddie and Beth. He saw it in how she spoke to them. How she wiped away their tears.

There was no doubt in his mind that her motivation had been to keep them safe.

Still, just because she gained his respect, it didn't mean he had to trust her.

Mary stopped her horse and he pulled up next to her.

"This looks like a good spot," she said, turning to face him.

When she smiled, he chided the light feeling it stirred in him. He refused to give in to the growing feelings for her. She would only hurt him like Dahlia had.

He looked away. The spot she picked was still a good distance from the herd—close enough to see the cattle and the cowboys, but far enough away to be safe. The small cluster of trees nearby would provide shade but not enough cover for someone to watch them. Though he doubted they would sit in the shade. The air still held enough of a chill that it would be nice to sit in the open sun.

"Ma'am, sure does look like a good place for a picnic."

Warren dismounted and tied his horse to one of the trees. Then he took Beth from Mary's arms and set her gently on the ground. He reached up and placed his hands on Mary's waist.

Then he paused. Energy surged through him, causing him to

forget anything but the way she felt in his hands. He lowered her to the ground and released her as soon as her feet touched the ground.

She smiled at him.

"Thank you, Warren."

Those words. She kept thanking him. Many times over the last five weeks.

When he stood guard while she helped Hannah with laundry. When he read a book while she taught her children. Even when he stood outside the outhouse waiting for her to reappear. Always, she thanked him with those same words.

Perhaps that had more to do with breaking down his resolve than anything else.

Stirring from his thoughts, he helped Eddie down from his horse. Then he tied the rest of the horses to a tree. He retrieved the blanket and food from his saddle bags and moved to where Mary stood in the sun. Eddie darted off.

"Stay close!"

"Can I go too?" Beth tugged on her hand.

Mary nodded. Her eyes stayed glued to her children as they chased each other a few yards away while Warren spread out the blanket.

"He was an awful man, you know."

Warren's eyes darted to her face, not certain she was speaking to him until she tore her gaze from her children for a few seconds.

"I'm sure I've told you before that he was... Reuben was abusive."

"Yes."

She turned to face him now. Her eyes darkened with intensity and fear. "More than just forceful. He was brutal."

Warren swallowed hard. Fear and worry marched across her face.

"I want you to know that I had no idea he was in Arizona. I didn't know."

Her eyes begged him to understand and he felt another place in his heart start to thaw.

She looked back out toward her playing children.

"He had my parents murdered."

The words were so matter-of-fact that he struggled to understand.

"I didn't know when I married him what kind of evil man he was. He was so good at lying, manipulating, deceiving everyone. Even his own father couldn't see his real nature.

"No, it was years later that I began to suspect. A rumor here. A whisper there."

She stopped. Then she took his offered hand and sat down on the blanket he spread out for the picnic.

As he took a seat next to her he studied her carefully. Fear. It always lingered beneath the surface of her demeanor. She never seemed to relax fully. Not even when she smiled.

"Beth isn't mine, you know."

"What?"

Mary turned to look at him. "A long time after Reuben disappeared, his…" She looked back toward her children. "A saloon girl came to see me. She told me this awful story. That I gave birth to another son. Stillborn. Just days before she gave birth to Beth. I was so weak. I didn't know that Reuben switched the children. He buried my son and replaced him with the saloon girl's daughter. His daughter. Not mine."

Warren's heart squeezed tight in his chest. That same protective feeling from before swelled within his chest. What kind of man would do such things?

"All I ever hoped for was to be free from him. Had I known he was in Arizona, I would have stayed in Texas—no matter how hard life got. I never wanted to see him again."

Compassion forced his hand toward her. Gently his fingers curled around her delicate hands. When she looked at him this time, all he could think about was wrapping her in his arms and keeping her from any more pain.

His gaze dropped to her lips.

She pulled her hands from his and scooted away from him. Pink dusted her cheeks.

"I don't want your sympathy, Warren. I just want you to believe me—to trust me."

The words shackled his conscience. Oh, he would let himself like her. He would allow the obvious attraction. But trust? That would be much, much harder to come by.

Mary stood. She needed to put more space between her and Warren. Brushing at her skirt, she hoped she hid her shaky hands. His gentle touch unnerved her—so foreign from the way Reuben touched her.

She saw that look in his eye. She traced his gaze as he looked at her lips. Unless she was completely misunderstanding his actions, Warren Cahill fancied her.

Shaking her head slightly, she walked closer to her children as they danced and played. She couldn't let Warren have feelings for her. She didn't trust the papers that Reuben gave her. Were they real? Was she really free from him? Or were they forgeries?

No, she couldn't let Warren get close. Not until she knew for sure.

Maybe she could ask Will to have his attorney look at them? It seemed over the past week that Will softened toward her. Maybe he would be willing to do this one thing.

She sighed. When had her life become so twisted?

"Hungry?"

Warren's voice from behind her stirred her thoughts.

"Eddie, Beth, come sit for a few minutes."

"Aw, Ma!"

"Let them play," Warren said. "They can eat when they finish working out all their energy."

When she turned back toward the blanket, she caught the glint in his eyes. The breath rushed from her lungs and she was grateful for his hand as he helped her take a seat.

He handed her some bread and cheese. She took them and broke off pieces.

"I was married."

The confession didn't come as a surprise. She remembered him mentioning it before.

"She… She divorced me."

A frown wrinkled her forehead. Was Warren heavy handed too? Why else would his wife have left him?

Warren rushed to explain. "Dahlia hated the ranch. She was a social girl and I never should have married her. Or, I never should have taken her from the city."

"I don't understand."

"She became quite... Morose. On the ranch. She hated it. She came to hate me."

Mary gave him her full attention now, as he opened and closed his mouth several times.

"One day, I woke to find a letter from her. She said that an old beau had written to her. He still loved her and wanted her to come back to him."

He picked at some lint on his pants.

"She did. A few months later I received divorce papers in the mail. A few months after that, I heard through a mutual friend that she married him."

"I'm sorry," she whispered.

Eddie and Beth rushed toward them. Eddie bolted for Mary and swung his arms around her, knocking her off balance. She shot an arm behind her to keep from falling into Warren. She certainly didn't want to encourage him.

"I love you, Mama," Eddie said.

Then in a flash he let go and flopped down on the blanket.

"I love—" Her voice cracked. "I love you, too."

She blinked back the tears. It was the first time Eddie hugged her since the night Will accused her of helping Reuben. Perhaps everyone's suspicions were relaxing. She sensed it from Warren, Will, and now her son.

The chill in the air sent a shiver down her spine.

"Time to go," Warren said a short time later as he jumped to his feet.

She packed up the leftovers while he folded the blanket and tied it to his saddle. Then he helped her and the children get settled on the horses.

Leading the way back to the ranch, she felt hopeful again. Maybe Reuben wouldn't really strike. Maybe they were all safe. And maybe Colter Ranch could truly become her home.

Chapter 16

Hannah smiled as she hung a shirt on the line. Mary seemed in good spirits since her picnic outing with the children yesterday. Not for the first time, she wondered if Mary and Warren might have growing feelings for one another.

The idea settled well in her thoughts. With the divorce papers Mary had from Reuben, it seemed there was no reason she couldn't find a new husband. Though, Hannah supposed others might not accept it. Even she might not have been so willing to if Mary had not shared some stories of Reuben's ruthlessness. But, the more she got to know Mary, the more she wanted her to find peace and a new life.

After all, isn't that what she and Will had done? Adam and Julia? Even Caroline and Thomas? All of them had found a new life that included a home and love with a godly spouse. How could she stand up and piously deny that same dream for Mary?

"Did you have a good time with Warren yesterday?" she asked, testing the waters.

"Shhh," Mary responded as she shoved another garment toward Hannah.

She lowered her voice. "Well?"

Mary moved closer and glanced over her shoulder toward where Warren stood not more than ten yards away. "He's just guarding me. The outing was for the children."

Hannah smiled. "Yes, but you still enjoyed it."

Red colored Mary's cheeks, answering for her. She decided not to pursue the topic more.

"Mama!" Beth's voice carried across the yard from the porch, though they couldn't see her. "Eddie took my slate."

"I better go see what's happening." Mary moved towards the house. Warren followed behind.

A minute later, Eddie came running past her, being chased by an unsteady James. Just when she thought about abandoning the laundry to follow after her son, Samuel fussed from the basket. She leaned over and picked him up.

"Don't make a sound."

Hannah froze at the unfamiliar voice as she clutched Samuel close. She turned to face a man she'd never seen before. Her eyes dropped to the revolver he pointed at Eddie's head. Another man held a squirming James in a tight grip, hand clamped over her son's mouth.

Fear gripped her heart. Instinct kicked in and she filled her lungs with air, ready to scream.

Pete Vance saw Mrs. Colter's intake of breath and didn't hesitate. He hit her with the back of his hand, causing her to stumble. He grabbed her arm seconds before she fell to the ground.

"I said don't make a sound."

He ushered her forward toward a cluster of trees where he and his men tied their horses.

"Get on the horse." He gave her a little push forward.

She stood in front of the horse but made no move to mount it. He had a hard time believing she didn't ride. She was a rancher's wife.

"The baby," she said when he gave her a second shove.

He took the fussy child from her arms. Once she mounted the horse, he thrust the infant up toward her.

The men with him already mounted and had each of the boys on the saddle with them. Pete mounted his horse, leaving the remaining one for the last man that should be along in a minute. As quietly as possible, they set off due west.

He pulled his horse up next to Mrs. Colter.

"You don't try anything stupid and nothing will happen to your sons. Do as you're told and you might make it out of here alive."

She nodded.

"I'll be right behind ya, so I'll know if you try something. Now get a move on it."

Mrs. Colter shifted the reins to her other hand, holding the baby close. Then she kicked the horse into a faster pace to keep up with the men in front of her. Pete brought up the rear.

When they were in the cover of the mountain switchbacks, he looked back down at the ranch. Only one rider followed. That would be his man. Robert Garrett would be right pleased to see the fruition of his plan.

Warren felt uneasy as he watched Mary go over lessons with Beth. She had sent Eddie and James outside to keep Hannah company while she got Beth back on track with her studies.

He glanced out the window in the dining room. Nothing. He couldn't see the laundry wash basin from here. Just part of the laundry line. Clothes swayed back and forth in the wind.

From this vantage point he couldn't really see Hannah or the boys.

He frowned.

"What's wrong?" Mary asked, stepping closer to the window.

Shaking his head, he said, "Don't know."

He tried a different angle. Still couldn't see them. Then he moved into the kitchen. That window was smaller, but he could see the wash basin from it.

"I don't see Hannah and the boys."

Warren moved from the kitchen toward the front of the house. Mary followed behind him.

"Wait here."

He drew his Colt .45 and cautiously opened the front door.

As soon as he stepped over the threshold, he felt a hard blow to the back of his head. Nausea rolled over him. His vision swam. He heard Mary's scream. Then everything went black.

Mary stood shaking as she watched Warren's body slump in the doorway. The shadow of a figure darted across the porch. She stood frozen for a few seconds before Beth tugged on her hand.

"Mama, is Mr. Warren dead?"

Confusion swirled in her mind. Warren couldn't see Hannah. The boys. Warren was on the floor.

Help. She needed to get help.

Her eyes scanned the area around her. Where was the rifle?

Then she remembered that they had taken it outside with them. It was near the wash basin.

Think, Mary.

The dinner bell!

She paused at Warren's body to check his injuries. From best she could tell, he was unconscious.

Stepping over his body, she rushed to the dinner bell hanging from the porch. She rang it with all her might. Hitting each side of the triangle in methodical movements, she continued to ring the bell. No one came immediately so she kept ringing.

Her arm hurt, so she switched hands. Though not as smooth, the loud clanging bell rang out across the valley.

Ben Shepherd was the first to arrive. "What." He gasped for air. "Happened?"

She kept ringing.

"Mary, what happened?" He grabbed her wrist to stop the ringing.

"Hannah. Eddie. James."

"Where are they?"

"Gone." She didn't know for sure. But, since they hadn't come running at the sound of the bell, she knew. They were gone.

Betty arrived next, followed by Julia.

"Oh, dear! Is Warren okay?" Betty kneeled by his still form.

"Yes. I think so."

A wagon came into sight at the top of the hill. Will was back.

Numb. Frightened. Mary sank to the steps of the porch. Her son was gone. How would she tell Will his wife and children were too?

"Samuel!" she screamed and darted from the porch around the side of the house. Maybe he was still in the basket.

She dropped to her knees next to the basket and pushed the small blankets around with her hands. He was gone too.

Her son. Her sister-in-law. Her nephews.

Lord, please don't let them die. Please don't let Will blame me for this.

Will heard the bell before the wagon cleared the top of the road overlooking the valley below. Something was very wrong. Had he not been the one driving the wagon, he would have pressed his horse for a full gallop. Instead he was stuck with the unbearably slow pace of the horse and wagon.

In the distance he saw several riders moving toward the ranch house from the herd. The boys must have heard the commotion above the noise of the cattle. He slapped the reins down on the horse's back trying to get as much speed as he could from the wagon laden with heavy supplies.

Why had he gone to town today? He should have stayed behind. Adam could have handled the meeting with the express line. And one of his men could have gotten the supplies. Then he would have been there to prevent…

He didn't even know what happened yet.

As the wagon neared the ranch house his heart stopped at the scene. Warren lay on the front porch, not moving. Mary rocked back and forth on the stairs of the porch hugging her arms around her. Her face was sickly pale. Betty hovered over Warren. Julia paced back and forth, rifle in hand. Ben stood nearby, also with his rifle in hand.

"Hannah!"

Where was she?

"Hannah!" He yanked back on the reins, set the brake, and jumped down from the wagon.

As he started toward the ranch house, Ben caught his arm.

"Hannah!"

"Will. She's gone."

His heart split in two inside his chest. He fell to his knees. The tears came unbidden. She couldn't be gone. His lifeblood. His soul mate.

"He took them." Julia's stiff voice came from the porch. "Hannah. James. Samuel. Eddie."

The pain squeezing his heart hurt worse than if he'd been trampled in a stampede. His entire family. Taken from him.

"Where's Catherine?" Adam asked, the fear evident in his voice.

"She's inside, sleeping," Julia replied.

Will took a deep breath. Falling apart wasn't helping his family. He had to pull himself together. Slowly he stood to his full height. Anger simmered beneath the surface.

"What happened?"

Ben answered, "Best we can tell some riders came in and took Hannah, James, Samuel, and Eddie. When Warren suspected something was wrong, he came out. Got knocked up the side of the head."

"Who took them?" He directed the question at Mary. "Who!"

Julia answered. "You know it was him."

"Reuben." His brother's name dropped from his lips as his fear swallowed all sense of stability.

Then the anger rushed him again. He would not let Reuben take his family without a fight.

"Gather the men. We're going after them."

"Will." Ben's soft spoken word stopped him. "It's almost dark. We should wait until morning."

Will clenched a fist as his side. "He's got my wife. My sons."

Adam came up next to him. "Ben's right. It'll be dark soon. We should use that time to figure out which way they went. Then at dawn we can ride after them."

Rage burned in his veins, fiercer than anything he felt before. He was not going to wait. He was not going to leave Hannah defenseless with those men. His mind imagined what they would do to her.

His feet pounded a steady rhythm to the barn. He grabbed his saddle and started towards Jackson's stall. Ben stood with arms folded across his chest in front of the stall.

"Step aside."

"When yer pa died, I made him a promise."

Will stopped.

"I promised to take care of ya. Watch yer back. Keep ya from doing something foolish."

Dropping the saddle, Will sank to the ground.

"He took my *wife*. He took my sons." He looked up at Ben, begging his old friend to understand. "I can't just leave them."

"I ain't asking ya to. Just get yer head on straight. Be ye of clear mind."

His heart broke again as two truths washed over him. He wasn't of clear mind right now. And, he forgot to call on God.

Lord, give me wisdom. Protect my family. Keep them safe. Show me what to do.

Then the answer came. *Dawn.*

Will stood and picked up his saddle from the ground. He stowed it back in its place. When he turned around, Ben pulled him into a quick hug.

"Son, let's go look around before sunset."

As they neared the ranch house, several of his men were waiting.

"Covington," Ben said. "Go get the sheriff."

Will watched numbly as the men set about looking for signs of what happened. He couldn't concentrate. All he could think of was Hannah. Her blue eyes. Strawberry blonde hair. The feel of her in his arms.

He couldn't lose her.

"Will, why don't you come in for a bit?" Betty suggested from the doorway. "Help me get Warren to a chair."

Warren groaned and sat up. Will moved to help him up and the two shuffled behind Betty. Once in the dining room, Warren slid into a chair. He propped his elbows on the table and rested his head in his hands.

Will took the seat next to him. He looked out the window. Dusk was falling. Hawk moved past the window carefully studying the ground. They would help him. His men would help.

"Commit your way to the Lord," Betty said from the kitchen. "Trust him and he will do this: He will make your righteousness shine like the dawn, the justice of your cause like the noonday sun."

Tears leaked from the corner of his eyes. *Lord, let it be true. Let me find her.*

The silent tears progressed to full on sobs. Betty came out from the kitchen and laid a gentle hand on his shoulder. She set a cup of coffee in front of him.

"Be still before the Lord. Wait patiently for him."

She rubbed small circles on his back until the emotion wasted from him.

"Will, the Lord is with you. Trust him. He knows where she is. He sees her and has her under his protection. Wait for Him."

He nodded and wiped the moisture from his eyes as what was left of his family gathered around the table for a meal. It seemed so empty without Hannah.

Chapter 17

Hannah looked around after she dismounted the horse. They were stopping for the night, which meant these men felt secure—confident that they hadn't been followed.

As dusk turned to darkness, she debated about what to do. This rocky area of the mountain would make it difficult for Will to know which way they went. She laid Samuel on the ground next to her feet and studied her clothing. A simple brown work dress. Her apron. One petticoat that seemed to do little against the growing chill in the air.

Perhaps she could fashion a sling for Samuel from her apron and then have enough material left over to drop some pieces along the way as markers for Will.

"Aunt Hannah," Eddie said as he snuggled up to her side. "Are they going to kill us?"

She glared up at the ring leader. Pete, she thought the others called him. He met her gaze with an unreadable expression.

"No, Eddie."

Pete's eyes narrowed as if to challenge her statement.

"Are… you sure?"

She kissed Eddie on the top of his head and whispered. "Yes, I'm sure. God says that he'll never leave us or forsake us. He is watching over us now. He won't let anything happen. Just be strong and trust him."

Eddie nodded.

"Mama!" James shifted in her lap. "Hungry!"

She sighed and wondered if these men planned to share any of their food with them. She set James on the ground and told Eddie to watch both of the boys. Then she stood and approached Pete.

With determination, she decided a firm request might be the way to approach him. "Will you watch the children while I go relieve myself?"

Pete narrowed his eyes and looked her up and down for a few seconds. "Avery! Escort the lady to the privy will you?"

"Sure thing boss." He laughed. "It'll be my pleasure."

"And keep yer hands to yerself. Don't get no stupid ideas. Garrett won't take kindly if any harm comes to her on the trail."

Avery grabbed her upper arm and led her away from the campfire. "Find a spot and be quick about it."

She moved a few feet away from him to crouch behind a large rock. Once she was out of sight, she took off her apron. She coughed to mask the sound of tearing fabric. She hid a few smaller strips in the pockets of her dress, then fashioned the larger piece into a sling over her shoulder for Samuel.

"I'm finished," she announced moving around the rock back toward Avery.

He gave her a nudge forward then he followed behind her.

Once back at the campfire, she used the sling to provide some cover while she nursed Samuel. Pete watched her with great interest.

"Must be odd, nursing Larson's baby. You have one of your own?"

Did he think Samuel was Catherine, Julia's baby?

She hesitated, then decided it would be best not to clarify that Samuel was her son. She nodded in response.

Pete frowned. Then he stood and walked toward the horses. He untied a few blankets from the back of the saddles and tossed two her way.

"One for the boys. One for you. Soon as yer done with the little one, get some sleep."

She nodded again. Then turned her attention to the children. "Eddie, you and James take this one."

"Yes ma'am."

She gave his arm a gentle squeeze. "Remember what I said."

He nodded.

Lord, please protect us. Keep us safe. Stay right here with us.

Will tossed and turned all night. It was so cold without Hannah.

So empty. Every time he dosed off, he woke with a start.

He prayed and prayed every time he woke up. He couldn't think of what else to do.

Long before dawn, he dressed and made his way down the stairs. The soft glow of a lamp emanated from the living room. Mary sat staring off at nothing in particular, shawl wrapped around her shoulders.

She looked up as he took a seat.

"Why would he take Eddie?" Her voice croaked.

Up until that moment, Will realized he'd been so consumed with his own grief that he forgot her son was missing too.

He cleared his throat. "I don't know. Hannah, James, and Samuel make sense. He's after me."

Mary frowned. "Maybe he wants his son after all."

She turned fear filled eyes towards him.

"Bring them back, Will. Please. Bring them all back."

Tears threatened his eyes again. He pinched the bridge of his nose in the hopes that they might not fall this time. "I want nothing else."

"Even if you have to kill him."

Icy eyes gave finality to her words. She would choose her son over her husband.

Will swallowed hard as Mary rose and headed to the kitchen. If he were called upon to make a choice between Reuben and his family, could he do it?

He shook his head to dislodge the thought. Best to focus on getting ready. Then he started gathering ammunition for his revolver and rifle. As he recalled the conversation with the sheriff, his jaw twitched.

"I can deputize you and your men, but I can't leave right now," said the sheriff. "Got too much going on in town."

So, Will, Warren, Jed, and Hawk were deputized. They would head out with the law on their side—just not with the law at their side.

"Your horse is ready." Warren's voice pulled him from his thoughts.

Mary made small bundles of food for each of them. She also set out breakfast plates. Will sat at the table. Warren, Hawk, Jed, and

Ben joined him.

He couldn't eat much, his stomach was in knots. Hannah was out there. She needed him.

"Sure you don't want me to ride with ya?" Ben asked.

Will shook his head. "I need you and Adam here. In case they try anything while we're gone."

Ben gave a curt nod and dropped the subject.

Warren rubbed the sore spot on the back of his head. The bump had almost disappeared from yesterday. Good thing too. If Will thought he wasn't in top shape, he probably would have left him behind.

He glanced over at Mary. Her eyes were glassy and red rimmed. She moved the food around on her plate, but ate nothing. Then she pulled her shawl tighter, as if taking comfort from its warmth.

Compassion took control of his thoughts. She must be worried about Eddie. Just one look at those violet eyes and it was clear her heart was broken.

The urge to hold her concerned him. It wasn't the first time. Probably wouldn't be the last. Yet, he still felt guarded around her. Cautious. Her reaction to losing her son should have been enough to convince him that she was so very different from Dahlia.

Still, he was reluctant.

He finished the last bite of his breakfast and excused himself, taking the bundle of food she prepared for their trip out to his saddle bags.

For the first time in years, he sent a prayer heavenward. *Lord, protect them. Let us find them.*

It felt awkward to let the words echo in his mind. Even though he went to church and occasionally picked up his Bible, he hadn't spoken to God much—not since Dahlia left.

The old emotions beat against his chest. Grief. Sorrow. Loneliness. Raw pain.

Why had she left him? How easily she tossed him and her vows aside!

He could have done some things differently. But, she'd been the one to give up. She's the one who ran.

But, even with all the pain she caused him, if she had been taken like Hannah had, he would have come for her.

Heck, he had gone after her. Once. Though she told him not to. Only to find his heart shredded at the end of the journey.

"Warren."

Mary's soft voice drew him from the memories. He didn't look at her right away—not until he had a chance to wipe the emotion from his face.

When he turned to face her, she said, "Find my son. Bring back Eddie."

A sob choked out anything else she may have been ready to say. He opened his arms and welcomed her close. He gently rubbed her back. She belonged there, with him.

He took in a sharp breath and almost pushed her away. But, he didn't really want to.

Instead, he lifted her chin so he could look into her eyes.

"I'll bring your son back. I promise."

As the hope filled her eyes, he inwardly kicked himself. He swore he'd never make a promise to a woman again.

Slowly he released her. The woman who elicited a promise from him—one he meant and had every intention of keeping.

She stepped away and returned to the porch as the rest of the men mounted their horses.

"Let's go," Will said as Warren mounted his horse.

With a glance over his shoulder, he nodded to Mary. She gave a small wave. As he turned back toward the trail, he knew the image would stay with him just as much as the promise would.

Hawk led the way, kicking his horse into a fast trot until they reached the base of the mountain. Then he slowed the pace to a walk.

Warren's eyes darted back and forth over the trail in front of him. He imagined Hawk was studying the path carefully.

After several hours, they came upon the remnants of a campfire. He dismounted for a closer look.

"Probably them," he said.

Hawk confirmed his opinion. "The fire is fresh. From last night. We're definitely headed the right way."

A few minutes later they came to a fork in the trail. Hawk dismounted and studied the ground and brush for a long time. Finally, he came back toward Warren and Will.

"I'm not sure, Boss. They could have gone either way. Could have gone one way and then back tracked."

Warren glanced at Will. The stress was etched deeply on his face. This was too personal for him.

"Hey, I got something!" Jed hollered from up the trail.

He rode back and handed Will a small piece of fabric.

Chapter 18

Will's stomach tightened as he took the small piece of fabric from Jed's outstretched hand. It was part of Hannah's apron.

Fear pounded in his chest. Had something happened to her? Was she hurt? What about the boys? Maybe one of them was injured.

"Hmm." Hawk studied the fabric. "I think Mrs. Colter did this."

Will's gaze shot his direction. He frowned.

"I think she's leaving us a sign of which way to go."

Warren agreed.

Hope sprouted from his heart, shading the fear that was there only moments before. His dear sweet Hannah was helping him. *Thank you, Lord.*

"Let's go." He motioned toward the trail where the piece was found.

Hours stretched. They found more signs of the party, but so far hadn't come close enough to see them.

Regret pushed forward. He should have left yesterday. Immediately. He shouldn't have waited. Hannah and his boys needed him. They needed him to come for them.

But, he hadn't found them yet.

As the sun started to set, Warren suggested they stop for the night. Will held back his arguments. It made sense, even if everything within him compelled him to move forward. He had to find her. Soon.

Mary took down the laundry that she and Hannah hung yesterday. She should have taken it down already. But, her sorrow made all her movements slower than normal today.

Her son was missing. The grandson her parents never met.

For a brief second she thought she shouldn't travel down that road of hurt. Then she decided she would. It felt good to remember that she once had a normal life.

Her father's brooding expression came to mind.

"He's so much older than you," Father had said. "You're only sixteen. There is still plenty of time for you to court."

"Nonsense," Mother argued. "Twelve years difference is still reasonable. He's a wealthy man from a well-respected family. Mary would make him a fine wife."

"Still, there's no need to rush."

"Aren't you eager for a grandson?" Mary teased. "The boy you never had."

Father sighed. "Not so eager as to marry you off quickly. Are you that ready to be out of my house?"

"No!" Mary jumped to her feet and ran to where he was sitting in his favorite cushioned chair. She wrapped her arms around his neck and gave him a brief hug. "I'm not eager to leave. I just meant that I know how much you wished I was a boy. If I'm married, perhaps I will grace you with a grandson."

"Sweet Mary-girl. There is plenty of time for that."

As she thought back on the long forgotten conversation now, she wondered if her father sensed something or knew something about Reuben. Why had he been so hesitant?

Just a few short weeks later, Reuben asked for her hand and murdered her parents. Had Father known of Reuben's intentions? Or had Reuben ordered him killed before he could object?

She liked to imagine that if her father knew the kind of man Reuben really was, that he would have stopped everything. He would have protected her.

Sighing heavily, she lifted the laundry basket from the ground and carried it into the house. As a parent, she was learning that she could never protect her children from everything. She tried to protect them from Reuben. Now he had her son and there was nothing she could do about it.

"Mama, when is Eddie coming back?" Beth asked as she set the basket down on the dining room table. "I miss him."

Tears burned her eyes but she willed them away.

"Soon, honey. Soon."

Please Warren. Keep your promise to me. Bring me back my son.

"I been praying like Miss Betty said. I asked God to bring Eddie back."

Mary moved to where Beth sat with her slate. She kneeled and pulled her little girl into her arms as the conviction of her words penetrated her heart.

As she released her daughter from the embrace, she also released the small willingness to consider asking for God to intervene. Surely, He had long ago forgotten her.

Pete Vance hummed a saloon tune to himself as he brought up the rear of the convoy. Avery was doing a fine job moving around and setting up possible misleads. If Colter was on their tail, he'd be mighty confused or lost by now.

Hooking up with Robert Garrett had been one of the best opportunities to come along in years. The man had cash and lots of it. And he needed a loyal man with Pete's talents.

He smiled as he thought about the rather large and accumulating stash of gold waiting for him back at Garrett's ranch. He'd been compensated nicely for managing the rustling operation. Spying on Colter helped line his pockets more. Delivering Mrs. Colter, her two brats, and the Larson baby was the last step.

Then he'd cash out and part ways with Garrett.

It wasn't that he had anything against Garrett. He just didn't like staying in one place too long. His Pete Vance disguise was starting to become a bit too recognizable. But, he had to stick with it for a few more days until this job was done. Then he'd put on a new identity.

As he daydreamed about a nice new suit and a wealthier persona, Mrs. Colter caught his eye. She had glanced over her shoulder then quickly looked back toward the horse in front of her.

He scanned the ground around them. A small white piece of fabric lay on the side of the road.

His anger boiled to the surface. He kicked his horse to catch up with Mrs. Colter.

When he was right beside her, he didn't wait for her to acknowledge him. Instead, he smacked her hard on the face. She started to lose balance on the horse and he reached out and steadied her, applying pressure on her arm.

"Stop your horse."

She complied.

"Git down."

She secured the baby in the sling around her shoulder before dismounting.

He dismounted his horse. Then he dragged her back to where the piece of fabric lay on the ground.

"Pick it up."

When she hesitated, he shoved her to the ground. He drew his revolver and pointed it at her.

She didn't move.

He cocked the gun then slowly pulled the trigger.

Hannah screamed as the sound of the gun shot rang in her ears.

"I said pick it up."

With shaky fingers she retrieved the piece of fabric from the ground. Pete took it from her. Then, without warning, he smacked her hard on the side of her head. A second welt puffed her skin, bringing with it searing heat.

"Next time you do something stupid like that, one of those boys of yours is going to suffer the consequences."

He grabbed her arm and pulled her back to her horse.

"Empty your pockets. I want every last scrap."

She did as he commanded this time without hesitation.

"Boss," Avery said, stopping his horse near them. "I thought you said Garrett didn't want no marks on her."

"Mind yer own business and keep it moving. We'll catch up in a minute."

As Avery directed his horse away, Hannah's breathing stilled. The look in Pete's eye frightened her.

Never will I leave you.

Then peace. *Lord, protect me.*

The features on Pete's face softened ever so slightly.

"Get on your horse."

As she did, he added, "And don't think of doing something so stupid again. Garrett wants you and the kids alive. Not unscathed. Until now, I been protecting you from these wolves. If you want to keep it that way, then you best behave."

Hannah nodded. Then she kicked her horse to a trot to catch up with the others.

Something was very odd about Pete. Oh, she believed that he would harm her again, now that she'd been caught. Yet, it seemed as if he didn't want to.

Then there was his language. When he was agitated, it came out as some strange mix of well-educated and common. Words like "unscathed" didn't seem to fit with the simple words he used at camp the night before.

He was definitely well-educated, she decided, and the rest was just a disguise.

Not that it mattered. She and her children and Eddie were this man's prisoner. He was intent on taking her to Robert Garrett's ranch. At least now she knew the destination.

Chapter 19

Four days.

Will clenched his jaw. They still hadn't found Hannah. They'd been wandering through the desert mountains for four unbearable days.

Hawk approached him as he dismounted his horse.

"I'm not sure which way they went," Hawk said. "Jed and I scouted all three branches of the trail. They all show recent tracks."

"Could be they are doubling back," Warren said. "Trying to confuse us."

Will nodded. The tightness in his gut squeezed harder. He couldn't leave her. He had to find her.

"Sun's pretty low. Maybe we should camp here for the night. See if we can't figure out which way they went," Warren suggested.

Will cleared his throat. "Alright."

Only it wasn't alright. Nothing was. And time was running out. They had to find them before they got to Reuben's ranch.

He didn't want to think of what might happen if they didn't. He knew what Reuben did to men who got on his wrong side. Shoot, he knew what Reuben did to Julia and what he suspected he had done repeatedly to Mary—his own wife.

Tears threatened again and he turned toward his horse to hide them.

Will's mind churned with all the possible ways Reuben might take revenge. He might kill James, or Samuel, or both. Maybe even Hannah. He could—Will swallowed hard—rape his wife. He could sell her to a brothel in another town. Make her disappear. Kill her.

The pain tore through his chest. He wouldn't let any of that happen, God willing.

Commit your way to the Lord. He will make the justice of your cause like the noonday sun.

It was so hard. Hard to trust God to protect Hannah. That had always been his job. He protected his family—his sister, his wife, his sons.

The reality of his failure struck him so hard he almost stumbled. Instead, he threw the saddle on the ground and took a seat.

He failed to protect Julia and Mary from Reuben. Now, he failed to protect his wife and sons from him.

Trust me.

Will inhaled deeply. Juniper tickled his nose as he closed his eyes. *I've never really protected anyone, have I?*

No. It is I.

Lord, forgive me. And watch over Hannah, James, Samuel, and Eddie. Bring them home unharmed.

A hand on his shoulder caused him to open his eyes. It was Jed.

"Boss, I just wanted to say I'm sorry. I know it's hard to… You know… Um…"

Will nodded. He knew. Jed lost his entire family to an Indian attack years ago. That pain was visible in his eyes now. He knew exactly what Will was feeling.

"I never did thank you for taking a chance on me three years ago. I… You and the missus are the only family I've got now."

Hawk joined the conversation. "Me, too. We want to find them for you, Boss."

Will cleared his throat to dislodge the emotions. "Thanks. I know you're doing your best."

"I been praying for us to find them," Jed said.

At Will's surprised expression, he added, "Been talking to Ben a lot lately. He's been helping me understand that it ain't God's fault that I lost my family."

Will reached out and squeezed Jed's shoulder. "That's good. And thank you for your prayers."

"Well, we still got some daylight left, so I'm gonna look around a little more. See if I can't figure out which way they went."

As Jed left, Hawk followed him, leaving Will alone to ponder just how much these young men had changed in the last three and a half years.

Warren listened to the conversation as he started a fire. Jed's admission hit his heart deeper than he thought it should. Though he hadn't been with Will from the beginning, he sensed what Jed had—the Colters weren't just his employers, they were his family.

He wanted that family back safe and sound regardless of the promise he made Mary. That promise only solidified his resolve in times where he thought they lost the trail, or like now, where he thought it might be better for Will if they turned back and came up with a plan to go to Garrett's ranch.

I'll bring them back, Mary. He promised.

He shifted his thoughts to her. How was she holding up? What about little Beth?

A brief image floated across his mind. Him. Mary was with him. So was Eddie and Beth. Only they weren't on Colter Ranch. They were on his ranch—a new ranch.

The ranch he hoped to start soon with the money he'd been saving for years. It wouldn't be big or fancy. But, he didn't want it to be. All he ever wanted was a simple ranch with a few hundred head, maybe one or two men working with him.

With a wife at his side and children around his table.

He almost had the dream once. With Dahlia. With his son.

Yeah, he could empathize with Will's pain. The only thing that hurt worse than losing your whole family, was never getting them back.

Another thing Jed said rolled around in his mind. He didn't blame God anymore for losing his family.

Warren hated to admit that was his attitude. He blamed God for Dahlia leaving. It was easier than admitting his faults. He knew she wasn't same after Lee's birth. Her mind went someplace dark, on the edge of sanity. It didn't help that he was working from sun up until well after sun down trying to build his ranch. She faced too many hours alone.

She hadn't been strong enough to handle it and she snapped.

The sound of Jed and Hawk returning pulled him from the stormy memories.

"Best we can tell," Jed said. "They headed south."

"Isn't Perry Quinn's ranch down the mountain?" Warren asked.

Will nodded.

"Maybe we should just head down there tomorrow and regroup."

"I don't know," Will said.

"We think they're headed to Garrett's ranch, right?"

Will nodded again.

"So it would make sense if we stopped this cat and mouse game and just planned our offense at his ranch."

"What about Hannah and the boys?"

Warren rubbed his chin. "I don't think he'll do anything right away. Whatever he does, he'll make sure you know it. He wants you to follow them and get frustrated. If we stop playing the game, then we can come up with a solid plan to rescue them."

Will sighed heavily. "You're right. This wandering around guessing which trail they took is getting old. Let's head down to Quinn's ranch in the morning."

"Let's get some shut eye, boys," Warren said to Hawk and Jed.

Sometime in the wee hours of the morning, Warren woke with a start. There it was again. The eerie scream of a mountain lion. Only much too close to camp.

Slowly he sat up and waited for his eyes to adjust to the early dawn light. He looked around camp. The food bag sat near Jed. Warren bit back a curse. He forgot to string it up in a tree.

In a flash, the animal leaped onto Jed, bringing him wide awake in a second. The mountain lion clamped down on the cowboy's arm with his teeth, while swiping at his body with his extended claws.

"Help!" Jed screamed as he tried to reach for his gun. Pain etched his face as the cat kept hold of his arm.

Warren jumped to his feet, trying to scare the mountain lion away. When he wasn't successful, he grabbed the food bag and tossed it from the camp area.

Unfortunately, the cat did not take the bait.

Jed got his feet up under the cat's belly and began to kick furiously. Hawk and Will were now awake.

"Shoot it," Will said.

Warren hesitated. It was a risky shot. If he missed, he could accidentally kill Jed. There was no room for error.

"Shoot it!"

He whipped his revolver from its holder and fired on instinct, barely taking time to think about the shot. The large cat relaxed and fell limp on Jed's body.

"Get it off!" Jed yelled.

Hawk and Will picked up the dead mountain lion and tossed it aside.

Warren took a deep breath. The last time he was in a position to make a tough shot, it hadn't ended well. Maybe God was on his side after all.

"Bandages."

The single word from Will jolted him from his momentary peace. He dug through his saddle bag and found something that would work. As he stepped closer, he saw the mess that was Jed's arm. At one spot, he thought he saw clear to the bone.

Hawk took the bandages and began cleaning and wrapping Jed's arm. By now, Jed passed out from the pain. Will checked the rest of the cowboy for other signs of injury.

"Look like it's just his arm. But it's bad."

Warren nodded. Looked like they had a second reason to abandon the search. If they didn't, he wasn't too sure Jed would survive.

Commit your way to the Lord. He will make the justice of your cause like the noonday sun.

Will clenched his jaw to keep his anger in check. He didn't understand. They were close to finding Hannah. He could feel it.

Now this. They had to give up and get Jed some medical care. His arm—he swallowed back the bile—it was bad.

Trust me.

"I'm trying to," he whispered as he mounted his horse. *I'm trying.*

Trust me.

He shook his head as he directed his horse behind Jed's so he would be able to see if the young man woke up. His limp body was slung over the back of his horse. They tied him to it so he wouldn't fall off.

How can I trust you? Hannah and the boys are gone. Jed is hurt. We have to stop. Surely God wouldn't ask him to forget about his family.

Trust me.

Will sucked in a deep breath and blew it out slowly. "Okay, Lord," he whispered. "I'll trust you. But you have to keep them safe."

The next few hours were tense as they carefully picked their way down the side of the mountain. At last, they made it to the valley floor.

Jed stirred a few times, but not enough to cause them to stop.

When Perry Quinn's ranch became a soft gray outline on the horizon, Will sent up another prayer. *Show me what to do.*

As they approached the house, a rider came in from the herd and met them. It was Perry Quinn.

"Colter." His voice sounded surprised. "What brings you out our way?"

"Perry. It's a long story. And we got an injured man. Mind if we head inside?"

"Sure. Thinking you'll need a doctor?"

"If you happen to have one handy."

"I'll get one of the boys to ride out to fetch Mrs. Van Dyke. She'd be the closest we have to a doctor around here."

Will nodded and dismounted his horse as Perry rode back to his herd. Warren and Hawk took Jed inside. He stirred briefly before relaxing onto the bed.

"Let's hope Mrs. Van Dyke will be able to help," Warren said.

Will hoped so too.

Two hours later Mrs. Van Dyke left. She gave Jed some medicine and left more for him to take. She stitched up part of his arm and wrapped it. She told him Jed would recover in time. Would definitely have some nasty scars, but she didn't see any permanent damage.

He breathed a sigh of relief.

As Perry started preparing supper, Will sat at the small table.

"How's your wife?" Perry asked.

"Missing. That's why we're here. She and my sons and nephew have been kidnapped."

"Got any idea by who?"

"Reu—" Will stopped himself. Perry wouldn't know his brother by his real name. "Robert Garrett."

"Garrett? Are you sure?"

"Positive. I believe he's really after me."

"Why's that?"

"Let's just say, he and I have some history."

Warren came in followed by Hawk and the rest of Perry's men.

"So what's the plan?" Perry asked. "And how can we help?"

Chapter 20

Garrett Ranch

February 27, 1867

Robert Garrett smiled as he sat down at the dining table alone. The smell of beef roast mingled with roasted potatoes and carrots. With little fanfare, he dug into the hearty meal. This cook seemed to understand his preferences much better than the last.

A knock sounded at the door. He swallowed the bite of roast. "Come in!" he hollered, before shoving the next bite in his mouth.

"Evening, Mr. Garrett."

A finely dressed gentleman entered his home.

Robert frowned, not recognizing the man.

"Mind if I join you. I believe we've some business to discuss."

He narrowed his eyes. "And you are?"

"You know me most recently by another name. Pete Vance."

Robert nearly choked on a potato. He looked the gentleman up and down. Then he stared at the eyes. Gray, steely eyes. "You got me this time, Mr. ?"

"Come on, now, Robert. Surely you know a name is meaningless to men like us. Pete will be just fine for the time being."

He motioned for Pete to take a seat. Then he rang a bell. When the cook appeared, he asked for another plate for his guest.

After the food was delivered, Pete discussed the reason for his visit. "Avery is guarding them now. They're out in the small shack as you requested."

"Good, good. Were you followed?"

"At first. Lost them the last day. I suspect they gave up."

Robert shook his head. "Not if I know Colter." He was counting on him following. His plan wouldn't be complete until Colter showed up and witnessed with his own eyes the wrath of Reuben Colter.

"About my payment—"

"Why don't you stick around for a few days? Enjoy my hospitality."

"Thank you for the offer, but I really must be on my way. I'm expected in California in a few days."

Robert frowned. "I didn't realize our contract was up."

"I delivered the woman and children as you requested. That was the end of our agreement."

He pounded his fist on the table. He had been counting on Pete sticking around for a few more days. This was a terrible slip up.

"I insist that you stay."

Pete lifted the napkin from his lap and wiped his lips. He laid the napkin on the table. Then his hand disappeared below the table. The sound of a revolver cocking echoed in the quiet room.

"Mr. Garrett, it's been a pleasure doing business with you, but I would greatly appreciate getting paid now."

Robert threw his napkin down and stood. With heavy steps he walked from the room, conscious of Pete's gun pointed at his back. He made his way to the parlor where his desk sat. He took a seat and unlocked a drawer.

Retrieving a stack of bills from it, he counted out payment.

Pete waved the gun at him. "I think one or two extra bills are in order, Mr. Garrett. For my trouble."

He frowned and begrudgingly added two more large bills to the stack.

Pete took the bills and stowed them in his vest pocket. "A pleasure."

Then Pete nodded and hurried out the front door. Robert ran to the open door and watched as the man and horse galloped away.

"Never trust a crook," he muttered to himself as he slammed the door shut.

He returned to the table and finished his meal. A nice after-dinner drink lifted his spirits. It was time to welcome his guests.

Removing his fine clothes, he donned a plain pair of trousers and gray button down shirt. He found his ratty hat and placed it firmly on his head. Grabbing a lantern, he headed out the door to the stables.

Twenty minutes later, he pulled to a stop in front of the small shack that contained his prize. He greeted Avery and tossed him the reins. A smile twitched at his lips as he opened the door. Will Colter would be sorry he took the Star C from him.

As the door opened, Hannah motioned for Eddie and James to stand behind her. Samuel remained quiet from his resting place in the makeshift bassinet set on the table.

"Mrs. Colter."

"Mr. Garrett." She kept her tone even.

"I hope you are finding the accommodations adequate."

She held back a snort of disgust as a rat scurried across the floor behind Robert Garrett.

"Avery!"

The young man entered behind Robert. "Take the boys outside."

"No!" Hannah lurched toward James as Avery grabbed his wrist.

"Mama!"

Hannah gasped as Robert slapped her son in the face.

"Keep them quiet while I talk to their mother."

Avery pulled the boys from the room and closed the door behind him.

Hannah swallowed hard. Robert removed his hat and approached her.

Fear not, for I am with you. Never will I leave you. Never will I forsake you.

She held on to the dear words as her fear threatened to bubble over.

"Lovely, Hannah."

Robert reached out to touch her bruised cheek.

"Gave Pete some trouble, huh?"

She didn't move or answer.

His hand moved from her cheek to her hair. Slowly he began removing the hair pins. When her hair cascaded around her shoulders, he ran his fingers through it.

"Robert—"

He grabbed a fistful of hair and yanked, stopping any more words from escaping. When he spoke, his drawl matched that of her husband.

"My brother has picked a pretty wife."

Lustful eyes burned into her soul.

"I wonder, Hannah, if you please him in every way."

Lord please. Don't let him—

He pulled her forcefully towards him. Then he lowered his head and kissed her. Her stomach revolted. She turned her head and coughed.

Shoving her backward, he pushed her onto the bed. She squirmed, fearing what he might do.

He moved forward but didn't touch her again.

"Sweet. Just what Will would like."

He stared at her for several minutes. Her heart raced at the thoughts she saw crossing his mind. Then without warning, he moved toward the door.

"Enjoy your stay." He slammed the door closed behind him.

Reuben spat in disgust as he left the shack. He couldn't do it. She looked too… Motherly. The way she reacted to Avery taking her sons away. It reminded him too much of his own mother.

Maybe with a few more drinks he would feel differently. He had to take her. It would kill Will slowly, knowing his brother violated his wife. He must do it if he wanted to see this plan to completion.

"Papa?"

Reuben stopped and turned slowly.

"What do you want me to do with these two?" Avery asked.

"What is this! That is not Colter's boy!" No. It was his son. His son that should be safe with his mother back on a ranch hundreds of miles away.

"I don't know," Avery said. "Pete said we were to grab the two boys and the baby. That's what we done."

Reuben threw the door open again. He moved to the small child in the bassinet on the table. As he removed the child's diaper,

Hannah grabbed his arm and tried to stop him. He smacked her across the face, knocking her to the ground.

He finished removing the diaper.

"Nooooo!" He screamed at the top of his lungs in a fit of rage. The baby was a boy. Not Larson's girl.

"Who is this child?" His anger burned as he turned on Hannah.

"My son. Samuel."

He cursed. "You idiot!"

He turned toward Avery. "You got the wrong kid. You were supposed to bring these two," he pointed to Samuel and James, "and Larson's baby. Not him." He pointed to Eddie. "Not HIM!"

"Papa."

Again Eddie spoke. Reuben erupted in a fit of rage. He grabbed the boy by the collar and shoved him against the wall. "Shut up! Shut up! I am not your papa! Do you hear me?"

Eddie nodded.

When Reuben released him, the child slumped to the floor. He ran from the small shack and mounted his horse. Kicking the animal for a gallop, he covered the distance to his home quickly.

Once inside the comfort of his home, he paced back and forth across the parlor.

Eddie was here. He wasn't supposed to be anywhere nearby. He was supposed to be on Colter Ranch. That was part of his plan.

Kill Colter's sons, but leave him with his nephew—his brother's son—to inherit his ranch. It would be the ultimate revenge. Knowing that Will would live the rest of his days forced to raise Reuben's son and to leave him the ranch. It was the only way he could make sure Will lost everything. It was the only way to make him pay.

Now the plan was in shambles. He didn't have Larson's daughter. So he couldn't raise her for a few years until she was old enough to go to a brothel as he planned. Larson wouldn't feel any pain for stealing Julia away. He would get off free.

And Will. He'd still feel the pain, but the ultimate revenge—his ranch for the Star C—would never happen. Not now.

Eddie wasn't supposed to be here.

Think, Reuben, think.

He would still kill James and Samuel. But not until Will arrived.

His wife, on the other hand, could be taken care of tonight. He moved toward whiskey bottle and began drinking. He had to get up the nerve to do it. No matter what.

Chapter 21

Hannah kept the lamp burning on low throughout the night. Eddie and James were both terrified. It took an hour or more to get them to lie down and even longer to finally sleep.

Samuel fussed and she adjusted him in her arms. She couldn't sleep. She was scared too.

Never will I leave you. Never will I forsake you.

She believed the promise, but she knew that dark and evil things still happened to the most faithful. This was Reuben—the man who raped his sister. He had no boundaries.

Fear not. I am with you.

She closed her eyes and leaned her head back against the wall. *I know, Lord. I know you are bigger and stronger and more powerful than Reuben. Please rescue us. Keep us safe.*

A dull pain in her neck brought her eyes open. Early dawn light filtered through the one window in the small shack. She stood and carried Samuel to the bed, laying him next to the other two boys.

She stretched and worked out the kinks in her muscles. If they were still here tonight, she'd be sure to sleep in the bed and not accidentally fall asleep in the chair.

Crossing the room, she opened the small door to the stove. Small embers burned. She found another log inside the room and tossed it in.

Then she scanned the shelves on the wall. Beans. Beans. Beans. Not many choices. Her gaze caught on one different item. Grits.

She sighed. It was better than starving. She found a pan—only one—and began making grits for breakfast. She rationed the amount she made, just in case. She had no idea how long they might be here or if Reuben would provide them with more food.

Reuben. After his sinister actions last night, she banished Robert Garrett from her mind. This man was definitely Reuben, Will's brother.

When he left, she half expected him to return in the middle of the night. But he didn't. She hadn't seen him since he realized he had the wrong children. Well, not all of them were wrong.

Thank you, Lord, that Catherine is safe.

Voices came from outside. She moved near the door to listen to what was going on. Another man came to relieve Avery. Neither bothered her or the children.

She stayed by the door until the sound of Avery riding off faded.

Surely Will was coming for her. Hope swelled. He would come for her. She was certain of it. He would do anything to rescue her. She just needed to stay strong until he came.

And it wouldn't hurt to take stock of what was available in the shack. She might even be able to fashion a crude weapon if needed.

Will swiped his hand down his face. Their plan was solid. The best they could hope for. Unfortunately, they were still half a day's ride out. It would be almost dark by the time they got there. The earliest he would be able to free Hannah would be tomorrow.

A knife sliced through him. Tomorrow seemed too long. She'd been gone almost a week now. There was no telling what Reuben had already done.

Was any of his family left to rescue?

What still didn't make sense to him was that he took Eddie. Hannah and the boys made sense. He was after Will. But, Eddie?

He shook his head.

Then it dawned on him. What if Eddie was taken by mistake?

He thought back to when Eddie was born. Reuben loved his son—if he loved anyone. His son meant a lot to him.

Maybe it was good for Will that Eddie had been taken. Reuben wouldn't let anything happen to him.

He sighed in frustration. Who was he kidding? Will couldn't harm Eddie. Not even to save his family. It just wasn't something he was willing to do.

There had to be a way to get everyone back unharmed without

anyone dying.

Images of different scenarios crossed his mind. Each one ended with Reuben lying limp on the ground. *Please, Lord, I don't think I can take his life if I have to. He's my brother.*

No matter how much they fought growing up, or their extreme tension as adults, Reuben was still his brother. He was still family.

Why had he taken the boys and Hannah? What was his plan? Was it just to make him suffer? Or was there some bigger purpose in Reuben's mind?

Was it possible his brother blamed him for the loss of the Star C?

From what Mary said, it sounded entirely possible, though completely false. It was Reuben's debt to Hiram Norton that led him to his schemes about Julia's future—and ultimately to the loss of the ranch. It had nothing to do with Will leaving.

Commit your way to the Lord. He will make the justice of your cause like the noonday sun.

He may never know why Reuben was doing this. But, God would resolve it. Of this, Will was certain.

Mary couldn't concentrate, she realized after reading Beth's answers on her slate for the fourth time. She sighed heavily and set it aside.

"Why don't you go play with your dolly in the living room for a while?"

Beth smiled and jumped up from the table. Then she stopped. "Mama, when is Eddie coming home? I miss him."

A sob caught in her throat but she swallowed it away before answering. "I don't know sweetheart. Uncle Will is doing his best to find him. He's probably already found him and is headed home even now."

Beth nodded and ran off to the living room, satisfied with the lies.

Mary collapsed into a chair, folded her arms on the table, and rested her head on them. Eddie had been missing for almost a week.

There was no word from Will.

She closed her eyes as her mind imagined dozens of scenarios. Eddie was dead. Eddie refused to come home, choosing his father over her. Will and his men were dead, having been ambushed by Reuben's men. Warren was dead.

Her heart crashed to the floor with the thought. She would never know if something more could have been there. If, just maybe, he could have cared for her as much as she was coming to care for him.

A gentle touch to her shoulder brought her head up. Betty rubbed circles on her back.

"Dear, the Lord has them all in his care. He will take care of them."

Mary nodded, though her heart didn't agree. How many times had she called on God to rescue her from Reuben, only to be left disappointed?

Betty moved to sit next to her. "He is still with them, dear. Watching over them. Just like he was always with you."

She frowned and found her words. "He didn't watch over me. Do you have any idea the horrors I was subjected to? How can you say he watched over me?"

"You made it here. You are a wonderful mother to your children. And you still have a caring and sweet heart. That's how I know the Lord watched over you."

Mary bit the inside of her lip. She didn't want to believe it. For some reason, she thought if God were so loving, he we wouldn't let all these evil things happen to her.

"I know, dear. It's hard to wrap our minds around the Father. His ways are not our ways, so we don't always understand why he lets some awful things happen to us."

She was fighting to maintain her composure. The pain was too raw. Too real. The number of times Reuben took her body—used it for his will—caused her stomach to revolt. That was something God could have stopped.

Years of bruises, physical and emotional scars, reminders of his brutality—that could have all been prevented. Her parents' murders. The loss of a son she never knew. So many evil, hurtful things. The night at his hotel in Prescott.

The tears began slowly. One trickling down her cheeks. Then

another slowly forming a path from her tear duct to her chin. Then another. Soon, the dam burst.

Betty remained silent, but kept her hand on Mary's shoulder as she relived years of pain—of lost dreams, lost hope.

Her one and only hope all this time was that she would be free from Reuben. Permanently free.

"Lord, Jesus," Betty prayed with a soft welcoming voice. "Mary has a lot of hurt, but you already know this. You've been right there by her side through every painful moment and every joyous one. You know her heart's desire. You have always seen every tear she's cried in the heart beat it was shed. Help her, Lord, to see just how deeply you care for her. How you have been there every day—even in the darkest moments. Reassure her of your love. Melt away her resistance to you. Help her lean into the arms you've had open wide every second of every day. In your precious and blessed name. Amen."

A wave of warmth spread through Mary's body. At some point during the prayer her eyes closed. She saw images of hope through the darkest times. When her mind left and settled into peaceful memories of her family as Reuben did as he wished. It was what kept her sane. Had that been God's way of sheltering her heart?

She hadn't realized it until now. Her heart was fine. It had always been fine. It had been sheltered from the abuse. It had been preserved and filled with love overflowing for her children. It bloomed under the praise of her father-in-law or under the kindness of her brother-in-law.

For each act of violence Reuben inflicted upon her, there had been an opposite act of kindness or compassion from the others around her. Hope had always been there in the way God made himself tangible through her father-in-law, through Will, through Julia, Maggie and George, and so many others.

He was here sitting right next to her in this motherly woman as she stood and squeezed Mary to her side. It felt like a hug from the Almighty himself.

Peace sent healing waves lapping over her heart—gentle, like the slight rocking of a rowboat coming to rest in the center of a lake, reaching and pushing at the same time. She gave herself over to the motion of her heart as each hurt and horror were drowned in waves of love. Back and forth. One gentle wave after another.

This is what love looked like. Forgiveness. Refreshment.

Slowly every corner of her heart repaired.

She felt different. She couldn't explain it. She didn't understand it.

But she knew. He had always been with her. He protected the most sacred part of her heart, never letting it be damaged beyond repair. He always left her with hope.

Hope was still with her now.

She opened her eyes and smiled up into Betty's face. In that second she knew—her son was safe and would be coming home soon.

And so was Warren.

Chapter 22

Dawn's colorful display streaked across the sky. From his prone position on the ground, Will stared up at the sight and allowed it to fill his soul.

I commit this day to you, Lord. Whatever happens, it is yours.

A hesitation—a briefly lived fear—popped into his mind. He quickly eradicated it and repeated the prayer. *Whatever happens, no matter what, this day is yours.*

The sounds of men stirring drew him from his silent meditation. He sat up, knowing they were only an hour from Robert Garrett's ranch and he still had one very important thing to do.

As Warren started breakfast, he gathered his nerve. These men had a right to know exactly what they were getting into. Food was passed around. Will took none. Instead, he cleared his throat.

"I think it's time I explain who Robert Garrett is."

Perry raised an eyebrow. Hawk nodded. The rest of Perry's men and Warren made no visible reaction to his statement.

"Three and a half years ago, my father passed. He left my older brother, Reuben, the ranch in Texas, but he provided cattle and financial resources for me to start over. Some of you came West with me and have been by my side making Colter Ranch what it is today.

"As I've come to understand, Reuben got into some serious debt. His idea for getting out of that debt was to sell my sister's hand in marriage to the highest bidder. He almost got what he wanted.

"Instead, Julia ran away. She came to Colter Ranch, leaving Reuben's plans in ruin.

"See, I know my brother's true nature. He is one who blames others for his failures and he seeks revenge. Somehow, in his mind he sees the loss of the Star C ranch as my fault.

"Now he is looking to get even."

Will looked down at his boots and kicked a small rock away from him. He hated the position Reuben put him in.

"He came to Arizona and assumed a new identity—that of Robert Garrett. He fooled me and my family with his changed appearance and northern accent. We welcomed him into our home and conducted business with him—never suspecting his real identity until his wife revealed it.

"I see now that was all part of his plan to learn more about us.

"We believe that he hired the men who took my wife and my sons and my nephew. We believe he has them somewhere on his ranch.

"He is—" Will cringed inwardly at his next choice of words, despite the truth in them. "An evil man. He won't hesitate to kill every one of us if he needs to. He has no limits to what lines he will cross."

Warren spoke up. "He even had his wife's parents' murdered so she would be forced to marry him. That's the kind of man we're dealing with."

Will couldn't breathe. How could Warren know? Even *he* didn't know about that.

Warren continued, "We don't know his plans—if he intends murder again or something else. But, we need to stop him today."

"No matter what," Will said. "He must be stopped. It ends today."

"We'll get them back," Hawk said.

The rest of the men added similar comments.

Will nodded, unable to smile. His heart was too heavy. He feared what it would take. He agonized over the choices he didn't want to make, but would likely be required to before the sun set.

I'm coming Hannah.

As soon as breakfast finished, Perry and Hawk mounted up to scout out Garrett's ranch. The rest of the men lagged behind. Will wanted to know exactly where Hannah and the children were before they chanced getting too close to the ranch. The closer they got, the more chance there was that Reuben would be alerted.

Two hours later, Perry and Hawk found them at their temporary hiding place.

"We found them," Perry said.

Will let go of the breath he barely remembered taking.

"He has them in a small shack at the edge of his pastures."

Hawk said, "Just one man is guarding the place. There might be another one inside. We couldn't get close enough to see in."

"I think our best bet is to come at the place from the west," Perry said. "It's the back side of the shack and there are some brush and low trees we can use for cover."

"Let's ride," Will said, as his stomach churned. *Let justice prevail.*

James had been fussy all morning. Though his vocabulary was still small, the word he kept repeating over and over broke Hannah's heart. "Papa. Papa."

"He's coming, little one," she whispered more for her own reassurance than for his.

They had been in the small shack for two days now. Other than trips to the outhouse, or when Reuben visited her, none of them had been allowed to leave.

Eddie vacillated between antsy and moody. Over the few months Mary and her children had been on the ranch, Hannah recognized where Eddie's moodiness came from—his missing father.

"Why doesn't Papa take me with him when he leaves?" Eddie asked without warning.

Hannah sighed. She wasn't sure she knew. Reuben acted both pleased and angry that Eddie was here.

"I don't know."

Eddie let the matter drop.

Twice now Reuben had come to the shack. The first time she feared his sinister intent. She thought he might treat her as he had Julia. But for some reason, he hadn't.

The second time he came, he was obviously drunk. It had been rather late. The children were already asleep. Amazingly, when he burst through the door, he hadn't woken any of them. She pretended to be asleep whenever he looked her direction.

He approached the bed and stood over her for several minutes. He didn't touch her or wake her. In her heart, she prayed fervently.

Lord, protect me.

Then, unexpectedly, he reached out and laid a blanket over her shoulders. She was sure he had come to the cabin for another purpose entirely.

"Mama," he had whispered. "I miss you."

Then he stepped back away from her and the bed. He kneeled next to where Eddie was sleeping. He reached out his hand and brushed the hair back from Eddie's forehead. He stayed there for a long time. She forced her sleepy mind to stay alert until he left.

When he did, it was without another word. He simply stood and walked toward the door. Then he closed it softly behind him.

She had no idea why God spared her Reuben's wrath when Julia and Mary had to suffer the worst of it. Hannah was certain Reuben's intention was not to spare her. Yet, he had.

Samuel cried from the makeshift bassinet. She stood and walked over to him. For a few seconds, she watched him. So oblivious he was to the danger they were in. So dependent and trusting. What would he do if something happened to her?

The thought brought a tear to her eyes. She didn't want him growing up without her.

Her hands flew toward him, cradling him gently, but swiftly toward her chest. He needed her. He would always need her.

Lord, protect me, if for no other reason than my children need me.

When she finished nursing Samuel, she wrapped him in his blanket and held him close for a little longer. James started his chant again.

"Papa. Papa. Papa."

"I know James. I miss your papa, too. He's coming. Soon."

"Papa. Papa. Papa."

"Shut up!" Eddie screamed. "Shut up!"

"Eddie—"

"He ain't comin'. Your papa ain't coming!"

James moved next to where she sat. Tears stained his eyes as he clung to her skirt.

"Eddie, sit down."

He didn't move.

"Sit down."

When he still didn't move, she stood. He finally sat. She placed Samuel back in the bassinet and extracted her skirt from James's tight hold. Then she went to kneel next to Eddie.

He crossed his arms when she approached. Anger burned in his eyes.

"I'm sorry your papa hasn't taken you up to the ranch house."

His eyes narrowed. "I hate him."

"Eddie, don't say that."

"It's true. He's a mean man. He doesn't love me or Beth. He never wanted us."

Hannah's heart broke. "You don't know that."

"If he loved us, why did he leave? Why didn't he come back? Why doesn't he come back for me now?"

Every question he asked deserved an answer. But not from her.

She opened her arms and waited for him to accept her embrace. Slowly, reluctantly, Eddie came. She circled her arms around him and rocked back and forth, praying the anger would leave him.

As he relaxed against her hold, he said, "I just want to go home. I miss Mama. I even miss Beth."

"I know you do. So do I. But, do you remember what I told you that first day?"

He shrugged his shoulders.

"God promised he would never leave us. That's how I know your Uncle Will is coming. He's coming because God is sending him to find us and bring us back home. Don't forget it and don't doubt it."

Eddie nodded as he wiggled from her hug. His anger faded.

She wondered for how long.

Reuben dismounted his horse in front of the shack. So far there had been no sightings of anyone watching the place. If he was going to see his plan through, he needed to deal with Hannah now.

He bit back a curse, frustrated at his inability to do so before now. He came here last night with every intention of bedding her.

Only for the second time, he couldn't do it. For some reason, she reminded him far too much of his mother, though she looked nothing like her. When he saw her sleeping there so peacefully, it reminded him of when he'd been scared as a child. He would sneak into his parents' room and stand in front of where his mother lay sleeping. As a very small child, he climbed into bed with her. But as he grew older, simply watching her sleep brought him comfort.

The memory of it overwhelmed him last night as he watched Hannah.

Today was a new day. He had to carry out this part of his plan. It would hurt Will in the worst way possible, so he had to do it.

"Avery, take the children and go for a walk," he said as he approached him.

"Sure thing, Boss."

Reuben waited as Avery retrieved the oldest two children and they started walking toward a small cluster of palo verde trees. Then he opened the door.

When she turned around and faced him, images of her sleeping pushed to the front of his mind. He tried to force them away, but they wouldn't budge.

It didn't matter. He could do this.

He moved toward her and crushed her to him. When she didn't resist, he hesitated. He didn't have time for this.

Narrowing his eyes, he tapped into his hatred for Will. She was an extension of him. Any pain he inflicted on her would be felt by Will. He lowered his head to her mouth and took another kiss from her forcefully. When she stiffened in his arms, it fueled his fire.

He pushed her away and shoved her on the bed.

She closed her eyes—the action confused him. Her lips moved, but no sound came. Then he realized she was praying.

"Prayers won't save you now."

She moved toward him. In a flash, she brought her arm up and a heavy object connected with his temple.

"Don't be so sure about that," she said.

His head throbbed and he dropped to his knees. She stepped around him and started toward the door. His foggy brain fought to keep up with her movements.

He stood and reached her just as the sound of gunfire erupted from the palo verde trees. He blinked trying to make sense of it.

Then he cursed. “William.”

Chapter 23

Warren was the first to see the man approach their hiding spot with the children. They saw Reuben on horseback when he rode up to the shack. No one else came with him.

He quickly moved next to Will. Lifting a finger to his lips for silence, he drew Will's attention. Then he pointed at the man walking with the children.

Eddie whined. "I have to pee."

The man appeared annoyed. "Go into those trees then."

"But—"

The man smacked Eddie on the head. "Go."

As Eddie approached, Will shifted his position so Eddie could see him but still out of the sight of the man. When he did, he looked back over his shoulder, then back at Will. Will motioned for him to keep coming forward.

Eddie did as he was told.

When he got to Will's side, Will moved Eddie away from the edge of the trees toward where the horses were. Warren kept his eyes on the man with James.

At a light tap on his shoulder, Warren looked at Will. With voice very low, he said, "I asked Eddie to keep quiet, stay low, and to stay with the horses."

Warren nodded.

"Come on boy! Be quick about it!" The man hollered.

After another minute passed, the man grew agitated.

"How long does it take to pee?" He released his hold on James and started walking toward the grove of trees.

When he got too close for comfort, Warren stood up and surprised him.

"What the…" The man drew his gun as a string of obscenities left his mouth.

He fired and Warren ducked. Another gun shot went off and the man fell to the ground.

"Tie him up," Will ordered.

"You shot my leg!" The man writhed on the ground.

"Just be glad he didn't kill you," Warren said. "Seeing as it's his wife you took."

Will rushed from the cover of the trees to retrieve James then he hurried back. Once under the safety of cover, he hugged his son tightly for several minutes.

Tears threatened the corners of Warren's eyes as he witnessed the scene, one he would never have with his own son.

"Papa. Papa. Papa." James babbled on.

"Stay with Eddie, okay?" Will said as he walked his son over to where Eddie sat near the horses.

"Colter!" Reuben's voice came from the distance.

The fear in Will's eyes connected with Warren's. In a second, they ran toward the shack.

"I have your wife!"

Warren said a little prayer as they dropped to their knees behind the shack out of the view of the window.

"Face me like a man!"

Will didn't move.

A baby's cries came from inside the shack. Warren noticed the tick in Will's jaw—a sure sign that sitting here doing nothing was killing him.

Footsteps sounded inside the cabin, followed by Reuben's muffled voice. "Make it be quiet."

After a minute, the baby quieted. Will still looked like he was ready to jump out of his skin.

By now, Perry and one of his men joined them behind the shack. The others were circling around to the far side, using the cover of the palo verde trees.

"William! Show your face. I know it's you!"

This time Reuben's voice came from the front of the shack.

"I'll kill her if you don't."

Will's grip tightened on his revolver. Warren hated seeing him so visibly stressed.

In a low whisper, Perry said, "Let's move over there." He pointed toward a dilapidated wagon. "It'll give us a clear view of the front."

Will nodded.

Warren led the way. As he darted from the cover, he held his breath, almost expecting a bullet to hit him. Nothing.

Three. Two. One.

He dove for the ground with a slow roll into his right shoulder, now obscured by the wagon.

Not a single shot was fired.

Once he got situated, he looked through a split in the wood at the bottom of the overturned wagon. The wheels and floor board faced the front of the shack. The inside of the bed faced him. It provided very good cover with a perfect line of sight.

The shadow of a man appeared in the doorway just as Will moved from the cover of the shack. Reuben fired a shot at Will but missed. When Perry started forward, Warren shot at the roof of the shack so he would not accidentally hit Hannah or the baby. The shot distracted Reuben long enough for Perry to make it safely to their hiding spot.

"Very sneaky, William. But, I still want to see your face!"

When Will started to rise, Warren grabbed his arm and pulled him down. "Don't do it. He'll put a bullet in you."

"He has Hannah. I have to."

Perry said, "This isn't the way. He'll just kill you."

Will sank back down on his knees.

The sound of footsteps drew their attention.

"I have your wife!"

Warren looked through the opening in the wood. Will gasped and Warren quickly figured out why. Half of Hannah's face was covered in deep purplish blue bruises.

He knew exactly how Will felt. Though he'd never seen Dahlia's face like that, he had seen her wrists, the long jagged marks she put there. Even now, the memory brought a flood of emotions to the surface. Helplessness. Anger. Fear.

What if she succeeded this time? What if he could do nothing to stop her? How could he get her to see that life was worth staying around for? He was worth it?

He swallowed hard. No, it probably wasn't the same as what Will was feeling. Someone else left the marks on his wife. It wasn't done by her hand.

Still, he knew the feeling of helplessness—knowing she needed him but being unable to save her.

Will never thought he'd want to murder his brother. But seeing his wife's battered face—wondering where else she might be hurt—sparked a deep rage within him. He would kill Reuben if he so much as thought about touching her again.

His eyes burned, but he clamped down his jaw so tightly that he thought he might break a tooth. He had to keep his emotions under control. He wouldn't be able to help her if he didn't.

"She's a very pretty thing, William. Never pictured you with someone like her."

Rage burned through his veins.

"Such soft skin."

He was going to kill him. With revolver drawn, Will started to peer over the top of the wagon. Warren's hand on his shoulder stopped him.

"He's goading you on," Warren whispered.

Will sank down again. He took a deep breath.

Commit your way to the Lord.

Revenge wasn't the way.

He will make the justice of your cause like the noonday sun.

He remembered his prayer from this morning. No matter what happened, he gave this day to the Lord.

A strange peace settled over him. Hannah would be fine. So would his sons. Somehow he just knew it.

He looked through the wood slats again. Her face looked painful. He saw the strong line of determination in the set of her jaw. She was strong, his amazing wife.

"I bet you are wondering how this is going to play out, William. Let me give you a hint." Reuben cocked his gun and pointed it at Hannah's head.

Will sucked in a quick breath of air.

Reuben positioned himself so only part of his right side was visible behind Hannah's body.

"See, William, you took my ranch. You stole my cattle. You destroyed everything I worked so hard to achieve."

Will could see the wild look in Reuben's eyes—one he'd never seen before. He wasn't sure what to expect.

"I had everything set up perfectly. And you had to go and ruin it."

He didn't understand what his brother was talking about, but chose to remain silent. That was usually the better way when dealing with Reuben.

"I thought Father had changed his will like we discussed. You know, a few days before the *accident*—"

The hair on Will's neck stood on end. Father died in a stampede. It had been an accident, right?

"He and I talked about you. It was time for you to move on. Father agreed with me—we could never share the ranch. You were plenty old enough to get your own place. He was going to talk to you."

Will's heart pounded so loud he swore it would drown out the sound of Reuben's taunting voice.

"He was even going to change the will. He was going to give me the Star C. Just me. Not you."

Fearful realization stung his heart. Reuben wouldn't have his own father murdered, would he?

"Once he came back from the meeting with Gainsley, I set everything in motion. I suggested he ride out with the herd that day. I had my men make sure he was positioned in the middle. They pressed the cattle in closer around him."

Will's heart imploded. It couldn't be.

"Then they got the cattle riled up. They did a good job of following orders. But, I didn't know Father would get the last word. He changed his will, alright. Only instead of giving you nothing, he gave you half of everything, except the land. That's not how it was supposed to happen."

A tear slid down Will's cheek. His brother murdered his father—so he could get the ranch. None of it made any sense. He hadn't seen any signs of it.

"At first, I thought stealing some of your cattle would bring me some satisfaction. The more I took the more I wanted."

Reuben yanked back on Hannah's hair causing her to whimper.

"You took what was most precious to me. Now it's time I returned the favor."

Will watched the scene unfold in slow motion, helpless to stop it.

Warren took a steadying breath. He watched as Reuben positioned himself for the shot. A thousand thoughts ran through his mind in a fraction of a second.

Here he was again. Called upon to make a difficult shot. If he missed, Hannah could die with Reuben. Or if he shot wide, a stray bullet could enter the shack, possibly hitting Samuel. If his timing was off, Reuben could get the shot off before his bullet hit its mark.

It was an impossible shot. He couldn't aim for the heart, as Hannah's shoulder covered it. He wasn't sure he could make a clean enough shot to hit him in the head.

Warren prayed—meaning it more than any prayer he'd prayed in his life up to this moment. *Lord, guide this bullet.*

Then he squeezed the trigger.

Enoch Fowler smiled from his hiding spot behind a palo verde tree. Neither Reuben or Will's men had seen him. Didn't matter if they had. He was here to do a job and he would do it.

As he tired of Reuben's mouth, he trained his rifle onto the center of Reuben's upper back. Could be the bullet would crash clear through Reuben's chest cavity and hit the little woman in front of him. Or could be it would miss her altogether. She was rather short.

Didn't matter.

Reuben hadn't been all that easy to find. What finally tipped him off was the number of trips he made to Prescott and to Colter Ranch. Seemed odd to Enoch that the man would buy so many horses and personally look them over. It was a job he could have left to his foreman.

He figured it out. Only one person had that much vested interest in visiting Colter Ranch often.

With one visit to Prescott, he learned all he needed to know about Robert Garrett. The man had an unquenchable thirst for women. Sounded a lot like what he knew of Reuben.

Then there was Mary Colter. Enoch heard about Robert Garrett's odd reaction to her arrival. Funny how much whores will tell about the loose lipped men they bed. Reuben really should learn to control his drunken tongue better.

Enoch snorted. Wouldn't matter in a few seconds anyway.

He squeezed the trigger on his rifle and watched as Reuben fell to the ground on top of the little lady.

He thought he counted a few other shots, but he wasn't going to stick around. It was clear Reuben was dead.

Now he had more important things to do—like getting himself out of there before someone discovered him. And figuring out how he was going to drag Mary Colter back to Texas to Hiram Norton. Wouldn't be easy.

Chapter 24

"Hannah!" Her name tore from Will's throat as he leaped over the side of the wagon.

There was so much blood. Too much blood to be just Reuben's.

He slid to a stop and dropped to his knees in one continuous motion.

"Hannah."

Fear lodged in his throat. She couldn't be dead. She couldn't.

A soft groan greeted his ears with the same melody sung by angels. Hope swelled as he pushed aside his brother's limp body.

"Will."

His name became the harmony to her gentle breathing.

"Hannah." Any further words were drowned out by his utter relief.

Gently, he pulled her into his arms, holding her cheek next to his beating heart. He breathed in the light scent of lavender as he buried his face in her hair. Rocking back and forth, he was only partially aware of the other men moving around them.

"He's dead," Warren said.

It didn't matter. His wife—his lifeblood—was safe. She was still with him.

"It hurts," she whispered.

His heart plummeted again as he released his hold. "Where?"

Then he saw it. A bullet grazed her right arm. He grabbed his handkerchief and pressed it against the wound. After a few seconds, he lifted the handkerchief and it appeared like it had stopped bleeding.

"Let's get you patched up."

He stood and helped her to her feet. Then he led her into the small shack. He checked on Samuel, who slept in a makeshift bassinet on the table before tending to her arm.

"Who shot him?" she asked.

Will was so relieved that he hadn't been the one to pull the trigger. Without thinking, he answered, "Warren. He took the shot."

"I hate him!"

Will glanced up to see Eddie running from the grove of palo verde trees headlong into Warren.

"I hate you! You killed my papa!"

Eddie pounded fists into Warren's chest.

"Will," Hannah said. "Bring him here."

He did as she asked, though Eddie fought against his grip.

"Can you take Samuel and give us a few minutes?"

Will wasn't ready to leave her side yet. He only just got her back. But after a quick look into her eyes, he understood that Eddie's wellbeing was important right now.

He lifted Samuel from the bassinet. He seemed so small in his giant arms. Then he stepped from the shack.

"Papa. Papa." James's happy cries greeted him.

He dropped to one knee. Holding Samuel in one arm, he folded James into the other. His family was safe. They were back with him again. *Thank you, Lord.*

When he loosened his hold on James, he stood. Warren sat leaning against the wagon that provided cover for them earlier. Will walked toward him.

"Sorry I couldn't—"

"It's okay," Will said. "I figured it would come to that."

Warren nodded.

"Thank you for saving Hannah."

"Glad to do it."

"How did you know you wouldn't hit her?"

Warren looked away. "I didn't."

Will slapped him on the shoulder. "Thanks again."

Though he still had Samuel in his arms and James tagging close by, Will glanced over at Reuben's lifeless stare.

No matter how the day turned out, grief still visited him. His brother was dead. It's not what he wanted. But, somehow after Reuben's confession about murdering his father, it seemed easier to accept. He had no idea that the stampede wasn't an accident. He had no idea Reuben harbored such deep anger against him.

He looked down into Samuel's sleeping face. Then he looked

down at James and tousled his hair. He longed for his sons to have a better relationship than he and Reuben had. Perhaps they would be better friends, especially being so close in age.

Hannah emerged from the shack with Eddie at her side. He looked so much like his father right now, with that same bitterness etched in his deep scowl. Clearly he was not handling this well.

His wife approached him. "Take me home, Will. Take me home."

He pulled her into one last embrace before they headed toward the horses. It was time to go.

After a brief exchange with Perry, who volunteered to stay behind to take care of Reuben's body and to notify Robert Garrett's men, Will helped his family onto horses and they started the long journey back home.

Warren's hand shook as he mounted his horse. He killed Will's brother—Mary's husband.

His gut tightened into a firm ball and bile rose in his throat. Everything changed for him in an instant. He killed a man. Something he swore he'd never do again.

Old memories hounded him, he tried to push them away, but he couldn't. This time he hit the intended target. And, he hit the right target when the mountain lion attacked Jed. But, long ago, as a young man, his aim cost his sister her life.

When he started his ranch, she came West to help him. Lydia cooked and cleaned—never complaining. That didn't surprise him. Life at the ranch was so much better for her than life had been under his father's brutal hand.

It was her eighteenth birthday, so he planned a special trip to town. He surprised her at breakfast. Even though he didn't have much money, he told her he was going to buy her material for a new dress. Whatever she wanted, she could have it. Then he was going to take her to dinner.

Only the trip hadn't gone as planned. On the way to town, they had a problem with the wagon. The wheel came loose. By the time someone came along and he was able to fix the wheel, Lydia suggested they return home and try again another day.

He was too stubborn. He had insisted that she would still have her birthday surprise. So he pressed on to town.

It was evening by the time they arrived. He took her to the mercantile and she had just enough time to pick out the fabric before the store closed for the night. Then, they headed to dinner at the boardinghouse.

They never made it.

On the way there, they had to pass a saloon. Some men who had obviously started drinking much earlier in the day exited the saloon right as he and Lydia passed by. One of the men grabbed her.

"Look at this pretty thing," he said as he cozied up next to her.

"Let her go," Warren said.

Before he fully understood what happened, the man twisted Lydia around and held a knife to her throat.

"Give me your money," the man said, suddenly sober. "I saw that bag of coin you pulled out at the mercantile. Give it to me."

Fear gripped Warren's heart. It was all the money he had to his name. He couldn't just let it go. Then, he saw the scene play out in his mind's eye. He had always been an accurate shot. He felt confident that he could hit the man, if he drew his weapon.

So he drew his gun.

The man pressed the knife closer to Lydia's neck.

"Give me your coin and I'll let her go."

Warren wasn't about to let that happen. Instead, he cocked the gun and aimed for the man's arm that held the knife. As he pulled back on the trigger, the man twisted his body, moving Lydia toward the spot where Warren aimed.

As she fell to the ground, the man and his friends hurried to their horses.

He rushed to her side and turned her over. The bullet, which was meant as a minor wound to the man, had pierced her skull. She was dead.

It was his fault and he vowed on Lydia's grave that he would never draw his weapon again.

Over time, the vow changed. More so after Dahlia left and he became a drifter. He had been in his fair share of gunfights over the years. But never again did he raise his weapon unless it was a sure shot.

Until it came to choosing between Reuben and Hannah—a scene that felt far too familiar for him to ignore.

Only this time, he hadn't been choosing between his pocket book and his sister. Instead, it was an easier choice—one meant to protect his boss's wife and even his boss. He spared Will from making a choice that would have eaten him up.

Now he was left with the consequences of that decision. He kicked his horse into motion at the tail end of the party as they headed back toward Prescott.

When they camped for the night, both Will and Hannah thanked him for saving her life.

All it took was one look at Eddie to remind him that there were still consequences to face. Eddie scowled his direction over his supper plate. As he walked passed Warren before bedding down for the night, he shouted out his hatred again.

How would Mary react when he gave her the news? What about when she saw how much her son hated him now?

Though he didn't want to think about it, he had more than enough time to think about it. They wouldn't arrive back on Colter ranch for several days yet—at least three or four.

He was glad he took the shot. He was glad that he saved Hannah's life. He just hoped that it didn't destroy any chance he had of winning Mary over.

As he closed his eyes, he realized that he wanted her heart more than anything.

Maybe Jed had the right idea. Maybe a prayer might help.

Lord, please keep her from hating me.

He couldn't figure out how to end it, so he left it at that. A little tiny flicker of hope sparked as he fell asleep.

Chapter 25

Colter Ranch

March 4, 1867

Mary could barely stand it. Ten days passed since she last saw her son. She felt peace every time she and Betty prayed for him—except for today. For some reason, uneasiness lingered in her heart. Something was wrong.

Or maybe it was more like her son was hurting. Safe, but hurting.

She shook her head as she pushed the thought away. She couldn't do anything to help him, other than pray and that's exactly what she'd been doing.

As she approached with a full bucket of water, Julia left the house. "Dishes are done."

Mary nodded and started up the porch.

"Mary," Julia said. "I'm…"

She turned toward her sister-in-law, setting the bucket on the porch, surprised that she seemed to have more to say. They had barely spoken more than a few polite words since Julia's birthday.

"I'm sorry I blamed you for what Reuben did. I know…" Julia kicked her booted toe in the dirt. "I know you suffered too."

Her heart lifted, but before Mary could respond, Julia turned and rushed toward the stables. It wasn't what she hoped for, but it was a beginning.

She grabbed the handle of the bucket and went inside. After adding soap to the water, she kneeled down with rag in hand, ready to mop the dirty floor. Thankfully, Betty and Ben had taken Beth into town with them this morning as they made their deliveries. It left her alone in the quiet house to think and clean.

As she scrubbed the floors, she thought of the news from town late last week when Ben took her to see Will's attorney. He looked over her divorce papers from Reuben and thought they were forgeries and would not hold up to scrutiny in court.

The news crushed her heart at first. She still wasn't free. She could not entertain ideas of any other man—of Warren. She tried to banish him from her heart. She was still married to Reuben. Still tied to him.

It hurt. After everything he took from her, Reuben continued to take her hope away. He had her son now. She was still bound to him by marriage vows, no matter how much she wanted them loosed.

But, through her morning prayers with Betty, she was learning to trust God again. She knew in her heart of hearts that she wouldn't have to go back to Reuben. She wouldn't have to live with him again. Though her marital status wasn't what she wanted, she didn't have to willingly subject herself to his abuse any longer.

If he did come for her, she would refuse to go with him and she knew that Will would protect her.

She attacked the floor with more vigor. She wondered if she asked Will if he would be willing to pay for proper divorce papers.

As soon as the thought came, she sent it scurrying. She already owed him too much. She couldn't add to it.

No, she would honor her vows and not seek a new husband. It was the right thing to do.

The door burst open startling her.

"Riders are coming," Adam said.

Mary stood slowly, wiping her hands on her apron. "Who?"

"Too far out to tell yet. But too many to be Betty and Ben."

A whisper of hope spoke to her heart. *Was Eddie coming home?*

She rushed to the door. Adam grabbed her arm.

"Wait. Let's wait until we can tell who they are."

She didn't want to wait. She couldn't wait. She knew it was them.

Though she wanted to rush out and greet them, she stayed behind Adam.

He peered through the front window. "A rider is moving away from the group."

She wrung her hands together in nervous anticipation.

"It's Warren."

The breath she was holding *whooshed* from her lips. When

Adam opened the door and stepped onto the porch, she followed him. She waited for Warren to dismount and tie his horse before she stepped off the porch.

"Where's Eddie? Is he okay?"

Warren's frown troubled her, but not as much as his presence unnerved her. She promised she would let go of any feelings she had for him. Yet, when she stood here face to face with him, she couldn't deny how glad she was to see him. Her eyes took in a quick accounting—until she was satisfied he was fine.

Then concern for her son took control again. "Eddie, is he...?"

For a brief second, Warren's heart danced at the sight of her. He noticed her eyes roaming over his body and the slight smile tugging at the corner of her lips when she found he wasn't hurt.

Then she masked everything. In a controlled tone and with a stoic face, she asked about her son again.

He hesitated for a brief moment. Eddie's attitude had not improved over the last four days. He didn't just blame Warren for his father's death, he hated him. Warren tried to talk to him several times, but Eddie wouldn't have it.

He even tried to get Eddie to ride with him this morning, picturing the joy on Mary's face when he delivered her son as he promised.

Instead, Eddie rode with Hawk, shrinking Warren's role to that of messenger.

"Eddie is fine," he said. His voice must have given away that there was something more, judging by the concern on her face.

"But?"

His shoulders rose and fell with a heavy sigh.

"Mary, perhaps we could sit down for a moment."

She narrowed her eyes. "You said Eddie is fine. Are you sure? What is it that you're not telling me?"

He swallowed hard. Every time he pictured telling her the news her husband was dead—that he killed him—he could never picture her reaction. He dreamed it would be softer with the knowledge that he saved her son.

But now? Looking into her lovely violet eyes, his courage waned. Perhaps he didn't need to mention who killed her husband.

"Warren?"

His heart turned over and upside down, squeezing hard against his chest. It was time to tell her. How would she react?

"Eddie is fine, like I said." He tried easing into the news. "He's not hurt. Just angry about everything that's happened." He looked away.

"I don't understand."

A light touch to his arm jolted his eyes back to hers.

"What's he angry about?"

Warren swallowed hard. "He doesn't understand why his father took him there. He's mad that I…"

He couldn't do it. He couldn't tell her his part in it, even though he knew she would find out soon enough.

"Your husband is dead."

The color drained from her face. He wrapped his arms around her and felt her weight press into him. She said nothing. Gradually, her weight shifted, like her legs gained the strength to stand on their own. Too soon, she moved from him.

"Reuben is dead?"

Warren nodded.

"He's dead."

He didn't nod again, sensing she understood, but was having trouble believing it.

"Are you sure? Did you see his dead body? Did you watch him return to the dust he came from?" Her voice rose to a shrill octave. Then she began pacing back and forth.

"Do you know how many times someone has told me they found his body?"

She grabbed his forearms and shook him. Her eyes begged him to understand.

"I need to know for sure. I need to know."

Warren wanted to pull her into his arms again, but his murderous deed stood in the way.

"I'm positive he's dead. Will confirmed it. He has someone bringing the body back so he can be buried at the ranch."

Any confusion in her vanished. "I don't want him on this ranch. Not when he was alive, and certainly not his dead body. I don't want that man anywhere near me or the children. I want his memory to rot as his body does."

The acid dripped from her voice, giving Warren deeper insight into just how much pain she endured at her husband's hand.

Before he could respond, the rest of the travelers returned. The fire in her eyes faded when she spotted her son.

"Eddie!"

Warren watched as an outsider from his vantage point in front of the porch. Mary clung to her son the second his feet hit the ground. She cried and smiled and thanked everyone for bringing her son back. Then she smothered Eddie with kisses until he squirmed.

She kept her arm around him as she walked up the steps past Warren. At the top she turned around and looked down at him.

"Thank you for keeping your promise."

Warren's heart smiled, though he kept it from his lips. "Ma'am."

She smiled softly at him. Something in her eyes told him that she held him in esteem. Perhaps he had already invaded part of her heart. Dare he hope for such a thing?

Then Eddie's words came in a firestorm, charring his hope. "He killed Papa."

Eddie spat at his feet, then turned and ran inside the house.

Warren watched as the shock on Mary's face gave way to horror. He knew then that he lost any chance he had with her.

Mary failed to mask her emotions in time. Warren's crestfallen expression confirmed it. Her horror was not directed at him.

No, it was Eddie's response that both shocked and horrified her. She couldn't understand his tone, his hatred of the man who killed his father. How was this same son who declared only a few months ago that he hated his father because of what he had done to her—to his mother?

None of it made sense.

Though she wanted to linger and set Warren's mind at ease, she turned and followed her son. He needed her.

She knocked softly on the door to his bedroom, thankful that Beth had missed the worst of the drama.

"Eddie?"

"Go away."

She drew in a breath then exhaled slowly. She waited a few more seconds before opening the door.

"Eddie, what's wrong?"

He sat on the floor in the corner of the room. Only a tuft of hair was visible over the bed. She closed the door behind her and moved to sit next to him. His arms were crossed over his knees and his head rested on his forearms. She couldn't hear the sound of crying, but she knew he was by the slight tremor in his body.

"Eddie?"

He stilled.

She waited.

"Warren killed Papa."

He lifted his head from his arms and turned fierce eyes toward her. Those same dark brown eyes as his father.

Reuben may be dead, but part of him lived on his son—her son.

Fear held her lips tightly shut. *Lord, please don't let him grow up to be anything like his father.*

"Papa wanted me. He did. I know it. He was going to take me with him. Then Warren killed him."

Mary reached out a hand to touch his shoulder. He shrugged her away.

"He wanted me. Papa wanted me."

The pain and longing in her son's voice brought tears to her eyes. If he only understood what Reuben had really wanted. Maybe he wouldn't harbor this anger toward Warren.

She couldn't bring herself to agree with what Eddie was saying. She knew better. Instead, she put her arm around his shoulders and offered silent comfort.

Perhaps in time, he would learn to see the truth.

Chapter 26

Home. No sight was as glorious to Hannah. She smiled at Will as he reined up his horse next to hers at the top of the hill. Well, maybe there was one sight more glorious—him.

As his gaze met hers, she noticed the sheen of tears in his eyes. "Welcome home, Hannah."

Moisture threatened her eyes as she read the unspoken words from her husband. Relief. Joy. Love.

His eyes drifted to the hole in her dress sleeve where her arm was bandaged.

"I—" His voice cracked. "I don't know what I would do without you. You are my life."

Love overflowed the boundaries of her heart. He nudged his horse closer and cupped her face in one hand. Gently he rubbed his thumb over her cheek.

"I love you, Will."

He looked at her for several more seconds. His eyes darted to her lips then back to her eyes. Slowly, a half-smile turned up one corner of his mouth. She knew that look and anticipated the eyebrow wiggle that followed.

"Let's get you home, so I can show you just how much I missed you."

She couldn't stop the giggle that erupted. She loved his sweet teasing and the way it made her heart dance.

She kicked her horse back into motion. "Stop dallying then," she shot back over her shoulder.

In a few minutes, they were back at the bottom of the valley. She reined in her horse and waited for him. He handed James down to Adam before dismounting. Once on the ground he came to her side and took Samuel from her arms and handed him to Julia. Then he lifted her from the horse. As soon as her feet touched ground, he wrapped his arms around her and held her close. She leaned into his embrace and savored the strength of his arms—the arms that rescued her.

When Samuel started to fuss, she reluctantly slid from Will's warmth. Taking Samuel in her arms, she accepted the greetings from Julia and Adam. Mary wasn't there, but neither was Eddie, so she assumed they had gone inside for a private moment.

"We'll see to the horses," Adam said. "Betty and Ben should be returning from town shortly."

Hannah smiled as Will scooped James into his arms. Then she led the way into the house.

She closed her eyes and took a deep breath. It smelled like home—a hint of pine mixed with the sweet smell of fresh baked apple pie. She savored the moment for a few breaths.

Slowly she opened her eyes.

Samuel fussed in her arms so she carried him into the kitchen. She sat in the small chair where she usually nursed him. Will hovered in the doorway with James.

"Can you take James up for a nap?" she asked.

Will came closer and kissed her on the forehead before he left.

Weariness settled over her shoulders, despite her joy at being home again. She went through the motions of nursing and burping Samuel, while she looked around the kitchen. It was time to start supper. Then there would be dishes to clean and a kitchen to right. No time to sit and soak up the comfort of home or to seek out the comfort of her husband's arms again.

She wanted nothing more right now than to be with him. There were too many close calls over the last ten days. She reached up and ran fingers over the scab on her cheek—where Pete struck her. Images of Reuben floated in her vision. The evil intent in his eyes. The threats.

Yet the Lord had been with her. He protected her and sent her husband to rescue her. She didn't suffer the full intent of Reuben's wrath.

She was home now. Safe.

"Dear!"

Hannah jumped at Betty's voice, aware that her skittish behavior was strange.

Betty moved to her side and pulled her into a huge hug.

"I'm so glad you're safe. I knew God was watching over you."

Hannah nodded and stepped back from the embrace. "Yes, he was."

She felt all the energy drain from her.

"Dear, why don't you go upstairs and rest? I'll take care of supper."

"Thank you, Betty."

"It's good to have you and the little ones home."

Hannah nodded and left the room. Slowly she made her way up the stairs. She noted both Will and James were fast asleep on the bed. She laid Samuel in his crib then crawled into bed next to her husband, letting the fears and stress of the past ten days seep away.

The next morning, Mary woke earlier than normal. Her mind taunted and tormented her. At supper, Will mentioned that he had the boys digging a grave for Reuben on the far side of the lake at the ranch. She said nothing at the time.

But her dreams had. She dreamed that she was walking along the lake. Warren was on one side. Beth and Eddie on the other. As she turned to look at Eddie, she realized he was a few years older, perhaps eleven.

When they walked past the grave, Reuben emerged. He struck a fatal blow to Eddie's chest. Then he came after her and Beth. She tripped and he caught her ankle, pulling her to him.

Then the dream merged with memories of nights with him. Her skin crawled just thinking about it. She still felt trapped by him.

She could not let Will bury Reuben at the ranch. It would be as if he were still there. She would always be looking over her shoulder, fearful that he could somehow return.

No, she had to convince Will that it would be better to bury him at the cemetery in town. Surely they had one. That way, if any of the family ever desired to visit his grave, they could. But, she wouldn't be subjected to his presence any more.

Mary dressed and headed down the stairs to start breakfast. When she stepped into the kitchen she was surprised to see Hannah already up.

"Couldn't sleep?" Hannah asked.

"No."

She moved to grab a basket from the shelf with the intent of gathering the eggs.

"How do you feel about… Reuben's grave being… well, here?"

Mary stopped and set the basket on the work table. She took a deep breath to steady herself.

"I'm not fond of the idea."

Hannah shook her head. "Me either."

When a frown passed over her face, Mary grew concerned. "He didn't… Did he hurt you?"

Hannah shook her head. "No, but I think there were a few times that's what he intended."

Mary blew out a loud breath. "I'm glad he didn't."

"Me, too."

Silence settled over them again. Hannah began slicing some bacon. Mary turned to grab the egg basket. She paused in the doorway.

"Did you say anything to Will?"

"Not about that," Hannah admitted. "He's pretty torn up about everything. Things Reuben said. That Reuben is dead. I didn't want to add something more."

"Please, don't let him bury Reuben here. Not on the ranch. It's too peaceful here—the one place he hasn't tarnished completely with his presence."

Hannah gave a slight nod then returned to her cooking.

As Mary left the warmth of the house for the chicken coop, she prayed that Will would change his mind. She would go crazy if he didn't.

She finished gathering the eggs and returned to the kitchen to help prepare the meal. In twenty minutes, the rest of the family joined them in the dining room.

After breakfast was served, Will started discussing the plans for the day. "Pastor Page will be out around ten."

"I don't want him here," Julia said through gritted teeth, sparing Mary the objection.

"Pastor?"

"No, Reuben. I don't want his body here."

"But, he's family," Will replied.

Julia bolted to her feet. "He lost that right when he did… When he…" She ran from the room. Adam stood and followed her.

Mary dropped her gaze to her plate before Will looked her direction.

"Will," Hannah said softly, "I know he was your brother, but—"

"I don't want him here either," Mary said. She lifted her head and locked her eyes on Will's. She hoped her reasons could be left unsaid.

Emotions marched across his forehead. Regret. Grief. Sadness.

"I'm not comfortable with it either," Hannah said.

Will turned shocked eyes toward her. "I thought you said he didn't—"

She shook her head. "He didn't. But, I don't want any reminders of what he almost did or of him taking us away."

Will's struggle was obvious. He opened his mouth several times to say something then he closed it. Mary felt bad for him, but not bad enough to back down from her position.

"You don't understand what it was like," she said. "To live with that constant fear. This ranch—it's a place of peace and comfort. For me. For Julia. For Hannah. Burying him here takes that away."

"I… I don't know what to say," Will said.

Eddie threw down his fork. "Say that he can be buried here. He's my father. He deserves to be with family!"

Mary nearly choked on her food. She hadn't expected Eddie to fight her on this.

"Beth," Eddie said, nudging her with his palm, "Where do you want Papa buried?"

Beth turned wide eyes toward her then she looked back at Eddie. "Who is Papa?"

Mary's heart rose and sank at the same time. Beth didn't remember him. She had been only three or four when he left.

"You're all traitors! You can't do this! Papa deserves to be with family!"

Eddie jumped up from the table and stormed up the stairs.

Mary turned her gaze toward Will.

He shook his head over and over again. He looked to Hannah, to

Mary, to Ben.

Ben said, "I think yer womenfolk come before the dead."

Will shook his head once more. After several minutes, he spoke, "I'll ride into town this morning to make the arrangements to have him buried there."

Then he stood, leaving his breakfast untouched. He walked from the room with heavy steps.

While she was relieved, Mary felt sorry for Will. She understood what he was trying to do. He wanted to honor a man who deserved no honor. He wanted to make up for the lost years. Yes, she understood what his intention was, but she was glad he changed his mind. There was no way she could live here under Reuben's shadow.

She was finally free.

On March 6, 1867, Will loaded up his family—all of them, including Julia and Mary and their children—and headed into town to pay his final respects to his brother.

He never anticipated such resistance to where they would bury Reuben. It broke his heart that even in death Reuben seemed to be dividing them still.

Regardless of Reuben's lack of morals, he was still his brother. He still deserved a proper burial with respect.

Mary hadn't looked at him all morning. Neither had Julia. Though both were here and wearing black. He doubted that Mary would wear it after today, despite the fact that Reuben was her husband and she should be in mourning for a year.

It was the look on Hannah's face yesterday morning that finally convinced him to change his mind. The fear in her eyes coupled with her restless sleep, led him to believe that either Reuben had violated her or he came much closer to doing so than she let on.

Ben was right. His womenfolk—his wife, sister, and sister-in-law—were far more important than the dead.

Pastor Page began the ceremony. Will glanced over at Mary and her children. She stared off at nothing in particular. When Eddie recoiled from her touch, he motioned for the boy to come stand with him. Eddie quickly moved to his side.

Will could feel the anger emanating from him. This morning he seemed intent on steering clear of both Warren and his mother. He made a mental note to talk to him later, see if he couldn't help get to the bottom of that anger. The last thing he wanted to see was Eddie following in his father's footsteps.

As Pastor Page read the twenty-third Psalm, Will's grief overtook him. He couldn't hold it or the tears back. That was the passage his father loved—the one read at his funeral. His father died an early death at Reuben's hand.

Reuben's words echoed in his mind. *Father and I talked a few days before the accident.* An accident his brother orchestrated. An accident meant to leave him with nothing.

Yet, here he was trying to do the right thing by his brother. The brother who loathed him.

As Pastor Page led them in a prayer, Will dropped to his knees and covered his face with his hands. He grieved anew for the loss of his father. He grieved for the closeness he and Rebuen never had. He grieved for the damage to his family that Reuben inflicted—the damage to Julia, to Mary, to Hannah, to his sons. To Eddie.

He wasn't sure how long he kneeled there, but it was Julia's muttered words that broke him from his grief.

"Rot in hell, Reuben. You don't deserve to bear the Colter name."

Then she spat on his grave and turned toward her husband who stood holding her daughter.

Will hugged Eddie before standing, hoping the boy hadn't heard his aunt's words or noticed her reaction. He led Eddie back towards Mary. At the sight of her son, she wiped the frown from her face. She took his hand and led him to the wagon.

Hannah came up next to Will. When he tried to put his arm around her, she stiffened. "I didn't think you were that close to him."

Then she stepped away from him and climbed into the wagon.

"I wasn't," he whispered as he walked around to the other side.

Setting the wagon into motion, he mentally wished his brother farewell. It seemed even in death Reuben had the last word—tearing his family apart.

Chapter 27

Colter Ranch

April 8, 1867

Mary stood before her dresses. Her fingers hovered over the black one she'd worn most days for a little over a month. She drew her hand back without making a selection. The only reason she even wore it was because of tradition. Certainly, not for Reuben's sake.

She frowned at the dress as if it represented everything she despised about her late husband.

Then she sighed. In her afternoon chat with Betty yesterday, she thought she let some of that bitterness go. It was so hard to forget everything he had done to her. It was hard to forgive. But, Betty was right. She did need to forgive him—for her sake.

Maybe if she did she could move on.

She took her green dress off the hook and donned it. Already she felt lighter than yesterday. She smiled as she fashioned her hair in a chignon, pulling loose a few tendrils on the side. When she looked in the mirror, she was pleased with the results. Feminine and free.

Free.

Lord, I want to be truly free. Free from this heavy, dark past. I want a new life. Maybe one that includes love?

Dismissing the thought, she realized she was asking a bit much. Her best chance at love was Warren and he'd been distant since he returned with her son.

She knew he had been the one to pull the trigger that ended her husband's life. She heard the story from both Hannah and Will's point of view—and Eddie's. His account dripped with anger.

Regardless, she knew Warren did what he had to. She didn't hold anything against him. Yet, he'd been aloof—almost avoiding her.

Mary sighed and shrugged off the heavy thoughts. She had plenty of work waiting for her downstairs. It was time to face the day.

She helped Hannah and Rosa get breakfast ready for the family and the men. As Hannah began setting out some of the food, she stayed in the kitchen to check on the biscuits. Once they were done, she entered the dining room.

For some reason at the moment she walked in Warren looked her way. His gaze rested on hers for several seconds before his cheeks reddened and he dropped his gaze. Did he have a new shirt on? She didn't remember him wearing a blue one before. Or maybe she didn't remember how it brought out the blue in his eyes.

Hannah cleared her throat and Mary realized she still hadn't taken her seat.

"Sorry," she whispered, dropping the basket of biscuits onto the table and sinking into her usual chair.

She quickly folded her hands in her lap and waited as Will prayed for the meal. When he finished, the conversation buzzed around her.

"Mary, would you like to ride into town with Warren today?" Hannah asked.

She looked her direction. "Why?"

"I thought you might like a chance to do some shopping. Get more fabric for you or the children. I noticed Eddie's shoes looked a little small."

The old familiar feeling of guilt surfaced. She hated living off of Will's charity. "I'm sure we can make do with what we have."

"Come now," Hannah said. "You've been here five months and refused every time. Just take Eddie and Beth and get whatever you need. Warren will settle the account."

Adam teased Hannah. "Are you sure you're not just trying to get rid of her so you and Will can go riding?"

Hannah's cheeks colored pink.

Mary smiled. She'd take the children and give them the day, though she would try to get out of shopping if at all possible. "We'll go."

Eddie frowned and kicked at the legs of his chair, but said nothing. She could tell he was mad. Probably because Warren would be the one taking them. Secretly, she liked the idea of spending the day with him. She was twice as glad now that she chose the green dress instead of the black.

Warren wasn't sure how he felt about Will's request this morning to take Mary and the children to town. He was less sure after seeing her out of her widow's black. Why had she chosen today to wear that dress? She looked so lovely in it. Her eyes turned a deeper shade of violet. Her skin looked soft and pale—but in a pleasing way.

She glanced up at him and he quickly dropped his gaze to his food. He felt the heat rise to his cheeks.

He had done a good job of avoiding her since they returned from the kidnapping. Countless times he thought about apologizing for killing her husband. But, he never could think of the right words.

Then there was her son. All he had to do was make a noise and Eddie sent daggers his direction. To say Eddie held a grudge was putting it mildly.

As long as her son hated him, he didn't stand a chance of winning her heart—something that tugged at his own heart on a daily basis now.

He chided himself. He swore off women. Hadn't life with Dahlia been enough to convince him that even the happiest moments weren't worth the dark ones?

Pushing his plate away from him, he excused himself with the pretense of getting the horse and wagon ready. In truth, he needed a few minutes to clear his head before the ride into town.

He couldn't give in to the feelings stirring deep within. He couldn't dwell on her pretty smile or her soft spoken ways or what a wonderful mother she was. He tried to make that dream a reality once and his heart still bore the deep scars from it. Long ago he traded in the desire for a family and replaced it with a single-minded goal—building his own ranch again. He was so close to realizing his dream and this attraction to her was getting in the way.

It was so tempting. When he lay in bed at night, trying to fall asleep, he imagined Mary at his side. What would it be like to share his home and his life with her?

Grunting, he tried to still his mind as he harnessed the horse to the wagon. This endless rant in his head ended the same way every time—with the resolve to distance himself.

Except Will and Hannah did a good job of making his resolve waver by putting him in this position.

He climbed up onto the wagon seat and pulled it around to the front of the ranch house. Mary and the children stood waiting. When Warren climbed down, Eddie immediately jumped up into the back of the wagon. Warren lifted Beth into the back to sit near her brother. Then he took Mary's hand and helped her up. Her gloved fingers curled around his hand, sending a strong current through him. It was the first time he touched her since they day he brought her son home.

As soon as she was settled, he released his hand, eager to fill it with the reins instead—anything to replace the sensation.

He started the wagon into motion up the hill.

"Do you have business to attend to in town?" Mary asked.

"Naw. Just here to help you."

"Oh."

She grew quiet and he wondered what she was thinking.

"I'm sorry to inconvenience you. Really, we're fine. We can make do with what we have."

He glanced over and watched her hands as she fidgeted with the ribbon on her reticule. She seemed nervous.

"Will made it clear we aren't to come back empty handed."

"I see."

The rest of the trip passed with Beth leaning forward and peppering him with a dozen questions. She wanted to know more about the cattle. How long did he work for her uncle? Had he always lived here? Was he ever a little boy?

He thought the questions were sweet, though he did try to give some vague answers on the touchier subjects.

"Here we are," Warren announced. "Hardy's Mercantile."

Mary almost leaped down from the wagon without waiting for him. She was so nervous around him and she didn't know why. He had been really quiet until Beth got him talking. She smiled. Sweet, curious Beth.

Instead, she waited for him to help her down. There it was again—a little flutter as her hand closed around his strong one. She thanked him as he reached over the side to get Beth and help her down.

When she pushed the door open, she was greeted by a familiar face.

"Morning, Mary," Caroline Larson—no, it was Anderson now—greeted her. She was still getting used to little Caroline being married.

"What brings you to town?"

"I guess we need some shoes and fabric for clothes. I'm surprised to see you here," Mary said.

"Oh, I'm just filling in for a few hours this morning while Abraham runs some errands. Let's see, which one of you," she said, leaning over and tweaking Beth's nose, "needs some new shoes."

"Both," Warren replied.

Mary cringed inwardly, but stepped aside as Caroline led the children over to the shoes. She watched silently as Caroline measured Beth's feet first. Caroline indulged the dozen or so questions Beth asked.

Then Mary noticed the way Beth wiggled her toes once they were free from her existing shoes. Guilt pressed in again. How had she missed noticing that both her children needed new shoes?

Eddie's pants climbed halfway up his shins when he sat down to have his feet measured. When had he out grown them? Why hadn't she noticed?

She was a terrible mother.

"She's chatty today," Warren said from behind her, rescuing her from more self-recrimination.

Mary cleared her throat, hoping to hide her inner turmoil. "Yes, she is."

"They look like they're in good hands. Why don't you look around?"

She glanced over her shoulder.

“We’re not going back empty handed,” Warren said. “So you can stop the arguing in your head.”

He flashed a grin before moving to another aisle.

As her heart settled down again, she watched him for a few seconds. She could see his head over the top of the shelves. His gaze remained intensely glued to whatever was on the shelf in front of him. Then he slowly lifted his gaze and looked at her. This time he gave her a soft smile that brightened her soul from the inside out.

He was a handsome man and so completely opposite from Reuben in appearance and demeanor. His blue eyes sparkled with tamed laughter. A ring of sandy brown hair peeked out from under the edge of his brown cowboy hat. When he smiled, his cheeks formed lines like that of a pair of parentheses.

When his gaze dropped, she willed her feet to move toward the fabrics at the other end of the store, though her mind stayed on the man who caught her attention. Could she trust him? Was he really just like he seemed—kind, gentle, and good natured? Or had he fooled her just like Reuben did?

The thought sent shivers down her spine. She had to get past this.

Her fingers touched some brown fabric that would work well for a new pair of trousers for Eddie. Then a soft pink calico caught her attention. She envisioned a new dress for herself and a matching smaller version for Beth. She finally let go of her pride and picked several more bolts of fabric before carrying them up to the front counter.

Warren saw the pink fabric Mary picked out. Old habits resurfaced as he stood in front of a row of ribbons. Countless times he surprised Dahlia with a small token of his affection—a ribbon for her hair, a trinket of some kind. Now, it was Mary that inspired the gesture.

He looked for something that would complement the pink fabric. Then he found it. His hand started to reach for it, but he quickly pulled it back.

Moving toward the counter where Mary and the children stood, he abandoned the ribbon. He waited as Caroline finished cutting the lengths of fabric. As the last package was wrapped in brown paper, he made his move.

"Why don't you and the children head over to Lancaster's? I'll settle the account, load the wagon, and meet you in a few minutes," Warren suggested.

"Oh. Thank you," she replied before ushering the children towards the front of the store.

"Would you like some of that ribbon?" Caroline asked.

Warren smiled. That was exactly what he wanted. "Enough for both Mary and Beth."

Caroline nodded and went to retrieve the item. Once she cut the appropriate lengths, she wrapped them in brown paper.

"That will go on my account," he said, pointing to the wrapped ribbon. "The rest goes on the Colter account."

She quickly had everything settled. He took the small wrapped ribbon and stuffed it in his pocket, confident that Mary would love the surprise. He just had to figure out when he would give it to her.

Chapter 28

After breakfast, Will paced back and forth in the living room while Hannah finished cleaning up. Though she agreed to let Betty and Ben watch the boys and she agreed to go riding with him this morning, she didn't seem very excited about it.

Nothing had been quite the same since the kidnapping and funeral. He couldn't remember the last time he made love to his wife. Not once since they returned.

She seemed distant.

His fears played over and over. Perhaps she had not been honest about what happened at that shack on Garrett's property.

He had to do something to erase this growing distance between him and his wife. It was slowly killing his heart. He wanted his wife's spirit back—her smile, her laughter, her intimacy.

"Finished," she announced from behind him.

He turned and noted the dark circles under her eyes. She looked weary, exhausted. He moved close, and grasped her hand, leading her to her favorite chair. She reluctantly sat.

"Please, tell me what happened at the shack."

She frowned and jumped up from the chair. "Stop asking about that. It's done. I just want to forget about it."

Hannah turned her back on him and walked over to the window. She crossed her arms and stared out.

Will knew he should let it go, but he couldn't. He followed her and stood behind her.

"Please talk to me. I miss you. I want you back."

She said nothing.

Not sure of what to do, but overwhelmed by the need to touch her, to reassure her in some way, he placed his arms around her and rested his chin on the top of her head. She stiffened at first.

The longer they stood there, the more she relaxed against him. He wished she would turn around and face him.

After several minutes, she finally spoke. "He did not do what you think. He wanted to. I could tell. But, something always stopped him."

He sensed there was more troubling her. Desperate for his wife to return, he pressed her. "What aren't you telling me, Hannah?"

She squirmed from his arms and turned to face him. Anger crinkled her forehead.

"Stop acting like I'm hiding something! Just. Let. It. Be."

Will backed away. He turned on his heel and headed toward the door.

"I'll go get the horses ready."

He slammed the door behind him and took off toward the barn.

Why was she angry at him? Why couldn't she just tell him what was going on? He missed her. He wanted her to open up to him again. Was it too much to ask?

Storming towards Jackson's stall, he stopped himself. Being angry at her wasn't going to help the situation. She was hurting and she didn't want to tell him. Though it hurt, he needed to be patient.

He hung his head and closed his eyes. *Lord, please help me know what to do to help her.*

Hannah blinked back the sting of tears. She had no idea why she lashed out at Will. She was just tired of him questioning her about what happened when his brother kidnapped her.

It was strange. During the whole thing, she felt that God was with her. She knew He would protect her.

But, since coming back home, she felt out of sorts.

Maybe it was Will's strange reaction to his brother's death. He seemed more upset about it than she thought he should. Reuben had his father killed, for goodness sake! Why Will seemed distant and still grieving made no sense to her.

She shook her head. No, her mood had more to do with her own fears. She didn't feel safe at home anymore. She never realized how easy it would be for someone to steal her or her children away from the ranch. No matter how much Will tried to protect them, he couldn't watch them all the time. He had a ranch to run.

Before now, she always felt safe. It was new and terrifying to have that security stripped away.

Footsteps on the porch alerted her that Will was ready for their ride. She wiped the tears from her eyes and tried to force a smile to her lips. She met him in the parlor as he opened the door.

He looked worried and tired.

Her heart softened. Would it be so bad to let him know how she felt?

She mentally shook off the thought. Wordlessly, she followed him from the porch to where the horses were tied. Then she accepted his help mounting the horse.

"Want to lead?" he asked.

Hannah nodded and kicked her horse into a slow trot. In the years since she first came to the ranch, she was getting better at riding horses. At first, she felt awkward and uncomfortable. It wasn't something she had done often growing up. She always rode in a wagon. But, with Will's patient instruction, she got better at it, to the point of even welcoming a ride from time to time.

Pointing the horse toward the lake, she took a deep breath. Fresh crisp air filled her lungs. The sun warmed her back. The coolness in the air slowly evaporated.

Once past the lake, she led the horse north along the base of the mountain—away from the route her kidnappers took. For some reason, learning the layout of the land closest to home suddenly became an overwhelming priority.

The herd was off to the east of where she rode. Billows of dust kicked up, hiding part of the herd. Even from this distance, she could tell the difference between many of the cowboys. Jed was rounding up a stray. Anyone watching him now would hardly believe he had been injured by a mountain lion. The only sign was a long ugly scar on his arm.

The thought struck her. She had scars too and she'd been hiding them from Betty, Will, and herself. It wasn't working. She just needed to accept them. They were her fears and they had become a part of her.

If she told Will, would it help?

Will rode up beside her. "This looks like a nice spot."

She glanced over her shoulder toward the ranch house, now a small gray dot in her vision. They traveled farther than she thought.

"This will do," she replied as she reined in her horse.

Will dismounted and tied his horse to a nearby tree. Then he helped her from hers and tied it as well.

He shook out a blanket and laid it on the ground. Then he helped her take a seat on it.

Hannah closed her eyes and turned her face towards the sun. If only it could warm her soul.

"I'm sorry for yelling this morning," she said.

Reaching out, he took her hand in his and squeezed it. Then he scooted closer to her, turning so he was behind her. He placed one leg by each side of her, bending his knees.

"Lean back," he said.

She let him pull her back against his torso and welcomed the warmth of his arms circling her waist.

Safe.

The word screamed in her ears. She felt safe in his arms as his legs acted like a fort on two sides, protecting her. She closed her eyes again and breathed deeply, this time getting a hint of horse and hay from his shirt sleeve.

She didn't know how long they sat there, but when she felt sleepy, she opened her eyes.

"Thank you," she said.

"For what?"

"Helping me feel safe again."

"Oh, Hannah." He buried his face against her neck and held her tighter. "I'm so sorry. I'm so, so sorry I didn't keep you safe."

Her walls crumbled and words loosened from her tongue. "I know you tried to, but you can't always be there."

She shifted her position so she could see his face in profile. "I just haven't felt safe since… I never realized before just how dangerous it could be out here. Kidnappers. Indians. Rustlers. All within a few hundred yards of my home." She shuddered. "It's all become too real and overwhelming."

Will released his arms from her waist and moved until she could see his entire face. Then he placed a finger under her chin and tilted her face up. "I didn't know."

His golden brown eyes locked onto hers. Pain. Regret. Love. He communicated so many emotions in those eyes.

Then he lowered his lips to hers. His soft, sweet kiss poured a healing balm over her heart. She was with him, here. Safe. With the same gentleness, she returned his kiss.

Will reined in the desire that sparked from his wife's heavenly kiss. Now was not the time to pursue his desire. Reluctantly, he ended the kiss, resting his forehead against hers.

She dropped her head to his chest and placed her arms around his waist. At her contented sigh, he wrapped his arms around her.

"Will?"

"Hmm?"

"At your brother's funeral, what were you thinking?"

He sucked in a deep breath then let it out slowly. "It was hard for me to accept that he had a hand in my father's death. Even after everything I know about him, it's just so hard to believe that he would kill his own father."

He coughed to hold back tears that threatened.

"If I had any notion he would do such a thing, I never would have left Julia with him. If I had known he was Robert Garrett, I would not have let him near the ranch or welcomed him into our home."

Sorrow and guilt slammed against his chest. "I'm sorry I didn't see him for who he really was. I'm sorry I put you—" His voice broke. "—and the boys in danger."

His failure taunted him again, just like it had many nights over the past month.

"Please forgive me."

Hannah didn't move, except to tighten her hold around him.

"You didn't know. But, if it makes you feel better, I forgive you."

Relief washed over Will. He needed to know she trusted him.

"You're a good man, husband, and father. There's no one else I would trust more than you."

He let out a choppy sigh.

"I love you, Hannah."

"I know."

She giggled and loosened her hold. Then she lifted her head and kissed him, her soft lips confirming her love for him.

This time, as he returned her kiss, he held nothing back. The wife he missed now returned and the distance between them vanished. They were together again. Complete and whole.

Another of life's storms had passed and they survived it.

Chapter 29

Colter Ranch

April 18, 1867

Warren glanced across the supper table at Mary. His heart pounded in his chest as the meal wound down. She smiled at him before Beth stole her attention.

All day he'd been waiting for the next few moments. When he woke up this morning, his hand brushed across the brown paper hiding the ribbons he bought for her and Beth over a week ago. He'd thought about when to give her the gift several times, but none seemed right.

This morning, he resolved he would do it before sunset. Now, he was running out of time.

He stayed seated as Adam and Julia left with little Catherine. He waited for Betty and Ben to take their leave as well.

"Something on your mind?" Will asked him, apparently noticing his reluctance to leave.

Warren swallowed, hoping his nervousness wasn't as obvious as it seemed. "I was hoping to have a word with Mary."

A soft smile graced her lips as she said, "Eddie, Beth, why don't you go play in the living room?"

"Ma!" Eddie whined.

Her smile faded, replaced with a steady frown. "Go."

Eddie glanced from her to Will, before getting up and doing as she asked.

Beth jumped down from her chair. "Can I play with Dollie now?"

"Yes, sweetheart. I'll be along in a few minutes."

"Thank you, Mama." Beth ran out of the room.

Will and Hannah excused themselves, leaving him alone with Mary. A brief moment of panic seized him as her smile returned.

What had he been thinking?

He cleared the panic from his throat. “Would you like to take a walk?”

Her face lit up and his heart danced. “Let me see if Hannah can watch the children.”

He stood as she did the same. He stayed nearby as she went into the kitchen. Whispers from the two women were indiscernible, but in less than a minute Mary returned.

“Ready,” she announced.

Warren led her to the parlor and waited as she wrapped her shawl around her narrow shoulders. Then he led her outside.

The sun was already dropping below the mountains, but there was still enough light left for a short walk near the lake so he led her that direction.

As they walked, she started the conversation. “Sometimes Eddie seems like he’s getting better. Then, like today, he’s as ornery as can be.”

“Is he still angry about his father?”

She grew quiet, and Warren wished he hadn’t asked the question. After several minutes, she spoke. “Yes. He’s young. He doesn’t understand. It’s strange to me. Sometimes, I think he’s forgotten what it was like to live under his father’s rule. I think he’s been longing for a real father for a long time.

“Even when we lived at the Star C, Reuben didn’t spend much time with Eddie. It was his grandfather that gave him attention. He was so young when he passed.

“Then Reuben disappeared. For two years we lived with no word. It’s been over four years since Eddie has had the attention and love of a father or grandfather. He’s hurting.

“What scares me the most is the bitterness I see in him. It’s frighteningly similar to his father.”

Her voice broke. She stopped walking and turned toward him. “I couldn’t bear it if he turned out like Reuben.”

Warren’s heart melted for her. “Maybe Will can spend more time with him?”

“He tries, but Eddie pushes him away.”

Mary started walking again, so he fell into step beside her.

“I’m sorry,” she said. “You had something you wanted to talk about. What was it?"

His hands grew sweaty and the words he rehearsed while watching the herd this morning suddenly vanished. He glanced over at Mary and wondered, yet again, how he could have ever thought she was anything like Dahlia. Just her concern for her son seemed to be more caring than Dahlia had in the last year of their marriage.

"You're nothing like her." The words coming from his lips startled him.

"Like who?" Mary asked.

"Dahlia, my wife."

"Why do you say that?"

Warren wanted to kick himself. This was not going at all like he planned. But, he was committed now.

He sighed. "My sister had been living with me, but passed away. I was so lonely and torn up over her death.

"Then, at the end of the drive to take the cattle to market, I met Dahlia. She was from a plantation near New Orleans. It was an accident that I even met her.

"She had been out in the city with some friends. One of them was dying to see the cowboys coming in to market. So she convinced Dahlia and their other friends to ride by the corrals. They were ignorant about the dangers. When their carriage horse spooked, the girls lost control of the carriage in the path of the cattle headed into the corrals. Most of the girls jumped down from the carriage and ran to safety.

"Dahlia didn't. She'd been frightened. She froze.

"I did what anyone would have done. Since I was on my horse, I rode over and grabbed her from the carriage, sweeping her onto my horse. Once we were safely out of the way, I helped her down.

"She clung to me. Then she looked up at me with those—" He stopped himself. Mary didn't need to know how much she looked like Dahlia. "She looked up at me and my heart melted. I kissed her."

He went silent for a minute, remembering his state of mind at the time. "I was young. Foolish. Lonely."

Warren sighed.

"Regardless, she was enamored, too. It wasn't until later that I realized she didn't care for me. She cared more for the idea of a cowboy rescuing her and carrying her off to his ranch. She had no idea what that even meant.

"We got married right away. And I did just that—I carried her off to my ranch.

"By the time reality set in, it was too late. She was already my wife. She was stuck—at least that's how she saw it."

Mary reached over and touched his arm. The kind act sent more of the story pouring from his mouth.

"I loved her. I really did. Despite everything, I loved her.

"I hated that she had such a hard time adapting to life on the ranch. I was out with the herd most days. Long hours. I saw her at breakfast every morning, and supper most nights. Sometimes, though, I didn't come home until late.

"If I had taken the time to get to know her before marrying her, I would have realized she would never fit in on a ranch. Her daddy was a wealthy plantation owner. She was a southern belle. She didn't know how to do much of anything. Not laundry, not cooking, not cleaning."

He stopped. This was not what he wanted to talk about. He wanted to tell Mary about his feelings for her, not relive the past that he swore he'd forget.

"What happened to her?"

The cold knife of rejection sliced through his heart as if Dahlia had left this morning.

"She left. After two years, she just up and left one morning. A note on the table greeted me when I got back home. She said she didn't love me. That she was going back to her daddy.

"Then three months later, I got divorce papers in the mail. Those papers included a plea not to fight it. She met a man she wanted to marry and that if I truly loved her, would I please just let her go."

The emotion burned in his chest. He kept the worst of the truth to himself—that she married the man who had been her beau before Warren showed up in her life. That she was stable and sane with him, bearing him many children. None of their children died. Not like his son.

"So you did?"

Warren shook himself from his ancient pain. "I let her go."

Mary stopped walking and turned toward him. The light was

fading faster now, reminding him of his purpose for this evening.

"I'm so sorry," she said.

"What is done is done."

He looked down at her. She—Mary—was beautiful. She captured his attention. No more thoughts of the past, he chided himself.

Reaching into his pocket, he pulled out the wrapped ribbons. "This is for you."

Mary's breath caught. She reached out and took the gift from Warren's extended hand. Then she unwrapped it and pulled two silky lengths of ribbon from the paper.

"I know it's hard to see, but they are pink—to match the dresses you're making. One is for you. The other is for Beth."

Her heart swirled with emotion as she ran the ribbons over her fingers. Not since her father was alive, had a man gotten her such a sweet and thoughtful gift. Certainly, Reuben never had.

"They are beautiful. Thank you."

She could hardly wait to get them inside into the light to see how they matched the pink fabric.

Then understanding began to dawn on her heart. Warren cared for her. He truly did. The gift was far too thoughtful for her to come to any other conclusion.

"I should probably get you back to the house," he said as he turned her that direction.

They walked in silence.

She thought about everything he said about his wife. There was more to the story than what he was telling her. She was sure of it. Yet, it didn't bother her. Not like Reuben's lies did. There was something about Warren's pain that seemed private, but real.

Glancing over at him, a smile graced her lips. He was so different from Reuben. So kind. Worthy of trust. Sincere.

She reached out for his hand. Without missing a step, he curled his fingers around hers. As they walked he rubbed his thumb across the back of her hand. The touch sent shivers up and down her spine.

"Well, ain't that just sweet."

Terror crawled through her gut as Warren turned at the sound of the voice—a voice she recognized. All the thoughts of freedom vanished as she turned toward the face of her enemy.

Chapter 30

Enoch Fowler laughed at the terror that crossed Mary Colter's face. He waited patiently over the last month after dropping her husband to the dust. Now was his time. His glory.

He pointed his cocked revolver at Warren's chest.

"Step away from the lady," he said.

He caught the slight jerk in Warren's arm as he moved his hand toward his gun belt.

"I wouldn't do that if I were you."

Warren's hand stilled.

Enoch smiled at Mary. "You been mighty hard to get alone these days little lady. Hiram Norton is gonna be right pleased that I'm bringing you home."

A sense of satisfaction settled over him. In a matter of minutes, he would have Mary Colter on a horse headed back to his boss in Texas. He'd get the big reward he had been hoping for. Norton would get the ultimate prize—Reuben's wife.

It didn't matter that Colter was dead. Norton would still want his widow. For some reason, unknown to him, his boss set his mind on having her. Probably some sense of getting back at Colter for everything he stole from him.

Enoch didn't care what Norton's motives were. He just wanted the money that came from keeping him happy.

All he had to do was put a bullet in Warren Cahill. Then he'd be home free.

Warren's eyes focused on the man before him. He wouldn't let him take Mary. She suffered enough under the harsh hand of her husband. No way would he let her suffer the same again—not while he had a breath within him.

His gaze darted toward the ranch house. If they made enough noise, there was a good chance someone would hear.

Running through all the possibilities in his mind, he decided the best thing would be to get Mary to stand behind him.

"I'm not going with you Enoch Fowler," she said.

Warren reached for her arm. "Get behind me."

Fowler glowered at him and pointed the gun toward her. "Don't move."

As his fingers grabbed her wrist, Warren yanked hard and maneuvered himself between her and the gun. A sound exploded in his ears seconds before he felt his flesh tear open in hot searing pain.

He heard Mary gasp behind him.

It was getting darker. The pain stronger. Pulsating.

His hand connected with his revolver. In one fluid motion, he ripped it from the holster, cocked it, and fired at the gray shadow of Enoch Fowler.

A grunt. Then a thud. Then silence.

Did he hit him?

Please Lord.

He was drifting. Swaying. Falling.

"Warren!"

His name tore from her throat as Enoch Fowler dropped to the ground dead.

Mary collapsed under Warren's weight as he fell back on her. Her back hit the ground hard. His body pressed the air from her lungs.

"Warren."

She shook him, but he didn't move. Was he dead? *Please, don't let him be dead.*

Footsteps sounded nearby. She felt his weight shift as someone rolled him off of her.

"Warren? Mary?" Will's voice invaded her shock.

"I'm fine. What about Warren?"

"Unconscious."

"Fowler?" Ben's question echoed in the growing darkness. "What's he doing here?"

Will helped Mary to her feet.

"Is he dead?" she asked.

"Yeah."

Warren groaned from his prone position on the ground. Relief washed over her heart. He wasn't dead.

"Let's get him inside," Will said.

Several men grabbed Warren's arms and legs. They lifted him from the ground and shuffled under his weight until they made it to the bunkhouse.

Will helped her up from the ground. "Are you alright?"

"Yes. I think so."

"Good. Go get Hannah and tell her Warren's been shot."

Mary stirred from her shock and rushed toward the ranch house. She threw open the door calling for Hannah.

As she stepped into the light, her gaze fell to the lovely pink ribbons in her hand. Only they weren't pink anymore. Warren's blood coated her hands, the ribbons, and the front of her dress. So much blood.

Hannah's gasp reminded her of her purpose. She dropped the stained ribbons on the table. Then she turned towards Hannah.

"Warren's been shot."

Hannah flew into motion, gathering a medical bag, bandages, and the like. Mary followed her, stopping in the living room.

"Eddie, take Beth and head over to your Aunt Julia's. Stay there until I come for you."

When he didn't move, she added, "Now!"

He jumped up and grabbed Beth's hand. "I hope he dies. He deserves it for killing Papa!"

"Not Mr. Warren!" Beth began to cry.

Mary instinctively reached out and slapped a hand across Eddie's face. "Don't you ever say something like that again."

Eddie stared at her in shock, rubbing his cheek with his hand.

"Go!"

He snapped out of his stupor and dragged his crying sister behind him across the yard to Julia's cabin.

Mary closed the door to the ranch house and hurried across the yard. Her hands shook. She never struck her son before. The look of disbelief on his face danced across her vision. *Forgive me, Eddie.* She hoped this night wouldn't drive him further away.

Taking a deep breath, she entered the bunkhouse. Hannah was bent over Warren's shirtless chest. She looked up as Mary approached.

"Here." She thrust a wet rag toward her. "Try to clean off his chest so I can find the wound."

Blood was everywhere. Mary held back a whimper. This was not good.

She began wiping the rag over his chest, arms, and shoulders.

Please Lord. Please don't take him.

"There," Hannah said, pointing at the hole in his left shoulder. She turned to Will. "Lift him up so I can see his back."

Will did.

"Looks like the bullet went clear through. Let's get him cleaned up and bandaged."

Mary followed each of Hannah's instructions. Between the two of them, they had him patched up in less than an hour. Then men carried him to his bunk.

When Mary started to help clean the table, Hannah sent her back to the ranch house. "Go home."

"Will he be okay?"

Hannah smiled. "Should be. Looks like the bullet missed everything important. Just left him with a nice little hole in his shoulder."

As Mary started to leave, Hannah added, "Don't worry about the children. I'll send Will to get them."

She nodded and numbly walked back to the house. Once there, she went into the dining room and grabbed the ribbons from the table. Warren's blood had dried. They were ruined.

Still, she folded them in her hand and took them up to her room. She stripped out of her blood stained dress and fell into bed.

The stress of the last few hours lingered, but eventually faded in the memory of Warren's hand clasped around hers. He saved her.

Before sleep claimed her, she sent one final prayer heavenward. *Lord, please help him heal.* Then she realized the prayer was for her son as much as it was for Warren.

Chapter 31

The next morning Mary woke as Beth crawled into bed with her. She opened her arms allowing her daughter to snuggle close.

"Mama, is Mr. Warren dead? I don't want him to be dead like Eddie said."

Mary placed a kiss on the top of her head. "No, sweetheart. Mr. Warren is not dead."

Unless he died overnight. She quickly chased the unwanted thought away.

"He's just hurt. Aunt Hannah says he'll be fine in a few weeks."

"Oh, good. I prayed for him."

"That's good. I'm sure Mr. Warren will be glad to hear that."

"Can we go see him?"

Mary took a second, wondering when Beth had become so attached to him. She wasn't sure she wanted her daughter to see him if he looked really bad. She didn't want her to worry. "Maybe later. He needs lots of rest."

"Okay."

For a few minutes, Beth was silent and Mary enjoyed holding her close. She loved her so much.

Slowly, she began to stretch and pull herself from the bed.

"Why don't you go get dressed and head down for breakfast?"

"Yes, Mama."

Beth jumped up from the bed, leaving the door wide open. As Mary stood and approached the door, Hannah appeared from across the hall.

"How is he?"

"I was just going to check," Hannah replied. "Do you want to come with me? Rosa can get breakfast started."

"Yes. I'll be down in a minute."

Mary closed the door and grabbed the first dress her hand touched. Quickly she twisted her hair back into a loose chignon. As she buttoned her boots, she tried to hold back her annoyance that there seemed to be twice as many buttons this morning.

In a few minutes, she joined Hannah in the parlor. When she opened the door, the morning air felt chillier than yesterday. She hoped it wasn't a sign of what they would find at the bunkhouse.

"Don't worry," Hannah said as she shut the door behind her. "None of the boys woke me last night, so that means he's fine."

After a few steps, Hannah asked, "How was your walk last night? I mean before everything."

Mary couldn't hold back her smile. "It was nice."

"Just nice?"

She giggled. "He gave me some ribbons that match the pink fabric I bought."

Hannah smiled. "That was very sweet."

"Only they got ruined."

"Oh, I'm sorry."

An idea popped into her head. She wanted to make something for Warren—something that would show him how much she appreciated him saving her last night.

"Do you have his measurements?"

Hannah stopped walking and turned to her with one eyebrow quirked.

"I'd like to make him a new shirt. He could use another one after last night."

Hannah smiled and started walking again. "I do. After breakfast, I'll look for the cards with everyone's measurements. That reminds me. I think Hawk hit another growth spurt. His sleeves looked a little short the other day. Probably need to have him measured again."

"I could do that this evening, after supper."

Hannah laughed. "You don't need to make up excuses to check on Warren."

Heat rushed her cheeks as Hannah knocked on the door to the bunkhouse.

Feet shuffled from behind the door.

"Just a minute," Jed called.

"Maybe we came a little too early," Mary said.

"Mrs. Boss," Jed greeted as he held the door open. "Mrs. Colter."

Inwardly, Mary cringed at her name. The only time she was reminded of it was when the cowboys were around or when she was in town. For some reason, being reminded of Reuben's name this morning bothered her.

She stepped into the bunkhouse. Several of the men sat around the table. Some already poured their first cup of coffee. Matthew had his head propped on his hand. Hawk yawned then nodded a greeting.

"How is he?" Hannah asked Jed as she moved toward Warren's bunk.

"Fine. Slept like a baby through the night."

"Good."

Mary moved to stand next to her. Her eyes roved over his relaxed face. He looked calm. Even serene.

"No sign of fever," Hannah said. "Let's see if we can sit him up to check his bandages."

"Here," Jed volunteered. "We'll move him to a chair."

As Jed and Snake maneuvered him to a chair near his bunk, Warren groaned, but didn't open his eyes.

Mary held a bowl in her hands to receive the bandages as Hannah removed them. Her eyes remained fixed on his closed eyes as she tried not to look at his chest. The thought sent heat pulsating against her cheeks.

Then, his eyelids moved. It was slight. She would have missed it, had she not been staring at them.

One popped open, revealing a silver blue eye. Then the other opened. He blinked several times.

"Mary."

Her breathing slowed when he whispered her name. This time, it was hers that left his lips first.

He winced and she could tell the pain entered his awareness.

"Almost done," Hannah said.

His gaze moved over her. "You're not hurt?"

"I'm fine," Mary whispered.

He closed his eyes and groaned against the pain.

"There," Hannah said. "Boys, please help him back to bed. Mary, would you give him some willow bark tea? I'm going to head back to the house."

Mary nodded and accepted the willow bark from Hannah's

hand. By the time she brewed a cup, Warren looked more than ready for it.

She scooted the chair close to his bunk. Then she leaned over and held the cup to his lips.

"Drink this."

He took a few sips. Then he stopped.

"That man."

"He's dead."

Warren's eyes glassed over in pain. She held the cup up, but he pushed it away.

"Who was he?"

"He worked for one of the men Reuben owed money to. Hiram Norton. For the last two years, anytime he heard rumor that Reuben was dead, he would come and try to get me to marry him."

Warren took another sip of the tea.

"He was the same lot as Reuben."

He leaned back and closed his eyes. Sensing he was ready to rest, Mary moved the cup away. He reached out and touched her hand.

With eyes still closed, he said, "Glad you're okay."

She didn't move until his hand relaxed and she was certain he fell asleep. Then, without regard for the audience of cowboys in the room, she leaned over and kissed his forehead.

"Thank you, Warren."

Warren faded in and out of consciousness most of the day. Every time he woke, he sensed Mary in the room, though he couldn't always see her. Each time he fell asleep, images of her filled his mind. She was in danger. She needed him.

As he woke again, the lingering dream bothered him. Mary and Dahlia melded into one. He was saving Mary from being trampled by cattle. Then he was saving Dahlia from a gunman by the lake. Reality was reversed in his dream. Mary had his dead son in her arms. Dahlia was here at the ranch.

He shook his head then opened his eyes. He didn't like the

tricks his dreams were playing on him.

Was it his dreams, or his heart?

The bunkhouse filled with noise as the cowboys returned home after the day's work. Warren listened without hearing.

Did his dreams mean something? Was it his heart trying to work out what he really felt for Mary?

He shifted his weight to move onto his side. Searing pain stopped him before he moved more than a little.

"You're awake."

Mary's soft voice cut through the noise. Then she appeared before him.

"Don't move. I have someone who wants to see you."

Little Beth's dark brown curls bounced as she leaned over him. "Mr. Warren?"

"Yes, Bethie?"

"You're not dead."

He laughed then stopped abruptly as pain shot through his left shoulder.

"I'm not dead." Though his arm felt like it.

"I told God I didn't want him to take you away."

"Thanks."

"Come on, Beth. Let's get Mr. Warren more tea."

Beth started to move away. Then she stopped and leaned real close to his ear. She whispered, "I told God not to take you 'cause I wanted you to be my papa."

She darted away so fast that Warren thought he imagined what she said. Her words warmed him from a place in his heart that he thought died with his son. The longing to be a father overwhelmed him. A lone tear trickled down his cheek. He lifted his hand to wipe it away.

"I'd like that," he whispered to himself, openly acknowledging the truth.

A few minutes later, Beth stood by her mother who brought him another cup of willow bark tea.

"Drink this," Mary said.

He didn't engage her in conversation. He drank all of the vile tasting liquid. Then he smiled at her and surrendered to sleep again.

This time his dreams were filled with images of Mary at his

side, holding his hand as they walked along the lake. Beth danced around him giggling.

“I love you, Papa.”

“He’s not your papa. He killed him, remember.” The bitter voice echoed in his dreams as Eddie’s scowl burned into his mind.

Chapter 32

Colter Ranch

May 3, 1867

Though his energy level wasn't quite back to normal, Warren was thrilled to be working again. He still favored his left arm, but he was getting used to mounting his horse one handed. Dismounting was always easier.

He held back a sigh as he led his gray gelding into the stables.

"Hey, Cahill," Jed greeted him. "How was last night?"

"Pedro had it under control. Probably didn't need to be out."

"So you're saying we can get by without Bates?"

"Guess so."

"Told ya," Hawk said, punching Jed in the arm.

"Stop that," Jed whined, rubbing his arm.

Warren moved his horse to his stall and away from the playful cowboys. Staying out with the herd all night usually left him in dour spirits. Today was worse. He was bone tired and it turned out that having one less man at night didn't make a difference.

Made him wonder if they had a few too many on hand during the day.

Well, if Will wasn't worried about it, then he wouldn't say anything. Besides, they'd need the extra help for branding.

"You look beat," Adam said as he entered the stall. "I'll take care of your horse for you."

Warren almost argued, but decided against it. He was tired.

Handing the brush to Adam, he thanked him and headed up to the bunkhouse. He pushed the door open and nodded to Rosa who was cleaning up the breakfast dishes from the day crew.

"Hungry?" she asked.

He shook his head and walked toward his bunk. After taking off his boots, hat, and gun belt, he flopped down on his bed and closed his eyes.

Mary missed Warren at breakfast this morning. Will said he rode out with the night herders last night and probably took breakfast at the bunkhouse. Still, the meal seemed quieter without him there—not that he talked much. He didn't. She had grown used to him sitting across from her most meals.

Humming as she worked, she finished the last stitch on the blue shirt meant just for him. She tied off the loose end of the thread. There. Done.

Running her fingers across the fabric, she tried to picture his reaction to the gift. She thought he would like it.

Careful not to crease the shirt, she folded it and laid it on the brown paper she laid out earlier. It seemed like such a small way to thank him for everything he'd done—for bringing Eddie back and for saving her from Enoch Fowler.

Secretly, when she was really honest with herself, she even thanked him for saving her from Reuben. Her stomach knotted at the thought. It wasn't right—to be glad that he was gone. But, she was.

She cut a length of string to secure the brown paper over the shirt. Then she picked it up and tucked it under one arm. She wondered if he would be awake or if she would have to leave it for him.

Shrugging off the thought, she hurried down the stairs. She hoped he would be awake. Mary really wanted to see him.

For the last week, other than at meals, she hadn't seen him at all. He had been very busy with one assignment or another. One day, Will had him drive to town with Ben. Another, he rode out with the herd. She worried he was pushing himself too hard too soon after being injured.

She opened the door and stepped out of the ranch house. The warm rays of the sun greeted her, lifting her mood. What a beautiful day it was. She wished her chores included laundry instead of being stuck inside cleaning the bunkhouse.

As she opened the door to the bunkhouse, soft snores met her ears. Warren lay on his stomach on his bunk, one arm hanging over the side and his feet dangled off of the edge. She smiled at the sight.

She set the wrapped shirt on the table. As quietly as possible, she moved the chairs from the table so she could sweep and mop that area of the floor. Without thinking, she hummed softly to herself as she cleaned the room.

The light melody invaded his dreams and slowly brought Warren awake. His left arm felt numb, so he rolled onto his back. As he did, the music stopped.

Exhaustion pulled him under again.

When he woke up later in the day, the fresh scent of a clean bunkhouse greeted his nostrils. He stretched slowly before rolling onto his side.

Remaining on his bunk, he looked around the main room. The floor was freshly cleaned. The fireplace was free from dust. A brown wrapped package caught his eye on the table.

Curiosity pulled him from his bunk. He crossed the room to the table and lifted up the wrapped package. A small piece of paper was tucked under the string with his name on it.

His heart picked up pace as he unfolded it.

Warren, thank you for the many things you have done for me. You brought my son home. You saved my life. This small gift hardly expresses my gratitude, but I hope you will eagerly accept it along with my thanks.

Fondly,

Mary

He swallowed hard as his fingers hovered over the string. He yanked on one end, pulling the bow apart and letting the string fall to the table. Gently, he lifted the blue shirt from the paper. He shook it out and held it in front of him with arms extended.

She made him a shirt.

Running his hand along one sleeve, he rested the sleeve on his arm. The length looked perfect. He quickly unbuttoned the wrinkled shirt he slept in and tossed it on his bunk. Then he put on the shirt Mary made for him.

He was right. The sleeve length was perfect.

As he buttoned up the shirt, the irony of receiving a letter from Mary was not lost on him. Unlike Dahlia's letter, hers held gratitude and hope.

Fondly. That's how she signed it. Any reservations he had about allowing himself to love her dimmed in light of that word. Fondly.

With the last button secured, Warren ran his hands down the front of the shirt. It fit him perfectly. When he moved his arms back and forth, it didn't pull across his chest like store bought shirts did. No, this one had been made to fit him and him alone.

The time it must have taken her to sew it. His heart melted as he unbuttoned the special gift.

His stomach growled and he looked at the clock on the mantle. Half past three.

Warren laid the shirt on his bunk and began washing up. Once he finished grooming, he put on the shirt from Mary. He still had time before she would start helping with supper. Maybe he could find her and take a short walk with her to thank her for the shirt.

He left the quiet of the bunkhouse and stepped out into the bright sun. Warm, but not so much that it would cause him to break a sweat yet.

The ranch house door flew open.

"Eddie!" Mary called after her son as he rounded the corner of the house. "Come back here!"

Eddie ignored his mother and kept running.

Mary followed after him.

Warren veered from his original course to catch up with them. But he stopped as he rounded the side of the house and saw Mary grab Eddie's wrist.

"Why are you being so difficult?" she asked him.

Both of them had their backs to him.

Eddie shook her hand off his arm then crossed his arms over his chest. "Why do you always change the subject when I talk about Papa?"

Warren's heart broke. How would she explain to her nine year old son what kind of father he had?

Her shoulders rose and dropped with her heavy sigh. "Do you remember living on the Star C?"

Eddie nodded.

"Do you remember what your papa was like after your grandpa died?"

Slowly Eddie nodded his head. "He pushed Aunt Julia."

"Yes."

"And he hurt you."

Mary's voice softened to a whisper. "Yes."

She laid a hand on his shoulder. Warren said a silent prayer.

"He was mean to me and to Aunt Julia and hurt us a lot."

Eddie nodded again.

"He hurt me so much that I don't want to remember it."

"But he loved me," Eddie cried. "He loved me."

Mary turned so her face was in profile to Warren's line of sight. He saw the pain there.

"Yes, in his own way he did."

"He was going to take me with him. I wanted to go with him. But Warren killed him!"

From his hiding place, Warren could feel Eddie's anger.

"I wish you would forgive him, son. He didn't mean to kill your papa."

"I can't. He killed Papa!"

"Eddie, your anger is going to make you into a mean man."

"I wish I were already a man so I could kill Warren like he killed Papa."

Then Eddie ran away from her.

Mary hugged her arms around her waist. She still hadn't seen that he'd witnessed the whole exchange. "I wish you would forgive him because I love him."

Warren would have run toward her and *swooped* her into his arms, showering her with kisses, if it weren't for the heaviness of the conversation he just overheard. Instead, he cleared his throat and walked toward her. Compassion would have to do.

For now.

Chapter 33

Mary turned at the sound behind her. Heat rushed to her cheeks as she watched Warren approach. Had he just heard her declaration of love?

He was wearing the shirt. Her heart flipped. Whether or not he heard her declaration, he certainly had to know she cared for him.

"Would you like to take a ride?" he asked, stopping in front of her.

"It's getting late. I need to help with supper."

He reached out and took her hand in his. "Please?"

The motion of his thumb rubbing across the back of her hand was enough to change her mind. She agreed.

As he went to fetch some horses, she returned inside and spoke to Hannah.

"Warren and I are going for a short ride."

Hannah smiled. "That's wonderful. I'll watch the children."

"Eddie took off around the lake. I'm sure he'll be fine."

"He's still angry isn't he?"

Mary nodded, afraid that her son would never let go of his hurt and even more afraid that he would grow into a man resembling his father.

"He doesn't understand what kind of man Reuben was. He only knows that he was his father and that he loved him. He doesn't understand that Reuben's love was conditional and would have pushed him into all manner of dark deeds once he got older."

"I'm so sorry. Do you think it would help to have Will talk to him?"

"Maybe. Anyway, Beth is playing in the living room. Warren and I will be back in time for supper."

"Go, have fun."

She thanked her before returning to the porch to wait for Warren. Excitement rose as he walked two horses up to the ranch house. He smiled at her and her heart sped up.

After he helped her onto her horse, doubt began to creep in. What if these sweet feelings faded? What if Warren turned out to be like Reuben? After all, Reuben seemed attentive and sweet when he courted her.

No. He wasn't like Reuben. She'd seen that in the way he talked about his wife. Though, something about how he talked about her bothered Mary. There were still some secrets—secrets she would have to uncover if she were to give her heart fully to him.

Warren led the way past the lake. She noticed Eddie on the other side skipping rocks. He seemed fine now. They kept riding up the path on the mountain for a few more minutes before Warren stopped his horse.

"Let's sit here for a bit," he suggested as he came to help her down from the horse.

His hands lingered on her waist and she looked up into his eyes. Such deep blue against the blue of his shirt. Her gaze dropped to his lips. They were full and so masculine. She wondered what it would be like to kiss him.

Her bold thoughts made her uncomfortable and she looked away. He kept his hands on her waist as he spoke.

"Thank you for the shirt."

Her gaze traveled back to find his. Those gorgeous eyes searched hers.

"No one has given me such a nice gift."

She giggled. "Surely someone has made you a shirt before."

"Oh, yeah. My mother. My sister."

His hand came up and cupped the side of her face. He brushed his thumb across her cheek.

"None were ever accompanied by such a heart-warming note."

Warmth spread across her face. "Thank you for saving me. For taking a bullet for me."

He pulled her closer, allowing the length of his body to lightly touch hers. Then he lowered his head and kissed her. The soft gentle movement of his lips against hers coaxed her to melt against him. She slid her arms around his neck as she kissed him back. His hands moved across her back with a light touch. Everything about this moment spoke of comforting sweetness.

Then he slowed the kiss until his lips stilled and he tilted his head back.

Her heavy eyelids peeked open as he trailed a finger down the side of her face. Desire danced in his eyes, but it was coupled with something she had never seen in Reuben's—love and respect.

"Mary," he whispered her name.

She buried her face against his shirt, to break the intensity of his gaze. He settled his arms around her waist.

Thoughts warred in her numb mind. *Could she trust him? Would he woo her and then change? Had his wife really left him because he was secretly a harsh man?*

Mary pushed back from him as her fear took root.

"What?" he asked. "What is it?"

She stepped away from him. One step. Two. Three.

"Tell me again, why your wife left."

He frowned.

She swallowed, hoping she could keep the tremor from her voice. "Why did she leave?"

"She didn't love me."

"Were you heavy handed with her?"

Warren bit his tongue as Mary's words doused cold water on his earlier desire. The sweet, light love he felt toward her a minute ago vanished as hurt pressed in.

"Don't you know me at all? How could you ask such a thing?"

She shook her head. "I don't know you. Not well. How do I know you aren't just playing with my heart to get something you want? How do I know you won't change later?"

He closed his eyes for a few seconds. Even though he understood where her fears were coming from, he couldn't help but feel his heart slicing in two.

"I was never heavy handed with her." He didn't have to be. She seemed intent on destroying herself and taking his heart with her.

"How can I know you won't turn out to be just like him?" She hugged her arms around her waist and fear swallowed up the sweet love that had rested on her face just a few moments ago.

Warren frowned. Kissing her had been a bad idea. She didn't know him at all—not if he listened to the crazy questions coming out of those luscious pink lips.

"How do I know you won't be like her? How do I know you won't grow morose and quiet?" He threw his arms up in the air in frustration. When she flinched, he slowly lowered them. He took a second to carefully remove any harshness from his tone.

"It's called trust. I have to trust you, Mary. You have to trust me."

"Then tell me."

"Tell you what?"

"The part of the story that you aren't telling me."

He frowned. Flashes of distant memories danced in his mind. Dahlia, white as a ghost. Her limp body draped over their bed. Bright red blood dripped from her arms staining the sheets. The musty smell of the room closed up too long. The ache in his ears from trying to listen for his son.

He turned back towards Mary. Surely she saw the raw pain on his face. "You don't know what you're asking of me."

She narrowed her eyes.

He clamped his lips shut.

She stepped toward her horse. "I think I hear the supper bell."

He strained his ears but heard nothing. Deciding their outing should end, he helped her onto her horse and led her back home. Neither said a word. When they reined in the horses in front of the ranch house, she slid from her horse before he could help her. Then she ran inside.

Giving up, he led the horses to the stable and took care of them before the supper bell rang.

Mary entered the ranch house. She forced a smile to her face as Hannah greeted her.

"Looks like the boys are on their way in," she said as she started to help set the table.

"Did you have a good ride with Warren?" Hannah asked.

"It was fine."

She reached for the basket of bread and hurried from the kitchen before Hannah could ask her anything else. She wasn't sure what she would say.

Emotions whirled in her heart. His soft kiss gave her such hope that he was different from Reuben—that she could trust him. Yet, when she asked about his former wife, Warren wouldn't tell her anything.

How could she trust him?

He's different.

She frowned at the voice in her head. What did it mean that Warren was different? Then it dawned on her. She never could have been that demanding of Reuben and not suffered harsh treatment for it.

Warren just frowned and became quiet. He didn't knock her on the ground for asking the question.

Will and Warren entered the dining room. Mary gathered her children and hurried them to the table. She wished she didn't have to sit across from him. It would be easier to get through the meal.

After Will said grace, Mary glanced up at Warren. His face remained passive. Throughout the rest of the meal, she could feel the tension across the table. If others noticed, they said nothing.

She'd never been more thankful for a meal to end. It wasn't until he left that she began to relax. Though, when she finally went to bed for the night, she was left with memories of his kiss warring with fears from her past.

Warren lay in his bunk in the dark bunkhouse, staring up at the bottom of the bunk above him. He wasn't sure when he decided he could trust Mary, but he did.

She loved him. He could tell from her kiss even if he hadn't overheard her declaration. And he loved her.

There were only two problems preventing him from asking her to be his wife—for that was what he wanted more than anything else.

The first problem was her late husband. Somehow he had to convince her that he was nothing like Reuben. He would never be like him. The second was that her son hated him and blamed him for his father's death.

He turned both issues over in his mind as minutes turned to hours. He had no answers. No definitive way to resolve either.

Trust me.

Warren bolted upright, bumping his head on the bunk above him. Would it hurt to trust God with these things? What was the worst that could happen? Her son still hated him and he would never be able to marry her. Well, that was where he was already.

He lay back down and closed his eyes. *Lord, you know my heart. Please work out Eddie's hatred. Please, help Mary let go of her past marriage.*

As the next few silent minutes ticked by, he wondered if God would really listen to his prayers. Maybe there was something more he needed to say. Maybe he had his own letting go to do.

Dahlia's passive face floated across his mind. They were at their son's graveside. Warren remembered that day. It was when he swore he would stop trusting everyone. God included.

Was he ready to release his fears?

He didn't feel ready, but he thought the words anyway. *Lord, I'm sorry I stopped trusting you. Forgive me and help me to change.*

Chapter 34

"Mary said Eddie is still angry about Warren killing his father," Hannah said as Will dressed for the day.

He heard the unspoken request in her tone of voice. "And you'd like me to talk to him?"

"I think it would help. I've seen the way he copies what you do."

Will held back a sigh because she was right. He needed to talk to his nephew. He was probably the only one that could help him. His meeting with Jacob Morgan could wait until the afternoon.

"You think he likes to fish?"

Hannah smiled. "I think he does if you do."

Maybe it was a crazy idea. In the entire four years he lived on this ranch, he never once went fishing. Some of the cowboys did. Occasionally, he'd even seen Betty and Ben take the boat out to the middle of the lake for an afternoon of fishing.

"After breakfast, I can take him fishing. Might be a good way to make sure he doesn't run."

She smiled at him and picked up Samuel from his crib. Then she gave Will a kiss on his cheek and headed downstairs with Samuel.

Will shook his head. He had no idea what he would say to Eddie. Then a slow smile stretched across his lips. He'd just try to think like Ben. Seemed he always had the right words to draw out a man's thoughts.

Before joining the family for breakfast he said a little prayer asking God to give him wisdom and words. Towards the end of the meal, he asked Mary if it would be okay for him to take Eddie fishing. Eddie's face lit up and she quickly agreed.

"You know how to fish?" Will asked as he led the way to the small dock and boat near Ben's cabin.

"Yeah. Ben taught me a few months back."

"Oh? Did you catch anything?"

"Naw. He said the fish were probably sleeping 'cause it was cold."

Will held the boat steady as Eddie climbed in. Then he climbed in and pushed the boat away from the small dock with one of the oars. As he rowed out to the center of the lake, he continued to pray for the right words to say.

"Uncle Will?"

"Yeah?"

"How come you ain't mad at Mr. Cahill for killing Papa?"

Will swallowed hard, not quite ready to broach the subject. *Wisdom.*

"How much did you see at the cabin on Rob—er, Reuben's ranch? Do you remember what your papa did?"

Eddie dropped his line in the water.

"You mean when he pushed Aunt Hannah on the bed and almost squashed Samuel?"

He nodded his head, not sure he could trust himself to hide his anger. Will dropped his line in the water to give himself time to calm down.

"Eddie, what happens when you hit your sister?"

He frowned. "I get in trouble. Mama sends me to my room or I have to do extra chores. Or if I get in really big trouble, Mama will spank me."

"See, some boys when they grow up, even though their Mama taught them what is wrong, they still do wrong things."

Eddie scrunched up his forehead in thought.

Will pressed on, hoping he was making sense to the nine year-old. "Your papa was that kind of man. Our mama and papa taught both him and me what was right and what was wrong. But, your papa kept doing wrong stuff later. Only some of the wrong things he did he hid from others."

"Like when he hurt Aunt Julia or Mama at night?"

Will's stomach churned at the thought of Eddie being aware of what Reuben did to Julia.

"Yes. Like that."

"He was going to hurt Aunt Hannah, too, wasn't he?"

Will nodded.

"Is that why Mr. Cahill killed him?"

"Your... Um... Mr. Cahill thought your papa was going to kill your aunt."

Eddie turned his attention toward his line in the water. He moved it back and forth. Will didn't have the heart to tell him to stop—especially since this trip had nothing to do with catching fish.

"Uncle Will?"

"Yeah?"

"Did my papa love me?"

The words sliced through Will's heart. He wasn't sure if Reuben was really capable of love.

"He told that man at the cabin that he didn't want me there. He got really mad and started yelling, like he did when we did something wrong. He told that man that I wasn't supposed to be there."

Will frowned. He had wondered why Reuben kidnapped his son. From everything Mary said, it seemed after Will left the Star C, Reuben practically ignored his children.

"I think he was mad at that man because he didn't want you to get hurt."

Will's line jerked and he tugged back on it. His empty hook flew out of the water, almost smacking him in the arm. Looked like the fish got just the bait. Eddie looked over his shoulder excitedly until he saw the empty hook. Then he turned his attention back to his line.

"Papa was a bad man, wasn't he? Like one of them outlaws the kids at school back home were always talking about."

"Yeah."

"I don't want to be like him. I don't want to make Mama cry."

Will's words lodged in his throat. It was the best thing he could have hoped to hear. He reached out and squeezed Eddie's shoulder.

"You don't have to be. You can be like your grandpa, instead."

"The one I was named after?"

"Yeah."

"Uncle Will?"

"Hmm?"

"Can you tell me about Grandpa Edward?"

Will chuckled. "I sure can."

"We got company," Will announced as he and Eddie returned from their fishing trip.

Mary looked over her son quickly while she listened to the conversation between Will and Hannah.

"Looks like wagons," he said.

"Do you suppose it's the Larsons?"

Mary's heart picked up pace. Was her friend Maggie finally here?

"Probably. In their last letter they thought they would arrive in early May. It's only the seventh now, so sounds about right."

Mary ignored the rest of the conversation and moved toward the window to look out. She couldn't tell from this distance yet.

"Mama?" Eddie tugged on her hand.

"Yes?"

"I decided I wanted to be like Grandpa when I grow up. Is that okay?"

She looked down and saw the excitement in his eyes. "Yes, sweetheart. That's just fine."

"Can I go out on the porch and wait for the wagons?"

"Sure. I'll come with you."

"Thanks!" He ran to the door and swung it open wide.

She followed behind him. Beth came next, followed by Will and his family. Looked like everyone was eager to greet their guests.

Mary thought back to Maggie's last letter. She apologized that they were so much later leaving than she expected. When Georgie took Will up on his offer to watch the land he selected, he decided to head back to Texas so he could marry his sweetheart there before bringing her out to Arizona. There had been a delay in the wedding, due to his future wife's uncle passing away. But, they finally held the wedding, and then left in late March.

From the stories Will told of his travel West, it sounded like the Larsons had made excellent time. They went the southern route, following the same roads as the stage. Seemed it was safer and more well-travelled than the route Will took. Though, from what he said, it sounded like a lot had changed in the Territory in the last four years.

Regardless, Mary was glad to have her friend here. A rider broke away from the group and headed toward the ranch house. It was Georgie Larson.

"Hope you have some extra supper on," he teased as he dismounted his horse. "Got a passel of hungry women folk coming."

Mary laughed. He wasn't kidding about the passel. With Maggie, and her three girls, plus Georgie's wife, they doubled the number of women on the ranch in one afternoon.

Another rider came in but from the direction of the herd. Warren stopped in front of the porch and dismounted. He smiled at Mary before greeting Georgie.

Soon, the wagons arrived and Mary was swept up in a flurry of activity. Someone suggested a bonfire, so she, Hannah, Betty, and Rosa started preparing food in the ranch house. Julia, Maggie, and Caroline—who came out with her husband about an hour after the rest of the Larsons—worked in Julia's kitchen.

"Will has some tables set up outside near the fire," Hannah said, coming back into the kitchen with several cowboys. She started handing them completed dishes of food to take out.

Mary grabbed the mashed potatoes and followed behind them. By the time she reached the front porch, she wished she had let the men carry the pot. It seemed to get heavier with each step.

"Here, let me take that," Warren said as he took the potatoes from her. "Where do you want them?"

She kept pace with him, walking close enough to catch the scent of horse wafting from him. It reminded her of how he smelled when he kissed her last week.

"Mary?"

"On the table by the platter of pork," she said as the heat rose to her cheeks.

When he set the pot on the table, he turned to face her. "Stay here. I'll go help bring down the rest."

"Thank you."

He flashed a sweet grin that curled her toes before he left.

"Sweet on someone?" Maggie teased as she came up next to Mary.

She felt her cheeks warm even more. "Maybe."

"He seems nice. Cowboy?"

"He's Will's foreman. Warren."

Maggie laughed. "Does he have a last name?"

Mary felt even more heat flame her cheeks. By now her entire face had to be red. "Cahill."

"Hmm. Mary Cahill. It has a nice ring to it."

"Maggie!"

"What? Where do you think my daughters get their match-making tendencies?"

Mary laughed. "Scheming is more accurate. And I'd keep an eye on that one."

She pointed toward the other end of the table where Maggie's daughter Missy stood surrounded by Matthew, Hawk, and Jed. Each of the three cowboys appeared instantly enamored.

Caroline joined their conversation. "And you thought I was trouble, Mama. I think Missy is going to be your biggest handful yet."

Maggie sighed and hugged Caroline to her side. "I seem to recall you being a handful at a much younger age. Now, where's that grandson of mine?"

As Maggie and Caroline walked away, Mary scanned the large crowd before her. Eddie and Beth were playing with Maggie's youngest two girls, Helen and Bethie. George, Will, Adam, and Ben were engaged in conversation. Hannah carried Samuel on her hip as James toddled down toward the blanket where Catherine sat under Julia's watchful eye. Cowboys that came with the Larsons intermingled with the Colter cowboys. Georgie and his wife Emmy sat on the porch away from the crowd. Betty joined Maggie and Caroline as they cooed over Caroline's son, Drew. Smiles adorned so many faces.

It reminded her of the big bonfires her father held on their ranch when she was growing up.

"You should join them," a deep voice sounded behind her. She didn't need to turn around to know it was Warren.

"Just taking it all in."

Rosa rang the dinner bell to let them know it was time to eat. Will's voice rose above the din as he said a beautiful prayer for the merging of two ranches. Mary wondered what he meant after the prayer closed and Warren led her to the buffet table.

"Did you hear the news?" he asked her.

"No."

"Will and George are combining their assets to form one big operation. Colter & Larson Ranch."

"You'll be the foreman of all of it?"

Warren shook his head.

Mary's heart sank. Did that mean he would be leaving?

"Georgie is going to be the foreman. I... Well, let's just say, I'm working on something else."

Even as Warren led her to a spot to sit down, she couldn't shake the feeling that he would be leaving the new Colter & Larson Ranch. She hated to admit just how much she didn't want that to happen.

Throughout the rest of the celebration, Mary moved around the crowd. She spent time with Maggie and her daughters. Despite her joy at seeing them again, the evening felt empty and her mind kept wandering back to what Warren said. He was working on something else.

As she climbed into bed for the night, she sent up a small prayer—a hope that he wouldn't go far. No matter where she stood with him, she couldn't bear it if he left.

Chapter 35

Mohave, Arizona Territory

May 20, 1867

Warren loaded the last of the supplies from Mohave into the wagon. Inwardly, he marveled at how things seemed different today than even a week ago. Will suggested he take on a supply load since they emptied their wagon of supplies in Mohave. He agreed to let Warren keep the entire purse for the return trip to Prescott, even though it was his wagon they were using.

"Have you given any more thought as to what you want to do?" Will asked.

He had, but decided to take a minute before answering. The sum he would make on this load would make up the last of what he figured he needed to start his own ranch. But, he wasn't sure that's what he wanted anymore.

Ever since the bonfire, he'd been thinking about approaching Will to see if he could become a part of the new Colter & Larson ranch. Granted, he wouldn't have nearly the number of cattle to contribute. But, he could build up his numbers quickly and in a few years be producing enough head to make his operation attractive to such a partnership. Perhaps he should wait until then before saying something.

"Thought I might start my own place."

"Really?" Will's voice sounded surprised. "Didn't think you'd be interested in having your own ranch."

"I used to have my own place back in Texas. Years ago."

"Huh? Didn't know that."

Silence fell and Warren found himself swaying to the shifting weight of the wagon. Will rode on horseback, keeping pace beside him.

Ben, Jed, and Hawk had left the day after they arrived in

Mohave, since their sole purpose of going was to drive cattle there. None were eager to stay away for long—but each for different reasons. Ben wanted to get back to his wife as soon as possible. Jed and Hawk seemed more concerned about letting Matthew have too much time alone with Missy Larson. Warren smiled. He suspected that one day the little red-head might come between the three friends.

"You gonna marry Mary?"

Will's question came so suddenly, Warren took a few seconds to absorb it. Then he sighed heavily. "I'd like to."

"But?"

"She's not sure she can trust me. She's afraid I'll woo her then change into someone like Rueben."

Will laughed.

"What's so funny?"

"Sounds crazy to me. I mean, you're nothing like him."

Even though Will's opinion relieved him, he wasn't sure Mary saw the difference.

"Anyway," Will said. "If you do decide to marry her and you can provide for her, Eddie, and Beth, then you have my blessing."

If he could provide for them. That was what weighed heavily on his mind for days now. No longer the foreman, but still a trusted member of Will's crew. The life of a cowboy wasn't the way to provide for an instant family. A new rancher just starting out—well, that hadn't worked so well for him the first time either.

"What about buying into Colter & Larson?" Will asked.

"Huh?"

"I'm guessing you've saved up some money if you're thinking about starting your own place. Why not just buy into our operation?"

"You'd let me do that?"

"Sure. We can give you shares of the company based on how much you contribute. And you know it's not just the ranching operation. It's also the meat company and the stables too."

"Yeah. What would George think of all of it?"

"Well, I'm sure he'd be fine with it. How much can you contribute?"

Warren told him.

Will let out a low whistle. "I suppose we'd need to make you a twenty-five percent partner for that."

"Twenty-five percent?" Had he heard correctly?

"Something right around that. We can talk to my attorney when we get back to Prescott to get a better idea. It'd be more if you had non-cash assets to contribute too."

"I don't. But twenty-five percent would be just fine."

"George and I have been talking about how things will change when the railroad gets here. Mind you, there's no definite time frame yet. But, the legislature has been talking about the railroads for the last few years. We want to be ready when it comes, whether it's in five years or fifteen years."

Warren always admired how Will thought ahead to the future—a great trait to have in a business partner.

"If you decide you want to partner with us, and you end up taking Mary as a wife, we could get you a house built nearby. That way all the cousins could grow up together."

"I think she'd like that."

The rest of the trip passed in silence. They made it more than halfway before stopping for the night.

Maybe it was time to talk to Mary again. Now he had something to offer. He had a job and would soon have a home. From Eddie's attitude these past two weeks, it looked like he had a change of heart towards him. He only had to worry about Mary's fears. Maybe, if she knew she would be close to family, it would help alleviate some of her fears.

Before he closed his eyes in sleep, he sent one more prayer heavenward. Then he thought about how he would ask her.

"Mary, can you take Ben some lemonade?" Hannah asked. "He's out on the front porch."

"Sure."

Mary stood from the table where the children sat with their studies. She went into the kitchen and squeezed some lemons for the tasty drink. In a matter of minutes, she had the beverage ready to serve.

Hannah enlisted Ben's help for the day so she could get the

fourth bedroom ready for her sons. She seemed excited to be moving them out of her room and thought Will would appreciate the surprise when he returned home tomorrow.

Mary smiled as she headed for the porch. She loved watching Hannah and Will's relationship. They seemed so in love.

A brief pang of jealousy replaced her smile. She wished she could have that kind of marriage.

Warren's face danced across her vision as she reached for the door knob. She paused. He seemed to love her. She loved him. Then why was it so hard to believe he was different from Reuben? That he wouldn't turn out to be a monster if she married him?

Where had that thought come from?

She frowned. It was what her heart wanted.

She pushed opened the door and set the tray on the small table next to the rocking chair where Ben sat.

"Thought I'd join you for a bit," she said, handing him one of the two glasses of lemonade.

"Sit. Enjoy the cool breeze with me," Ben said.

Mary sat in the other rocking chair and sipped on her lemonade. Ben took a big swig, draining the entire glass. Then he set the glass on the table.

"Ahhh. Delicious."

She smiled.

"Lookin' forward to Warren getting back tomorrow?"

Heat warmed her cheeks.

"I'd say ya are."

She didn't respond.

"Tell me, why ya runnin' from love?"

"Pardon?" she blurted out. What was Ben talking about?

"Seems to me that ya like Warren a lot. Why ya runnin' from it?"

"I'm not running."

"Aren't ya?"

She frowned.

Silence settled over them as her mind worked hard to reason through what Ben was saying. She did love Warren. She wished she could have what Will and Hannah had. But…

"I'm afraid he'll turn out to be like Reuben."

Ben's loud guffaw echoed across the valley.

"That's plain foolish."

Mary frowned again. "How so?"

He snorted. "Girl, I've know Reuben for a lifetime and Warren Cahill for a couple of years. The two men couldn't be more different 'n night and day. Warren ain't got a schemin', lyin' bone in his body."

Ben shifted in his chair to look her in the eye. Suddenly Mary was transported back to a time when she was a little girl and her father gave her that same look.

"Ya couldn't pick a better man than Warren Cahill. He'll treat ya right. Always. He ain't out to get somethin' from ya, like Reuben was. 'Sides, what ya got to offer him that he ain't already got?"

Ben was right. She didn't have any money or any land. She came with two children. That was it. All she could offer him was love.

Why *was* she running?

She shook her head.

"I can see ya thinkin' it through." Ben stood. "Best be gittin' back upstairs to help Hannah now. Thank ya fer the lemonade."

She smiled as he left. She should be thanking him for speaking plainly and helping set her heart in the right direction—back toward Warren, the man she loved.

Chapter 36

Warren woke early his first morning back on the ranch. He had a dozen different things that needed his attention and he planned on ignoring them for one more day.

Today was Mary's day.

When he and Will got back yesterday evening, they arrived after the family had dinner. So he ended up scrounging up some leftovers in the bunkhouse before Rosa cleaned up everything. Secretly, he wondered if Mary wished he would have gone up to the house instead.

A smiled stretched across his lips at the thought.

He flattened himself against the side of the house as Mary left with egg basket in hand. Then he snuck into the house and headed straight for the kitchen.

"Morning, Mrs. Colter. Rosa."

"Morning, Warren. What brings you here so early?" Hannah asked.

"I was hoping to ask a favor. I'd like to take Mary out for a picnic this afternoon and, I need something to take."

Hannah smiled. "I'll fix up something. Now go on. Get out of here before she gets back." She winked at him before turning her attention back to the meal preparation.

He hurried through the front door and back toward the barn. He would pick out the horses for them to ride. Then he stopped. Would it be too early to leave right after breakfast?

Shaking his head, he selected a horse for Mary. He had so much to tell her, the sooner he got started the better.

Once he had the horses ready to go, he led them to the hitching post in front of the house. Then he went inside for breakfast.

He arrived at his usual time, so she shouldn't be suspicious. He smiled at her before taking his seat, noticing the pink dusting the apples of her cheeks. She was wearing the pink dress today and the ribbon. How had she ever gotten it clean?

Will said grace then Adam stood.

"Everyone, we have an announcement," Adam said.

"I'm going to be an auntie!" Julia squealed.

All eyes turned toward them.

Adam continued, "Georgie and Emmy are expecting a child. They just told us at supper last night." Congratulations flowed around the table as Adam took his seat again.

Warren looked across the table at Mary. Was she too old to bear him a child? No. Will said she wasn't even thirty yet. Surely she would be able to have more children.

She looked up at him and smiled, almost as if she could read his thoughts. He quickly looked away.

As the meal concluded, he asked her if she would go for a ride and picnic with him. She didn't even hesitate. Instead, she asked Betty to watch her children then joined him on the front porch as quickly as possible.

"It's a lovely day," Mary said as Warren helped her up on the horse. "Perfect for a picnic."

He agreed and mounted his horse.

"I thought we could go back to the scenic outlook that we went to last time. I think we have some unfinished business to discuss."

Heat flamed her cheeks as she remembered the soft kiss he gave her there. It seemed like months ago. In reality it had been only a few weeks. She followed as he led the way.

When he looked at her this morning following Adam's announcement, she had the strangest sensation that he was thinking of her as the woman who would have his children. She admitted thinking of him as the father to hers—not just Eddie and Beth, but future children. Surely she would be able to have more.

Even if she couldn't, she knew she wanted to spend every day with him. The conversation with Ben two days ago really helped her think through what she really felt. She loved Warren Cahill and wanted to spend every day of her life with him.

Little nagging fears taunted her from time to time, but she brushed them aside. She believed he was a far different type of man than Reuben and she would trust God to keep him that way.

"Here we are," Warren announced.

He dismounted and came around to help her down. This time, he released his hold on her quickly. Then he grabbed a blanket and spread it out on the ground.

Once they were both seated, he started. "Last time you asked me to tell you about my wife and my son."

"Warren, wait. I was wrong to ask you."

He shook his head. "No. It's fine. I want you to know what happened. All of it. Though, I must warn you, it is not a pleasant story."

She nodded her head. Then she turned so she could clearly see his face. His gaze moved from hers to the horizon over her shoulder.

"I already told you part of what happened—how Dahlia and I met. That we married and she moved to the ranch.

"At first, we were both so enamored with each other that I couldn't see how much she was struggling or how lonely she was. Then, as work piled up, I started working later hours, neglecting her.

"About four months after we married, she confronted me one day. She screamed at me and told me how she could not take one more day in isolation. She needed other people around. She needed me.

"So, I arranged an outing for us. We spent a few days in town. She seemed to settle back into a normal state of mind. We spent every minute together for those few days.

"When we came back to the ranch, I returned to working late hours and she became sad and distant. Within a few months, we learned she was pregnant. She started to pull out of her despair as she looked forward to the baby's arrival.

"Our son was born on the fourth of March that year. I thought for certain she would find joy in motherhood.

"Only she didn't. Instead, she grew gloomy. More than once, she threatened to leave 'the screaming child' with me and let us fend for ourselves. She couldn't take it anymore. She wanted to leave. I told her she couldn't. She needed to be a mother for Lee. She needed to care for him and care for me.

"A few days later, I came home earlier than normal. When I entered the house, Lee's screams filled the air. Then I found her. She had taken a knife and cut long lines from her wrist halfway up her lower arm. Blood pooled on the floor by her chair.

"But, she wasn't dead. I got to her in time. The doctor said she had a sickness. Some women got it after giving birth. He thought it would go away in a few months.

"Only it didn't. Twice more I came home to a similar gruesome scene—except the third time, Lee's cries didn't greet me at the door. Silence permeated the house. I found him on the floor, next to the bed where she lay. He was dead. She wasn't very far from it either.

"After the doctor kept her alive and she recovered, we waited a few days before burying Lee. The doctor said he had stopped breathing.

"I didn't believe it. I knew she killed him. I told her so. I blamed her. She blamed me for getting her pregnant and making her stay on the ranch.

"A week later, I came home to the note she left saying she was going back to New Orleans. She didn't want me anymore.

"I followed her. I showed up at her family's plantation. I begged her to come home. I told her I would give up the ranch—everything—if she wanted. I could work for her father at the plantation."

Warren turned to look at her. His face showed just how deeply broken his heart was. Tears began pooling in her eyes.

"Dahlia refused me. Every option I gave her, she threw back at me. She didn't want me anymore. She told me to go back to Texas and forget about her. Pretend like we had never met.

"I couldn't do that. But, she left me no choice. I went back. Each time I visited Lee's grave, I began to imagine I was visiting hers too.

"Still, I held out hope for months that she might return—even after I received the divorce papers. I even held out hope after hearing she married another man."

Warren's words came to an abrupt stop. He let out a shaky breath.

"Mary, I know you suffered horrible things from Reuben. I know you will never speak of many of them. That's fine." He reached over and took her hand, sending her heart into double time. "I promise you, I am nothing like him. Just as you are nothing like Dahlia. We've both had painful pasts. We've had terrible marriages that have left us both scarred.

"But, the love I feel for you is real. I am not the same man I was when I met Dahlia. I'm stronger. I won't leave you alone, like I did with her. I will give you everything—the love you deserve and a home for your children."

She allowed his words to sink in to the deepest parts of her heart as he took her hands and lifted her to her feet. He gently ran his fingers down the side of her face to her arm to her hand again. Her heart opened even more to receive his love.

Then Warren dropped to one knee in front of her. She felt lightheaded in anticipation for his next words.

"If you trust me, then be my wife. Let me share life with you. Let me spend the rest of it loving you and being worthy of your trust."

The words she wanted to speak, lodged firmly in her throat. She knew, looking down into his silver blue eyes, this was the love she always hoped for—revealed in the heart of a man who treasured her more than she ever dreamed possible.

"Mary?"

She nodded. "Yes, Warren. Yes, I want to be your wife."

He stood to his feet and pulled her to him. This time his kiss was less restrained than before. It held promise and passion. Hope and healing. Love and life. All of it swept away her fears.

Warren Cahill was the man she believed him to be. The one she would love forever.

She returned his ardent kiss with equal longing, letting him know the depths of her love. As a groan rose in his throat, he pulled away.

"Mary. Sweet Mary. Can we wed soon?"

"I'm not sure," she teased. "Where will we live?"

He laughed. "I forgot to tell you, didn't I?"

She nodded.

"On Colter & Larson Ranch. Not as foreman, but as partner."

"What?"

"I'm a twenty-five percent partner in Colter & Larson Ranch.

All we have to do is tell Will where we want the house, and it'll be built."

Mary's shock started to wear off. "How?"

"I've been saving for years to start my own ranch. I was ready to go find some land and get started when Will told me about Colter & Larson Ranch and that I wouldn't be foreman any longer. On the trip back from Mohave, he suggested that I buy in as a partner."

She smiled and gave him a hug. "It sounds wonderful. When did you want to get married?"

"It will take a few weeks to build the house, even with all of the help we'll have. If we wait until the end of June, that will give us five weeks. The inside won't be finished, but if you're willing—"

"Yes. The end of June will be just fine with me."

The one thing Mary hadn't thought about was her wedding night. The morning had been a blur. The afternoon, festive and joyous. But now it was the night of the thirtieth of June.

Her husband of a few hours smiled as he led her to their new home.

"Hannah said that Eddie and Beth could stay with them for a few nights," Warren said as they stood on the front porch.

She swallowed hard and fidgeted with the lace handkerchief in her hands.

"Mary," he said softly as he took her hands in his. "You have nothing to fear. Remember, I'm not like he was."

"I—" Her voice cracked. "I know."

He opened the door and led her into the parlor. Then he turned and closed the door. He came close and slowly pulled her into his arms.

"This is me. Warren. The man who is insanely in love with you."

"I know," she whispered.

"Trust me."

His gaze connected with hers and she was reminded again of what he promised in front of the pastor and witnesses. He promised to love and cherish her. His eyes spoke another promise now—to be worthy of her trust.

Gently, he tilted her chin and lowered his lips. As he kissed her slowly at first, she let his hands roam over her back. She savored the taste of his lips and the feel of his touch. When she started to kiss him back, he kept the kiss going, but gently lifted her into his arms. He carried her to their room.

Then Warren Cahill showed her there was nothing to fear on her wedding night or any night after as long as it was with him.

Chapter 37

Prescott

July 4, 1867

"Eddie!" Mary called after her son as he darted away with the other boys his age.

"He'll be fine," Warren said as he reached for her hand.

She sighed. "I know."

"Papa, can I go play with Helen?" Beth said, tugging on Warren's hand.

He nodded.

Mary smiled. In less than a week, Beth fully accepted Warren as her father. It made sense, since she had little or no memory of her real father.

"You know what she said when I took that bullet for you?"

She raised an eyebrow at Warren's teasing tone.

"She told me she prayed to God and told him that He couldn't take me. She wanted me to be her papa." A bright grin spread across his handsome lips.

"And you believed her?"

"Yeah. But, I had my own reasons."

He leaned over and gave her a kiss on the cheek.

"Yuck!" Julia whined as she took a seat next to Mary. "I swear Catherine spits up more than she eats these days."

"But she's taking solid food now. That's good."

Julia rolled her eyes. "She doesn't have much choice."

"Why not?"

Julia glanced at Adam as he sat down next to her. "Go ahead."

"Shouldn't we wait for Will and Hannah?"

Adam laughed. "Since when do you wait for anything?"

Mary smiled as Julia swatted at Adam's hand.

"I'm pregnant. At least I think I am. Most of the signs are there.

But, it might be a little early to tell for sure."

Adam shook his head. "I'm sure she is. It's the only thing that explains her weird cravings. Did you see her with the pickles and eggs this morning? Talk about gross."

Julia pouted and Adam leaned over and placed a kiss on her cheek.

"I think it's cute," he said.

"What's cute?" Caroline asked as she and Thomas joined the growing crowd at the two tables the Colters and Larsons claimed at the town square for their large clan.

"Julia thinks she's pregnant," Mary said.

Caroline jumped up to her feet and squashed Julia with a huge hug. "So soon? Catherine's not even a year yet. I'm so jealous. I was hoping I'd have the next baby."

"You can hardly keep up with the one you have," Julia shot back.

"Well, if I had another one, Mama said she might send Missy to town to help."

"I'm not so sure that's a good idea," Adam said, pointing to where Missy stood with at least five men standing around her. Three of them were Colter cowboys.

"Oh, I don't know. It would keep her away from Matthew, Jed, and Hawk," Caroline said.

"Yeah, and it would put her much closer to all of the single eligible men in town," Julia said.

"Is this what I'm going to have to look forward to when Beth gets older?" Warren asked.

Mary shook her head. "No. She comes from much more refined stock."

Caroline burst out laughing. Julia followed. Adam smiled. Warren winked at her. He knew what she meant.

Soon Maggie and George joined the group. Then Georgie and Emmy arrived just before Betty and Ben. Betty's son Paul sat with them. Only Will and Hannah and their children were missing.

Mary scanned the crowd for her two children and found them both playing without a care in the world. So free.

Warren wrapped an arm around her waist loosely, sending another smile to her lips. He was a good husband and father. She looked forward to all the days ahead of them. Maybe some would be filled with new babies in their home.

Hannah took a deep breath then let it out slowly. It had taken too much effort to wrangle James this morning. At two years old, he was getting better at hiding and running away from her. It took her and Will working together to get him dressed and in the wagon.

On the trip to town, he kept standing up in the back of the wagon and tried to get Samuel to do the same. She was seconds from climbing in the back and using Will's lasso to tie her son down, when Will told him to sit down. She wondered if his father used the same quiet but firm voice to command authority in his home.

As the wagon crested the hill overlooking the town of Prescott, she couldn't stop the wave of nostalgia that washed over her. This was where she met Will. In fact, three years ago, she stood on the platform as he dazzled the crowd with his rope tricks—one of which involved her.

She smiled. Such sweet memories in this town.

Four years ago, she had never even heard of Prescott or the Arizona Territory or Will Colter, the man who became her second husband. Now, she left the memory of the first buried, not because she didn't love him—she had loved him very much—but because her life was so full with Will. They had two sons. Her hand moved to rest over her stomach. Maybe a third would be conceived soon? She was in no hurry. James and Samuel kept her busy enough.

So much had happened in four seemingly short years. Julia and Adam moved here then married and started their family. Thomas came. Then Caroline. Now Mary and the Larsons. Will's little ranch kept growing and growing, not just with cattle but with people—family.

Will pulled the wagon to a stop in front of Lancaster's Boardinghouse. He came around and helped her down. Then he handed her Samuel. He sat James on his shoulders. It was probably the best way he could figure out how to keep him from running off.

"There they are," Will said, taking her hand in his. "Big group huh?"

"Much bigger than our first Fourth of July."

He turned to face her. "Much. I was still fighting for you then."

She smiled. "You didn't really have to fight for me. You already had my heart."

"Yeah, but I didn't know it yet."

"What do you suppose the future will hold, Mr. Colter?" she teased.

"More babies. Ours. Theirs."

"What else?"

"More trials. Ours and theirs."

"What else?"

He leaned down and pressed his lips against hers, stealing a quick kiss.

"More love. Ours and theirs."

Heat pushed up through her cheeks.

"What else?"

He smiled. Then he turned to face the crowd of friends and family gathered. He put his arm around her and stepped forward.

"Mrs. Colter, all I can tell you is that no matter what else comes our way, we know God is with us through every smile and every tear. There will be both—that's just the way of things. But, I can tell you one more thing."

"Yes?"

"I'm glad he brought us together. You and me. And that he brought each of them together. Our family is strong, but our God is stronger."

"Well said, Mr. Colter. Now, shall we go grab a bite to eat and get ready for more of your rope tricks?"

"After you," he said with that devilish wiggle of his eyebrows.

She sighed. How she still loved this man.

Author's Note

Readers, I hope you have enjoyed travelling the West with the Andersons, Colters, and Larsons. While I'm sad to see this series come to an end, I have thoroughly enjoyed taking you on this journey.

By 1866 and 1867, the Arizona Territory was already changing and transforming from just a few short years earlier when Hannah and Will arrived. Stage travel became more readily available and offered an alternative to the longer wagon trains if passengers could travel lightly. I wondered just how difficult it might be for a single mother to manage her children on this type of journey.

I know many aspects of Mary's story were difficult and heart breaking. Many women didn't have the wonderful experiences like Hannah did. Instead, far too many stories more closely resembled Mary's. Even today, too many women live in bondage to a harsh spouse. If this is your situation, please seek help from your local church or shelter. There are many kind-hearted people in this world that would love to help you experience freedom.

If you are already free, but still healing from a past like Mary's, please know that there are many honorable and trustworthy men in this world—like Will and Adam and Warren. Don't lose hope.

With the close of this series, I would like to thank:

My husband – for sticking with me through all the ups and down of writing and marketing. You keep me steady.

My editors, Fae and Deana – you help me in so many ways.

My father – thanks for believing in me.

My Lord and Savior Jesus Christ – I write for an audience of one. May this book honor and glorify you.

Book Club Questions

1. If you were in Mary's situation, what would you have done?

2. How has this book challenged your thoughts about divorce? Do you believe there are good reasons for getting a divorce, or do you believe something else?

3. Will's love for Hannah grows even deeper in this book. How does he show it?

4. Do you believe someone as evil as Reuben deserves a second chance? Why or why not?

5. What was the most heart-wrenching scene for you?

Karen Baney, in addition to writing Christian historical and contemporary fiction novels, works as a Software Engineer. Spending over twenty years as an avid fan of the genre, Karen loves writing about territorial Arizona.

Her faith plays an important role both in her life and in her writing. She is active in various Bible studies throughout the year. Karen and her husband make their home in Gilbert, Arizona, with their two dogs. She also holds a Masters of Business Administration from Arizona State University.

For more information about Karen Baney, the history behind the books, or other books written by her, please visit www.karenbaney.com.

Other books by Karen Baney:

Prescott Pioneers Series
A Dream Unfolding
A Heart Renewed
A Life Restored
A Hope Revealed

Contemporary Novels
Nickels

CPSIA information can be obtained at www.ICGtesting.com
Printed in the USA
LVOW051149190612

286756LV00003B/8/P